The
PAINTER
of SOULS

Also by Philip Kazan

Appetite

The
PAINTER
of SOULS

Philip Kazan

PEGASUS BOOKS
NEW YORK LONDON

THE PAINTER OF SOULS

Pegasus Books LLC
80 Broad Street, 5th Floor
New York, NY 10004

Library of Congress Cataloging-in-Publication Data is available.

ISBN: 978-1-68177-123-6

10 9 8 7 6 5 4 3 2 1

Printed in the United States of America
Distributed by W. W. Norton & Company

For Flora

Prologue

September 1469

The man lying back on the dusty boards of the scaffold, high above the altar of Spoleto Cathedral, knows he is dying. The thought of his death, familiar as it has become, does not trouble him now, as he licks a stubby finger and touches the moist end carefully to a small, loose flake of gold leaf that is coming away from a beam of divine light. He is stretched out below God's raised right hand, with the great crowned head gazing down at him. The rainbow he painted last year, vivid bands shining against the sky's deepest ultramarine, arcs above him like a gold-studded doorway. He will be passing through that door soon: a few weeks, a month at the most. He wonders, idly, whether he hasn't made the rainbow too gaudy, whether death itself will be quite so colourful. 'Aren't we all dying anyway?' he mutters, and his words return to him in the dry rustle of the dome's echo. The fresco he has been working on since last year tells a story about death, after all.

It is cool and quiet under the cathedral's half-dome. He looks up at the Angelic Host, all those faces in serried rows ... He hadn't known, then, that he was dying, but still he had summoned this legion up out of their graves, summoning them back to life with brush and pigment. Friends: so many friends. If the good people of Spoleto only knew who these angels, so innocently holding up Heaven's rainbow, had really been. He chuckles. Beggars, thieves, tricksters. Whores. But honest, in their way: every one of them. His boyhood companions from the streets, the riverbank. He can only remember their faces through veils of driftwood smoke and river mist, through rippling curtains of summer heat. And in his memory they are all innocent, all fit to stand beside God. So what if he's made all of them blonde and curly and clean? At least he had told the truth when he painted himself into the crowd: plump, frowning, peppered with greying stubble, draped in the Carmelite robes he hardly ever wears these days. The only ugly face in this throng of painted wonders. Staring out at the good people of Spoleto, who will have to stare back at him until the Last Trumpet sounds, or until they get around to painting over him, whichever comes sooner. As a betting man, he would put money on the latter.

The thought makes him chuckle and then wince at the pain that follows like an obedient dog. When it subsides, he stretches his short legs out across the boards and sighs with contentment. He's suffered worse in his time. He can remember the wheel of the rack turning, the ropes cutting into wrists and ankles, the wet pop of his shoulder joints giving way, and then the tearing and the warm gush of blood. Well, at least they'd stopped turning the damned wheel when his belly had split and a purple loop of gut had slid out. The Executioner of Florence had even apologised – what a nerve! – for being a bit heavy-handed, and for nothing more than a forged signature on a contract. He remembers screaming, and the face of his benefactor squinting down at him along that uncompromising Medici nose, as a barber had stitched his belly together again. But it had never quite healed. It is killing him, slowly, now.

Faces. What else has his life been made of? Beautiful faces. And every one is beautiful, even the ugly, the angry, the despairing. He shifts, bites his lip as the pain in his belly bites him again. Still alive, though! He's reached sixty: a decent age. How strange that he has outlived most of those here. Like his beloved teacher, who left him so early. Here he is among these kneeling saints, old and bearded as he never got to be in life. That girl ... Cati!

God, how lovely she had been! That young man he'd last seen as a corpse, tumbled like flotsam among broken reeds.

His pain does not like to be ignored and he rolls over to avoid it. The scaffold is flimsy and the drop is long, but heights have never bothered him. He's spent half his life up ladders and crouching on narrow perches. But now, looking down into empty air, he feels a sudden, woozy lurch of vertigo. For a moment he doesn't see neat lines of empty pews but more faces, tight-packed, snarling up at him, spittle-flecked lips drawn back from bared teeth. There is someone beside him in this memory, framed in the carved stone of a tall, open window. And then he is alone. A rope hisses against stone as it uncoils, then jolts. The crowd howls.

Albertino, he thinks. I never forgot you. I never forgot any of you. His eyes are wet, but they always are, these days. Old age, and years of squinting in bad light. He looks up to where Albertino is dancing hand in hand with a companion behind the Virgin's shoulder. Where he should be. He grins. They would damn this old painter if they knew what he'd done: turned a blasphemer into an angel. He closes his eyes, sees the rope shift against the stone as its burden swings above the shrieking mob and wonders: should I have done it, this time, all the other times? Have I not been the greatest sinner of all? How have I escaped the rope?

He lies back, and there is the brightness of the rainbow, leaping across the starry sky like a comet's tail. Angels at my head, he thinks; angels at my feet. I have not sinned, not in my work. I have used my gift. And what a gift, what a miracle, to be given eyes that see the beauty in everything. To be given hands that can trace the lines of Creation, give them colour. Give them life. He closes his eyes. I'd do it again: bring all the lost souls home, strip away the ugliness and the horror. Even the worst of it is so beautiful. A miracle.

I

Aɴ ᴀᴘᴘʟᴇ-sᴇʟʟᴇʀ ʜᴀs ꜰᴀʟʟᴇɴ asleep at his pitch in the Santo
Spirito market. Slumped in the shade of a boarded-up doorway
on this hot September day, his head is propped in an angle of
wood and marble and his basket, which still holds a small hoard
of scarlet fruit, is slipping down between his knees.

Who falls asleep like that? The boy peers around the corner
of the alley, biting his lip. The fool has apples still to sell. How
could he be asleep? Or perhaps...The boy feels an uncomfortable thrill, but then a fly lands on the man's eyelid, only to be
swatted away by a fat, red hand. Not dead then; just lazy. And
a lazy fellow like that deserves what he gets. Dozing off in the
middle of the market...The boy's mouth is watering. He glances
up and down the narrow street, crammed with people buying
and selling, and steps out of the alley. Just then a couple of older
boys glide by. As they reach the sleeping man they both bend at
the waist, supple as herons, and come up with an apple in each
hand. Then they are gone. *Madonna!* But – he clenches his fists
with relief – the man is still snoring. The boy swallows hungrily
and pushes his way between two men who are carrying a load
of wooden planks. His mind is busy with calculations: can he
grab two apples with each hand? Should he just swipe the whole
basket? Yes! He can manage it. He'll just grab it, duck under the
melon-seller's stall and make for the Via Squazza. Staring at the
wicker handles, he can already feel his hands closing around
them...

'Eh! Giovanotto!' The voice is high and sharp-edged. The

boy knows, immediately, that it is aimed at him. The snoring apple-seller is so close...

'Young man!'

Distracted, the boy pauses. The apples are in reach. But he feels the pressure of someone's gaze on his back, and instead of reaching into the basket he spins around, smiling innocently, to face the four women who are glaring at him from next to the stall of Piero the honey-seller. Monna Gemma, Monna Dianora, Monna Filippa and Monna Antonia, each of them swathed in black from head to foot like the Madonna del Popolo, the ancient Madonna in Santa Maria del Carmine, who has a young, wide-eyed, kindly face that looks a little as if she is trying not to laugh. The Madonna had watched him being baptised, and take his first communion. She had been watching, too, as the funeral service was said over his father's body. Unlike the Madonna, though, the four widows are pale, stern and distinctly unamused. He stands in the middle of the street, grinning like a fool, and behind him he hears the apple-seller yawn and sit up.

'Good day to you, distinguished ladies,' the boy says, his imagined apples popping like soap bubbles. He throws in a bow for good measure. These are the *commesse*, after all: the rich widows who support the Carmine, who know everybody's business in this neighbourhood of the Green Dragon, who, very possibly, are studying the thoughts inside his head at this very moment, as if his skull were made of glass. 'Isn't the weather lovely?'

The tallest, oldest *commessa*, Monna Gemma, beckons him over. He obeys, still smiling desperately.

'How is your mother?' asks Monna Gemma.

'She's well, Monna. In... in her way.'

'Are you taking care of her?'

'No, Monna Gemma. You know my sister looks after Mamma. There's just enough for the two of them. I'm... staying with my Aunt Maria.'

'With Monna Lapaccia?' Monna Dianora raises an eyebrow.

'Curious that when I saw her yesterday in church, she made no mention of it.'

'She has a great deal on her mind, my lady!'

'We talked about her cat, boy. No mention of you.'

'Are you on your own again?' Monna Antonia is a little more gentle.

He shrugs. 'Why shouldn't I be? It suits me.'

'What would your father say?'

'I don't know, Monna.' He looks down, prods the edge of a cobble with a bare toe. 'I don't remember him very well. But I think he would give me some food.'

'Are you hungry? Of course you are.' Monna Dianora, studying him intently, looks a little more like the Madonna del Popolo. She must have been pretty once, the boy thinks, and sees the lines that would draw her face now, quite angular and hard for the thinning lips, the fine membranes visible in her eyelids, the puckered skin around her jaw; and then, in his mind, he softens the lines, makes her young. Gives her back her husband. Lifts the corners of her full lips into a cautious smile.

'I'm fine, Monna,' he says.

'But you could have made room for an apple or two.'

'Apples?' he says, innocently.

Monna Dianora shakes her head, sighs. 'Come along, boy,' she says. 'The brothers will feed you.'

'I can't ask the brothers again!'

'Nonsense!' snaps Monna Gemma. 'The brothers like you. The prior himself likes you, for some unearthly reason. And besides, it is their duty. We shall remind them of it, won't we, sisters?' Four black-draped heads nod. 'You are stubborn, Pippo. But there is good in you. If your mother cannot . . . Well, it does not matter, because you have the Carmine. Come along, then.'

The four women turn and begin to walk away from him up the street. The boy hesitates. He glances at the apple-seller, who is wide awake now, and rummaging in his basket, looking displeased. The man catches his eye, and the boy grins and shrugs.

'You were robbed,' he says. 'But you've only lost a couple.'

'If you ...' The man is scowling, struggling to his feet.

'It wasn't me!'

'I don't give a fuck,' the man growls, balling his fists. 'You would have.'

The boy lunges, grabs two apples and sprints off, dancing past a loaded handcart, rattling the sword of an overdressed *bravo*. He darts into the dark opening of an alley, his old leather satchel slapping the back of his thighs as he pounds along the cobbles. The man won't chase him for a couple of apples ... Even so, he only stops running when he reaches Borgo San Frediano, his own territory. Only a few short streets away, but he feels as if he has just left a foreign country. Everything here is familiar: every stone, every smell and sound. There is Pagolo, the cobbler, arguing with Signor Becci the lawyer. He waves, and the cobbler waves back, though the lawyer frowns. He greets some other passers-by, then settles himself on the steps of the empty house near the corner of Via di Cestello to eat his prizes. He bites into the reddest apple, which is crisp and sour. Sucking greedily at the juice, he watches the comings and goings on the street. He waves, calls out to people by name. This is the centre of his world: the middle of the parish of San Frediano, in the middle of the neighbourhood of the Green Dragon, in the heart of Oltrarno, the best quarter of this great city of Florence.

A few coins are tossed in his direction, almost worthless *denari*. Enough for him to buy some scraps from a friendly butcher, though. In a little while he will go down to the Arno and see if his friends are there. They will build a fire, cook food if they have it.

'Spare me a bite?' The soft voice at his side makes him jump. The girl has crept up on him.

'Cati! You scared me. What's going on?'

'Nothing.' She shrugs, settles down next to him in the door-way. She is a little taller than him, her hair tied back in an old piece of scavenged silk, freckles on her sunburned face. Through one of her ears is a piece of gold wire, roughly crimped into a circle.

'You look just like a queen today. The queen of...' He searches for an exotic kingdom, remembers someone talking about some merchant or other from a long way away. 'Scotland. *La Regina di Scozia.*' He holds up the apple he has been saving. 'For Her Majesty, I can spare two bites.'

She plucks it from his hand, opens her mouth as wide as it can go. With a crunch, half of the apple disappears. Juice runs from the corner of her mouth.

'Where is Scotland, then, Pippo?' she asks, her voice muffled by apple pulp.

'In Flanders, I think.' He frowns at his bisected prize. 'Cati, if you're going to do that...' She is watching him with her almond-shaped eyes over the jagged edge of the fruit. The irises are brown and gold. Beautiful. He sighs. 'Go on, just eat the bastard. I give it to you. A gift from the people of Florence.'

'Thank you! You're so sweet, Pippo.' She leans against him, takes another bite, delicate this time. Her dress of homespun cloth has been warmed by the sun and smells faintly of tarred rope. Caterina Serragli shouldn't really be sitting with him, the boy thinks. She is not an orphan. She doesn't need to beg. She has a mother and a father, and though they are as poor as dirt, because her papa is a labourer in a dye works, she is pretty enough, and clever enough, that she stands a chance of making a good marriage. All the more reason not to be soiling her reputation with an urchin like him. But he has always known Cati, as he has always known almost everybody in San Frediano.

'How's your mother?' she asks.

'You're the second person to ask me that this afternoon.'

'Well, how is she?'

The boy shrugs, looks away, pretending to study the jackdaws playing on the roof of the church of San Frediano.

'Just the same, then?' Cati finishes the apple, throws the core into the street.

'I suppose so. I haven't been over there for a while. I … I don't like to see her like that. And I can't do anything, can I? Besides, my sister worries about me more if she has me around. I don't like people worrying about me.'

'*I* worry about you.'

'No you don't.'

'I do! I don't like your friends: Albertino Rossi and that one who calls himself the Cockerel. And the others.' She wrinkles her nose and sniffs pointedly. The boy finds himself pleasantly involved in the way it makes her freckles shift. Her makeshift earring catches the sunlight.

'Too rough for you, my queen?'

'They are disgusting. They'll all end up hanging from a window in the Signoria.'

'With me alongside them, I expect.'

'Don't say such things! Those boys are no better than rats. They never even had fathers!'

'I don't either.'

'But you did, once! My papa still talks about your papa. He always says what a good man he was. Those little apes had whores for mothers and … and …'

'You shouldn't talk about them like that.'

'You see? You're sticking up for them, because you have a good heart. They would be talking all kinds of shit about you if they were sitting there.'

'What a foul mouth you have, Queen of Scotland,' says the boy, chuckling. 'But the lads aren't as bad as that. And we look after each other. That's what's important. We're like the Confraternity, don't you see?'

'Lord!' Cati is quite round-eyed at his presumption. The Confraternity of Saint Agnes is the thing that glues the whole of the Green Dragon neighbourhood together, a brotherhood of the quarter's most important, wealthiest and most capable men based in the Convent of Santa Maria del Carmine. The boy's father had been a member, once. A butcher with his own shop, he had spent his free hours at the Carmine, and the boy had marched at his side, no more than knee-high, in the great processions of the parish. But that had been a long, long time ago.

'Are you still doing your pictures?' Cati asks, pulling him out of his memories.

'Of course.' He pats his satchel. 'Someone gave me a *quattrino* for one yesterday. Probably because I drew his nose a little bit smaller than it really was.'

'Draw me, then.'

'You? What do you need a drawing for, Cati?'

She cocks her head. 'Aren't I pretty enough to have a picture? And ... I'll pay you.'

'A *quattrino*?' he asks, laughing. He knows she doesn't have such riches.

'A kiss.'

'Hmm ...' He make a show of considering, but he knows he is blushing to the tips of his ears. 'Done.'

He opens his satchel, takes out a rough pad of vellum pieces stitched together at the top with a leather thong. He has scavenged these precious scraps from across the city: from the rubbish heaps of lawyers and priests, from under the green baize tables of the money-lenders outside Orsanmichele. Next is a stained ball of cloth that has once been a gentleman's hand-kerchief. He unravels it carefully, to reveal a small, stoppered glass pot filled with ink, which he has made himself from lamp-black and oak galls. Last comes a goose quill stripped of all its feathers, its tip protected by a hollowed-out rabbit bone. These things, and the folding knife in the bottom of the bag, are his prize possessions – his only possessions, apart from the rags he is wearing. The tools of his trade. Cati leans back regally against the doorframe while he sets up his things, precisely, reverently. He uncaps the quill, dips it in the ink and makes his first line.

The boy does not have to watch his subjects carefully as he draws them. They are already imprinted on his sight, or at least the parts of them that matter. It is easy for him to catch the line of Cati's nose, the Cupid's bow of her upper lip, the tiny cleft in her chin. Though she is staring at him he draws her looking off to one side, with the indomitable calm that only the Queen of Scotland could possess. He considers his sketch, leaves out her freckles but tries to catch the splintered glow of her eyes. He has never gazed at her like this before. How strange: she is the same person, but she seems to have opened for him, like a rose. But that is what happens when he makes his pictures. His gift, which comes from God, as people never tire of explaining to him, is like that. Catching people's faces in his delicate, inky lines lets him see inside them, in a way. And lets his subjects have a glimpse as well: Heaven's gift, passed on. He does not really understand what happens. The paper and the ink are not something he has chosen. They have always, it seems, been in his hands.

'There.'

'Already?'

'It's been a little while. Didn't you hear the bells?' He takes out his knife and cuts the sheet free of the pad, holds it up for her to see.

'Oh, Pippo.' She reaches for it, but he shakes his head.

'It needs to dry for a minute.' He tilts the sheet against the light, blows on it and, satisfied, gives it to her. She gasps with pleasure.

'Do I really look like that?'

The boy feels himself blushing again. 'Yes.' He ducks his head, feeling her eyes on him, smelling the warm cloth of her dress, the faint cinnamon of her skin. How wonderful life is, he thinks. How unexpected. He puts away his tools, his mind wandering over the drawing that still hovers, fading, behind his eyes. As he is tying the laces of his satchel, she touches his arm.

'Ready for your payment?'

He grins, shuts his eyes and purses his lips, waiting. Life is good.

'No, not here.' She stands, grabs his hand and pulls him up off the step. 'Come on.' He follows her across the street, down past the church, up the narrow Via del Piaggione. Half the people on this street died in the plague and there is no-one about now. There is a little deserted courtyard through an iron gate and she pulls him into it. In the cool shadows she takes his face between her hot, dry hands and kisses him hard on the mouth.

'Lovely Pippo. You deserve more than a kiss. More than a *quattrino*. You made me beautiful. If I had a florin I'd give it to you.'

'But you *are* beautiful, Cati. I just showed you the truth.' He raises his inky fingers and brushes her cheek. She kisses him again, and this time her mouth opens. Time, measured by the sound of sparrows playing on a windowsill above them, ebbs. *I would do anything* ... he thinks. *I would do anything for this to last for* ...

'Bloody little heathens!' A man's voice, too loud. They both open their eyes, pull apart. She is still holding the drawing by a corner.

'You'd better go,' the boy stammers. Cati makes a face, grabs his ears and kisses him once more.

'You're not a heathen, Pippo,' she whispers. 'You are blessed.' And then she is gone. The boy looks around the corner, sees her brown dress disappearing towards the church. There is a red-faced, very drunk man with a sagging goitre leaning against the house opposite. 'Fornicators!' he shouts, his face contorted with rage, though the vigorous motion of one of his hands, thrust down inside his breeches, indicates something other than outrage.

'Looks like you were enjoying the show,' says the boy, edging through the gate. 'What about a florin for it, then?' The man isn't from this side of the river. There is a bag by his feet, with the green glass neck of a large wine flagon poking from it. Seeing that the man has his hand trapped down his breeches, he darts across the alley, grabs the bag and takes off after Cati with the man bellowing obscenities behind him. But when he reaches the Borgo she is nowhere to be seen. He sags, feeling like a pennant that has been blowing proudly in the breeze, only to fall when the wind drops. He could have kissed Cati all day. And all night...

'Porca di misere,' he mutters. He looks up and down the street, wondering if it might be worth setting up his drawing things by the church in the hope of snagging a late customer. But there is a crowd now, bustling purposefully homewards. The day is coming to its end. He depends on idlers for his trade, on the bored, or rich, or vain. These people are just hungry.

So he makes his way down to the river. The water is low, and the banks are still covered in their pelt of summer grass, though it has long since faded to pale gold. He walks upstream towards the Ponte alla Carraia. Fishermen are sitting on logs, staring at their limp lines and shouting at children splashing in the shallows. It is blissful beside the Arno at this time of day, before the whores begin to drift down to the water as the mist rises, before the sodomites arrive to angle for a conquest. He doesn't mind the whores or the sodomites, because they often buy drawings from him, but they attract the attentions of The Eight, the city's night police. It is dangerous to sleep down here, but on a summer's evening it becomes the taverna, the kitchen and the Signoria of the city's street children.

It doesn't take the boy long to find his friends. They have already lit a small fire beneath the bridge and are making a lot of noise over some game or other. He trots over and drops down into the circle of ragged boys.

'Evening, my boys!'

'Pippo lo Schizza!'

They all greet him: short, buck-toothed Nuzzio; Il Cucciolo – the Puppy, which they call him because he is always scratching at his ringworm-infested skin; Federico; the Little Cockerel, Il Gallettino, who will fight anybody over anything; Meo, tall for his age and thin, with knobbly knees and elbows; and Albertino, the tallest, with a shock of tight, curly blond hair and only one earlobe, the other having been bitten off years ago by the Cockerel over some insult neither of them can remember now.

'What do you bring?' demands Albertino. It is their ritual greeting. Grinning, the boy thumps the stolen bag down onto the sand and pulls out the flagon, which is almost half full. There is some greasy, slightly rancid bacon in the bottom of the bag, a welcome bonus. The children clap him on the back and begin to pass around the flagon. Nuzzio can barely raise it to his lips, it is so large and heavy.

'Nice! Where did you get it?' asks Federico.

'From a *segaiolo*,' says the boy, pumping his hollowed fist up and down in the air. The others roar.

'Were you drawing him, Pippo lo Schizza?' splutters the Puppy. *Pippo Who Draws*. The only name he has gone by for years now.

'No! I was kissing...' He stops himself. He shares everything with his friends, but something inside him says *not this.*

'*What?*' More hoots of laughter.

'I mean he was watching a couple having a kiss. A tart and her trick, behind San Frediano. I sneaked up and...'

'Good one!' Albertino grabs him around the neck and plants a noisy kiss on the top of his head.

The wine is gone long before the sun begins to sink towards the west. The bacon has been hacked up and toasted. There are some small fish to eat as well. Nuzzio has bread. There is a stolen melon. They are licking its juice from their hands, enjoying the slow, warm melting feeling of the wine in their guts, watching the swifts slice back and forth across the glassy river, listening to the noises of the city – the babble of voices, laughter, shouts, the hollow tap of hooves – when the older boys appear out of the long reeds upstream.

They say nothing, but rush at the little group around the fire, kicking, punching, tumbling the friends over into the grass. The boy tries to rise, sees a face he recognises before a shoe catches him in the ear and he sprawls. The gang from the Scala neighbourhood upriver, the tannery slums... His ear is ringing and there is blood running down his face. He feels the strap of his satchel being tugged and he grabs at it in desperation but another foot gets him in the stomach and stamps on his chest again and again until he lets go. Then the gang is gone, running back the way they came. Out of one ear, the boy can hear their shouts. He curls up around the pain in his body. When he finally rolls over and forces himself onto his knees, he finds Albertino staring into his face.

'They've killed Meo!' he is saying, his voice high and breaking.

'What?' Filippo mutters, stupidly. 'Where's my bag?'

'He's dead! The cuckolds, the *bardasse* ...'

Filippo turns his head, which hurts so much that his vision turns purple for a moment. Through the swirling, livid colours, he sees a bare leg, thin as a pole in a vineyard, and an arm with a limp hand, touching the swollen knee joint at an impossible angle. Bright-red blood is smeared across dirty skin.

'Come on, Filippo. We've got to get them.'

'Who, 'Tino?'

'The Scala. They've killed Meo. We're going to kill them all.' Albertino's eyes are wide, the pupils completely black. There is blood in his hair, and a ragged cut runs across his shoulder. 'We're going to kill them, right?'

'Right. Where are the others? Where's my bag?'

'What the fuck are you talking about? Come on, Pippo!' Albertino stumbles off into the reeds, heading upstream. Filippo watches him go. He can't think. His ears are roaring and there is a horrible aching in his groin. Still, he forces himself to stand.

There is no point, he knows. The Scala boys are all older than them, vicious and armed. He still stumbles up the narrow path through the reeds, following the trail of trampled stems, but when he finds his ink bottle, ground into the sand by a heel, nothing left but splinters and a sad, spreading pool of black, he sits down and weeps. He has nothing left, nothing at all.

But crying serves no purpose in the boy's world. He limps down to the water and looks at his reflection. His face is a mask of dried blood. He cleans himself off as best he can. By the time he has climbed up the bank and is edging along the wall of the Lanfredini family's tower, he is wondering what to do next. He needs to find a place to sleep. Then there will be the long, tedious business of collecting more scraps of paper. Making more ink – perhaps he can steal some? He ponders. Should he go to his Aunt Maria's house? But no, she will beat him for having been beaten. There is his mother's ... no. Not there. He finds himself limping west along Borgo San Frediano, because this is home, where he belongs. He has decided to go back to the deserted house where – it seems like a century ago – Cati had led him, and is crossing the bottom of Piazza dei Carmine when he hears familiar voices calling out to him from the square.

'Filippo Lippi!'

The black figures of the widows, the *commesse* of Saint Agnes, stand there like four ancient statues. He feels like running – he *should* run – but he is much too tired. Instead, as though they have netted him and are drawing him in, he trudges over to them, trying to muster a cheery smile.

'What a beautiful evening, reverend ladies,' he manages, swaying on his feet.

'What has happened to you?' Monna Gemma bends down, scowling.

'He smells of wine,' says Monna Filippa, darkly.

'But his head ...' Monna Antonia takes him by the collar, hauls him to her side and takes his head in her startlingly strong hands, bending it this way and that.

'You're hurt, Pippo.'

'I had an accident, Monna Antonia. I'll be fine.'

The widow straightens, says something in a low and urgent whisper to her companions.

'I think so,' says Monna Gemma. She reaches down and takes the boy's hand. And without another word they lead him up into the square, and the boy finds that he is glad to be going with them, held in the safety of their rustling black robes. They walk on towards the rough brick façade of Santa Maria del Carmine, deep orange in the last moments of daylight. Monna Dianora reaches down and pats his head softly. Then she sniffs, straightens her back. The boy decides that, after whatever is going to happen has happened, he will go into the church and sit in front of the Madonna. Then he will find some charcoal and draw the four widows, not as the people in the piazza are seeing them now, but as God sees them. You must always repay kindness, he knows, and that is all he has to give.

2

CHRIST IS STUCK. HE HANGS, swathed in red and white, midway between Heaven and earth. One of Heaven's seams splits and its newly dyed indigo cloth, heavy with a good hundred gilt stars, sags, revealing a wooden platform festooned with rope. Below, on earth, the maestro curses volubly and kicks the winch mechanism. There is a *clack*, Christ drops a foot or two and stops, shuddering in the dust motes.

'Oi!' shouts Christ.

'We'll have you down in a moment, Domenico!' The maestro's assistant shouts up to the young man who is clinging to the brightly decorated uprights of his elaborate cage which is turning gently, forty feet above the altar.

'I told you, maestro. The cogs have swelled. They need to be shaved down,' he says, wiping his nose with the back of his hand.

'Then you should have shaved them first, before we hoisted him!' The maestro clenches his jaw angrily, which makes his upper lip stick out further, his nose appear longer. The assistant pales, ducks his head and shouts at his own assistants, who hunch their shoulders stoically. Maestro Brunelleschi has been in a foul mood all day. *Too grand for the Ascension Day play this year*, they have been muttering to each other. He is in the middle of building the new Foundlings' Hospital, and this work, designing machinery for church theatricals, appears to be a little beneath him now that he is an *architect*.

The maestro turns to the rood screen, where a small army of carpenters is noisily building the frames that, with the addition of painted boards and some clever drapery, will become Mount Olive and Jerusalem. Brunelleschi sighs, still angry, and runs his eyes across the pattern of ropes and pulleys slung from the beams of Santa Maria del Carmine, which will cause Christ to rise smoothly, effortlessly over the gasping audience, and four adoring angels to swoop in from the sides and escort him into the highest, to the suspended tent of spangled cloth which conceals another cage, this one holding God Himself. Except that the musty damp of the Carmine has got into the wooden machinery, and the angels, life-size effigies of wire and leather and feathers – chicken feathers, though for the second year running Brunelleschi has demanded pheasant and peacock – are looking shabby. They will need to be touched up, or the spectacle will be ruined. Jerusalem is much improved – new paint, the buildings given a sense of perspective – but the angels are letting everything down.

The maestro has always loved the Ascension pageant that the Company of Sant'Agnese puts on every year with the Carmelites, and it had been a great honour when the company had first asked him to design some stage machinery for it. He had been immensely flattered. But now it is becoming an imposition. No, he must be grateful. They had honoured him when he had needed it most, having just lost the competition to make the Baptistery doors ... Just thinking of that makes him angrier still. He sees Lorenzo di Bicci, talking to one of the priors. Not the greatest painter in the world, Bicci ... Still, he should be capable of prettifying the angels. There is a groan of wood turning against wood, and Christ begins to descend towards the upstretched arms of Confraternity members and friars while ropes creak and men wrestle with the uncooperative winch.

Something smashes behind him. Growling, he spins around. One of the ingenious lamps he has designed to light the ascent to Heaven is now a spray of crystal splinters on the tiles.

'Mother of God!' Teeth clenched so tight that his ear is singing, the maestro rounds on the apprentice boys who have dropped

20

the lantern. His arms are waving, his mouth is open, but rage has stolen his voice. The boys, none of them yet shaving their cheeks, look stricken. At least one of them is ready to cry. He is soft-faced, almost girlish, with a head of floppy, straw-coloured hair and wide eyes that are beginning to fill with tears. His mouth is a perfect O of terror. Brunelleschi seizes him with his gaze, advances, clenching and unclenching his fists. Just in time, an older assistant lopes up with a broom, manages to insert himself politely between the maestro and his prey. Thwarted, Brunelleschi makes sharp points with the joints of his forefingers and grinds them into the throbbing flesh of his temples. He squeezes his eyes shut. He sees velvety crimson light: his ill humour, slopping around in the boiling kettle of his skull. He is not a violent man, not even a stern master, but today... He is being thwarted from all quarters. Someone must be made an example of. That soft-faced lump, that clumsy, worthless little... He opens his eyes, ready to dispense rough justice, but instead of his intended victim he sees a young friar kneeling on the floor, scratching at a drawing tablet.

Another useless lump! The maestro is at the boy's side in two abrupt strides. He bends down, reaching for the stylus, about to pluck it from the boy's stubby fingers and hurl it away, even though, as a friar, the boy is strictly speaking outside his control – *but for God's sake! Drawing!* – when he sees the face on the tablet.

An elongated heart. Little apricot-shaped chin, wide-set eyes, the centres black; a falling lock of wavy hair, a fringe of disordered curls. The mouth, turned down, as if startled by something, as if the boy cannot decide whether he is terrified, or blessed. And though it is nothing more than white paste, paste of chicken bone ash scraped away to reveal the black slate beneath, the face seems to be possessed of a faint, warm light. The ash, the slate might be a pane of rough glass through which the morning sun is shining. The maestro recognises the boy he had been about to ... what? Slap? Kick? Humiliate? In the name of the Holy Mother, what had he been thinking?

He finds himself squatting beside the boy. 'Did you do that?' he asks.

'Not very good, is it, maestro?'

'It's ... No, it is very good. What is your name?'

'I'm Filippo – like you, maestro.' The boy grins. He has a round head, which the tonsure, shaved into his coarse black hair, makes even more round. He lifts the stylus and scratches absently behind one of his small but protruding ears.

'How old are you, Fra Filippo?'

'Fourteen.' Filippo drops his head and looks sideways at Brunelleschi, conspiratorially. 'I should say *fifteen*, shouldn't I? That's the age people make their profession. But they let me in early. Don't tell them I told you.' He smiles again.

'Why did they do that?'

'It was the Confraternity that talked to the prior. Maestro Bicci himself.' Filippo nods in the direction of the artist, who is shouting up to a carpenter balanced on a ladder above Jerusalem. 'I think it's because they're short of brothers. A lot of them died of the plague. They'll take anybody these days!' He snorts with laughter. 'And I suppose they did it as a favour to my father.'

'Is your father one of the Confraternity, then?'

'My father ... Yes, he was. He died when I was six. Tommaso di Lippo.' The boy raises an eyebrow, though Brunelleschi has said nothing. 'No, sir, you would not have heard of him! He had a butcher's shop on the Ponte Vecchio.'

'But you didn't go into the Guild of Butchers?'

'Bless you, maestro! It ought to have been the thing, you are right. But after my father died, my poor mamma took ill. It fell to my sister to look after her, and I was put out of doors.'

'Dear me! Your own mother threw you out?'

'She took to her bed and has never been quite clear in her mind since. No, I left of my own accord. My Aunt Maria took me in, but she is ...' He makes a slapping gesture with the flat of his hand and turns his head from side to side, *left, right, left,* chuckling. 'There are calmer places in our city than Monna Lapaccia's house. Plenty of places to sleep. I drew people, and sometimes they gave me a bit of food. I let my aunt feed me sometimes, to make her feel better. And to be fair, sir, her *ribollita* is as good as any in Oltrarno.'

'And you always knew you would become a friar?'

'I had never thought of it. But life ...' He spreads his fingers, shrugs.

'So.' The maestro frowns. 'A butcher's son. An orphan ... A beggar?' The boy nods, genially. The maestro runs the tip of his finger carefully over the chalky surface of the tablet. 'You did not learn this in a butcher's shop, or on the streets of Oltrarno.'

'Well, sir, I did not exactly learn it anywhere. When I was small I supposed that everyone else could do it too, and when I grew bigger I discovered that wasn't true. So I take it to be a gift from Our Heavenly Father. He gives us all gifts, does he not?'

'Of course. But not often one as generous as this.'

'The Lord is always generous!' The boy looks up, and Brunelleschi takes the motion for piety, but Filippo is staring delightedly at Christ, who is swaying again in mid-air, looking decidedly green and gesturing angrily, obscenely, at the men handling the winch. 'He should do that tomorrow night. What a laugh!' He picks up the tablet that is resting in his lap. 'Matteo didn't drop your lantern, you know. The hooks in the rood screen ... The iron is rotten. They've been struggling with them all day. Too scared to tell you, maestro. They're only boys, after all.'

The maestro looks at the face that the young friar has drawn; feels, again, a strange sense of being illuminated. It is fleeting, but ... He stands up, finds that all the tension, the suppressed rage, has left his body.

'The hooks have rusted, you say? That does not surprise me. The Carmine is always so bloody damp. We must have new hooks, then.'

'Talk to Biagio over there.' The boy points casually to a thick-set, grey-bearded man who is half-entangled in a bolt of rose-coloured silk. 'He's a blacksmith.'

'I know he is.' The maestro looks down his long nose at the boy. 'Filippo, eh? Filippo what?'

'Lippi, sir. Filippo di Tommaso Lippi. I think you should have them get Christ down now. He looks like he's about to be sick.'

'Oh? Yes! What are they doing with that bloody cage...' But he is not angry any more. When he goes over to the winch, it is to peer into the wooden mechanism, to probe with a file, to nod at his assistants' nervously offered advice. Christ descends at last, and must be pacified with a glass of wine and a sweet cake. The maestro sees where a new gearing can be inserted into his machine, and decides to overhaul all the pageant machinery, a prospect that makes him feel quite excited. The blacksmith is spoken to, and the boys who broke the lantern get some kind words and are promoted to the pageant cast – as Sons of God, no less. The blond boy, Matteo, cannot meet the maestro's eye, but his friends take him kindly by the arms as they hurry off to get their orders from the prior. Maestro Brunelleschi has already forgotten all about them. He is drawing machines in his mind, toothed cogs and levers and hinges. The long body of the church is filled with hammering and sawing, laughter and orders. Time passes unnoticed.

★

The candles are lit, the choir begins to practise. Brunelleschi's new device, a ball encrusted with pieces of mirror, attached to a clockwork meat-turner, is set spinning in the light of the lanterns on the rood screen, and countless squares of light begin to dance and flit around the columns and ceiling ribs. Christ is hauled aloft once more, smoothly this time, and ascends to where His Father, an old Confraternity member chosen for his luxuriant white beard, is waiting to reach out His hand. It is late when Maestro Brunelleschi remembers something. He finds Bicci di Lorenzo regilding Christ's cage.

'There's a young friar. Filippo ... *Fra* Filippo, I suppose.'

The older artist looks up. He has flecks of gold in his beard. 'Lippi? Little Pippo? What about him? Has he defaced something important?'

'No, no! I was wondering ... Do you think he's up to retouching the angels?'

Bicci straightens, grins. The gold sparkles in the dancing light of the mirror ball. 'I think,' he says, 'that Filippo Lippi has been waiting his entire life to paint an angel.'

3

Filippo lies on his narrow straw mattress, looking up at the beams of the ceiling. His cell is small and white, and with the door closed, all the noises of the world are reduced to the sounds of his own body. The tune of his blood, pulsing gently in his ears. His breath, shushing in and out. The viscous clench as he swallows. The insinuating gurgle of his belly, neglected for almost twelve hours, though its owner has been asleep and awake, asleep and awake several times, has shuffled down chilly stone corridors and stairs, stood and knelt and sung and gone back to bed without so much as a grain of *farro* to eat. And of course, there is his *ucello*, standing to attention beneath his thin blanket of brown homespun, as if to greet him back into the waking world. With painfully won discipline he ignores it. He often dreams about the afternoon when Cati Serragli had stolen his apple, and kissed him, and from the lightness around his heart, and the stirrings down below, he guesses he has had that dream again. Resignedly, he waits for his flesh to subside.

In a moment, thinks Filippo, who is lying perfectly still, the bell will ring for Prime, the First Hour. Then the city bells will ring six of the clock. Fra Andrea, on the other side of this wall, will start to cough. Then the cell doors will open up and down the dormitory: click, clack, creak. He will rise while the bell is still ringing, pull the heavy white Carmelite cloak and mantle over his habit, which he has slept in and which is damp with sweat because the late July night has been warm, and step out into the corridor with all the others. He will join the silent procession down the stairs and through the cloister to the church. With the others, he will stand in the choir and say the creed: *Quicumque vult salvus esse, ante omnia opus est, ut teneat catholicam fidem.* He will join his rough, unworthy voice to theirs in the singing of the psalms, and the music, as unadorned as the walls of his cell, will rise and fall, enter and leave the pure silence. And as he has done perhaps a thousand times now, Filippo will find himself standing in the familiar damp air, breathing in the smell of unwashed wool and snuffed candles and yesterday's frankincense, thinking about the world just beyond the wall, which used to be his, but does not belong to him at all now.

There is chestnut bread, dense and heavy, for the breaking of the night's fast. Fortunately there is milk as well: though it is thin and watery, yesterday's second milking, when Filippo mashes the bread into it with his spoon it makes a kind of thick, earthy pottage. He sits, watching the other friars eat, listening to the only sounds, which are the clunk of wooden spoons in wooden bowls, sipping and chewing. Now and again a sandal scrapes against the floor tiles. Sometimes the calm is so great that the sound of a bench being pushed back will startle him. Perhaps, he thinks, when he has been here for another ten, twenty years, he will have forgotten every other kind of sound. It is already hard to believe that he has spent winter nights huddled in old sacks, listening to the Arno in flood, or to chunks of ice knocking against the piers of the bridges. That he has woken to the barking of dogs, or horses' hooves, and once to the screams of a young woman giving birth in an abandoned house. What had happened to that baby? And what had brought that woman there? He spoons bread and milk into his mouth. Strange that he should remember them. But they come and go, these memories, rising through the clear silence of the cloister like fish rising in still water.

He crumbles another piece of chestnut bread into his bowl. Eight times a day, the psalms soothe the outside world from his mind. But it always seeps back. As he chews his bread, men are opening up their shops, and stirring tanning vats, and shovelling up horse shit from the cobbles. The city's tarts — women, girls and boys — are washing themselves, and gentle ladies are having their hair braided and pinned. Someone is waking up in their own vomit, someone is preparing a legal brief, and someone else is trying to remember why their purse is empty. The air will be full of the scent of freshly baked bread. The dead are waiting to be buried. The living are falling in and out of love.

When he had first come to live in the cloister he had seen it as a strong-box sitting in the middle of the vast disorder of Florence, a tiny, protected fragment of calm and safety. He had felt very big, very noisy then, though he had been hardly more than a child: a dirty, clumsy giant invading the pristine world of the friars. These days he feels as if it is the cloister that is huge, and that the city clings to its fringes, dwarfed by the walls of the Carmine. When the friars raise their voices in song, the sounds of Florence are drowned out. When they pray, the city's sins are washed away. The Order has folded him in.

By nine of the clock, Filippo has been sitting in the chapter house for two hours, squinting at an ancient copy of *St Augustine: On Christian Doctrine*. It is a relief to file into the church for Terce. As he takes his place in the choir, he notices something quite out of the ordinary. The sound of voices is coming from the right-hand arm of the transept, laymen's voices with the edge of the city to them. Things are being dragged along the floor. Filippo cranes his neck, trying to see around the corner, but with no success. The sacristy is round there, and the back door to the chapter house, and a neglected chapel that, only a few weeks ago, has been freshly plastered. He hears the voice of the prior, Fra Pietro di Francesco, remonstrating gently. The noises stop. The precentor clears his throat discreetly and begins to recite, and the voices of the friars rise in answer.

After prayers are over, Filippo does not leave with the others. Instead he lingers, making sure that the prior and the sub-prior have gone back into the cloister, then peers around the corner of the transept. There are four men standing in the derelict chapel, in a blaze of lamplight that blends uneasily with what little sunshine is slipping in through the high, narrow window above the chapel's altar. A thick-set older man is lifting a wooden pole, which he leans against one wall. There are more poles on the floor, and a sheaf of them already leaning. Boards are stacked in front of the chapel, with coils of rope and various tools. A younger man, head tied up in a faded red scarf, is pointing to a point below the window. The other two have their backs to Filippo. One is of medium height, bearded and broad-shouldered, with wiry black hair poking out around a white carpenter's cap. The other man, with streaks of grey in his shoulder-length hair, is strikingly short. His head barely reaches the chin of his companion. The bearded man sees Filippo watching him and bows his head respectfully. Embarrassed, Filippo nods back and hurries past, to the stairs that lead up to the chapter house.

By Sext, the midday prayer, the back wall of the chapel has been covered in a scaffold of poles and boards. The muffled sound of hammering and sawing has been seeping up into the chapter house all morning. By None, three hours later, the scaffolding has crept halfway around the chapel, and the small man is high up, beside the window. By Vespers, the men have all left, but the scaffold has covered all three walls.

That night, between Matins and Lauds, he has a vivid dream about a ruined house. It seems to be on the outskirts of San Frediano, somewhere emptied by the plague and not yet refilled. The roof has fallen in and the building is nothing more than sagging walls and a tangle of beams and floorboards. But the timber is ink-black and the walls are pure, stark white. In his dream, Filippo is looking for a place to sleep, but as he clambers over the fallen timbers he realises that the family who had lived in the place are still there. He sees a lifeless foot, a tangle of dusty clothing, a shoe, all dull and dingy against the stark black and white. And then he sees the hand, pale and half-open, jutting from underneath two crossed beams. He goes closer, but he already recognises it, because it wears his mother's wedding ring. The bell that wakes him tolls through his dream like the *Vacca*, the great warning bell of Florence, booming for plague, or fire, or war. But it is only the bell for Lauds. As he joins his brothers in the corridor, shivering despite the July heat, he wonders what dreams are hovering around their tonsured heads. But he doubts there are any. He cannot imagine that his brother friars dream at all.

Filippo cannot see the scaffold-lined chapel from the choir but its presence distracts him and he misses some notes, though many voices are ragged at this hour of the night and no-one seems to notice. He goes back to his cell, sleeps soundly, wakes again, sings and prays. At breakfast he studies the other faces, wondering if any of them are as curious about the chapel as he is. *Did you see?* he wants to ask. *What is it? What are they doing?* But he doesn't dare.

The men are back again at Prime. Filippo lingers, trying to drag out the few paces between the choir and the chapter house steps. The short man and the young one are up on the top course of scaffolding, the others are busy with buckets next to the altar. As no-one has noticed him, Filippo sidles closer. He sees the young man's right arm moving, making swoops and precise curves in the half-moon space beside the window. The white plaster is collecting lines of reddish brown. Filippo squints, trying to make out the shapes behind the man's shifting body. Lines... Creases. Folds. The swag of a cloak, an arm. The man is drawing.

Filippo runs to the stairs, dashes up to the chapter house. The older friars, already sitting in front of their books, scowl at him. A finger is raised to pursed lips: a crushing rebuke indeed, but Filippo ignores it. He finds his book, sits in front of it, but he cannot read a word. All he can think of is the men in the chapel. Painters! There are painters in the Carmine!

After the midday prayer, Filippo sidles into the transept again. This time there is someone he recognises in the chapel: the tall, dapper figure of Bicci di Lorenzo, who is stooping slightly to talk to the short man. Bicci's curly blond beard is almost touching the top of the other man's head. Filippo tries to slip away but di Lorenzo catches sight of him.

'Fra Pippo!' says Bicci, beckoning him over. Filippo swallows and obeys. He likes Maestro Bicci, and is somewhat in awe of him. He is, after all, one of Florence's most admired painters. One of the leaders of the Confraternity, the painter had been a friend of his father's, and had made it his business to keep an eye out for Filippo in the years when he lived on the streets.

'Masolino, this is Fra Pippo Lippi,' Bicci says to the short man.

'I've seen you before,' the man called Masolino says, gravely. *Little Tom*, thinks Filippo. Not the most imaginative nickname. 'Does this interest you, what we are doing here?'

'I'm sure it does,' Bicci says. 'Fra Pippo draws — rather well, in fact. We have had many conversations about painting in our time, have we not, Pippo?'

'In the old days, maestro,' Filippo says. 'But not… Oh, I never thanked you for the angels!'

'Angels?' says Masolino, eyebrows arching. He has a strange face, very carefully proportioned and intense, like a satyr. His mouth and eyes, which are dark and penetrating, turn down slightly, and his thick brown hair has receded far back on his square head.

'For the Ascension pageant,' Bicci explains. 'Filippo Brunelleschi was complaining that the angels on Christ's platform were looking tatty. You know what a stickler he is. So I suggested young Fra Pippo here, and he did an excellent job. Exceeded my expectations — which were high,' he adds, patting Filippo's shoulder.

'Do you paint here in the cloister?' asks Masolino.

'No. There's no ... time.' He shrugs. 'There is study, and contemplation, and the daily offices.'

'Ah. But you miss it,' Masolino says. It is not a question, but a statement.

'Of course,' says Filippo. He can't help grinning: the little man is so serious, and yet so warm. 'I spent years drawing. It's how I kept myself fed.'

'Pippo had the misfortune to lose his father when he was very young, and made his life out on the streets,' Bicci explains.

'Ah! And the friars took you in?' asks Masolino, interested.

'By the grace of God, yes,' Filippo says. Then he can keep his thoughts to himself no longer. 'What are you doing here, sir? I mean, what...' He waves his arms at the walls, at the other artist, who is high up on the scaffolding, adding more detail to his drawing; to the carpenter, who is mending a ladder, to the man with wiry hair, who is studying a sketch on a piece of paper.

'Scenes from the life of Saint Peter,' says Masolino, and closes his mouth abruptly, as though that is sufficient, or too exciting for more words, or far too dull. The corners turn down like the mouth of a wise carp.

'You know Ser Felice Brancacci, Pippo?' says Bicci.

'Everyone knows the Brancaccis, maestro. Isn't Ser Felice the silk merchant who won that tournament?'

'That's the one. He has just come back from being our ambassador in Egypt and he's made himself – and Florence – a lot of money. This chapel has come into his hands, and he has decided to make it beautiful.' Filippo can't tell if Maestro Bicci approves or disapproves of this. The Brancaccis are an old and respected family in San Frediano, neither too poor nor too rich. Perhaps Maestro Bicci would have liked to go to Egypt himself. *Ah, of course: Maestro Bicci thinks he should have been asked to do the chapel.* He smiles to himself. Business.

'Are you working, maestro?' he asks.

'Oh, I'm busy. Very busy...'

'How's Lo Scheggia, Bicci?' The man up on the scaffolding

has turned away from his drawing and is squatting on the top platform. The Splinter? Filippo is puzzled.

'Coming along,' says Bicci, with a lift of the brows that might indicate that the opposite is true. 'A new apprentice,' he explains to Filippo. 'Real name is Giovanni, but he fancies himself to be a bit sharp.'

'Rubbish. It's because he's thin.' The man mixing plaster is grinning. 'But you're right. He does fancy himself.'

Filippo suddenly realises that he is late for his studies. 'I'm sorry, maestro, Ser Masolino,' he says, bowing to the painters. 'I ought to ... That is ...' Feeling himself starting to blush, Filippo bows again and hurries off.

He doesn't dare to venture beyond the choir for the rest of that day. The next day is Sunday, which is filled with prayer and meditation that keeps him out of the transept. It is not until after None on Monday that he slips away from the other friars and wanders with poorly feigned nonchalance into the transept.

There is no-one in the chapel of Felice Brancacci except the plasterer, who is sitting cross-legged, like a tailor, a half-unrolled scroll of vellum in his lap. He hears Filippo's sandals tapping on the floor, puts the scroll to one side and stands up. He is wearing a long, rather dirty white tunic spattered in places with knobs of dried plaster, and with streaks of paint.

'Good afternoon,' he says, and offers a hand. Filippo takes it, seeing that the man is young, only just into his twenties. The hand Filippo shakes is rough, a worker's hand.

'Tommaso di Ser Cassai,' he says.

'Filippo di Tommaso Lippi,' says Filippo. '*Fra*, I mean.'

'Of course. I'm delighted to meet you, young brother.' He has a hint of the country in his voice, or Arezzo, perhaps. He doesn't sound like a plasterer, though. Filippo studies the man's face, quickly, out of habit: it is quite long, and tapers down from a pelt of wiry black hair and a rounded brow to a rather weak chin. A large nose that looks as if it has been freshly modelled out of soft clay. Grey eyes. A plasterer's face, no doubt about it. But then the man grins and his features come to life. With a shock, Filippo sees that the other man's eyes are studying *him* with an almost frightening keenness. 'The Reverend Prior has been telling me that you like to draw.'

'Fra Pietro?' says Filippo, confused. Surely it had been Maestro Bicci who had been talking about him the other day. The thought of the prior, who is as craggy and as sharp-eyed as a red-tailed kite, discussing him with workmen...The thought of the prior thinking about him at all, in fact, fills him with horror.

'I'm an orphan – more or less,' he says, reluctantly. 'I expect the prior told you that I lived out on the streets for a while. And yes, I would earn a few coins or a bit of food from my drawings.'

'Kept you alive, then?'

'I suppose so. I'm still here, aren't I?'

'It's good when it keeps you from starving. We're not all so fortunate.'

'We?' Filippo looks Cassai up and down, sceptically. He seems well fed, his paint-dotted shoes are not the cheapest sort, the hose he is wearing beneath the dirty tunic are decent cloth, he wears a gold ring on one of his pigment-stained hands. 'Wait: you're a painter too?'

'What did you think I was?'

'A plasterer,' Filippo mumbles. Cassai blinks, then roars with laughter. Filippo can't help grinning as well.

'A good trade, plastering,' says Cassai. 'Alas, I have no skill in that direction. For my sins, yes, I am a painter of sorts.'

'And you are here to help with the frescoes. Of course! I'm an idiot.'

'To paint my designs. I am pleased with them. I'll be curious to hear your thoughts.'

'*Your* designs?' Filippo stares at the man. 'But you're...'

'Too scruffy?'

'No! I mean...' Filippo thinks of Maestro Bicci, who has grey in his beard; Maestro Chellini, who is a grandfather. 'I thought the artist was the short man...' He stops himself.

'My master, Tommaso Fini. Masolino. Yes, he is not the tallest man in Florence, and I can say that, because he is on the other side of the Arno right now and probably can't hear me. Hard to think of so much talent inside such a little vessel, but outward appearances...'

'He's your maestro, then, but you work together?'

Cassai shrugs. 'You can't be a pupil for ever. Well, I expect you'd like a better look at the wall, yes?'

'Really?'

'Why not? How are you on ladders?'

'Oh, ladders don't bother me!' Filippo almost runs to the end of the chapel, tucks the hem of his habit into the rope belt around his waist, and starts to climb. He has lived and played in building sites for half his life. It feels good to grip the rungs, feel the wood flex as he goes up. He scrambles onto the top platform. The scaffolding has a little give, a little sway, but it is solid. He finds his balance and stands up to face the half-painted saint who is gazing heavenward, the grey curls of his beard shiny with fresh paint. His face seems oddly familiar.

'Who is he?' Filippo says, without thinking.

'Saint Peter!' Cassai is looking up at him, fists on hips.

'I know it's *him*. I mean who did you use for the face? He's a real person, isn't he?'

'Well...Yes, you're right.' The artist swarms up the ladder with the grace of long practice, and kneels next to Filippo. 'How can you tell?'

'Because saints always look the same, don't they? Everyone paints them to look a certain way. And the Madonna, too. Yours looks like someone you might find in the market.'

'That doesn't sound promising,' says Cassai, scratching his chin.

'Well, I expect Saint Peter went to the market sometimes.' Filippo shrugs. Cassai looks up at him in surprise. Then he grins.

'Of course he did. I can't remember where I saw this face,

to tell you the truth. It probably *was* the market. I was going to base him on Giotto, you see: Giotto di Bondone, the greatest painter, who lived...'

'I know who Giotto is,' says Filippo.

'Do you, indeed? Well, there's a head of Saint Peter in Assisi, but then I saw this fellow.'

'It's good,' says Filippo.

'Thank you.'

'So what will the rest be?'

Cassai explains it all: Maestro Masolino is doing the main lunettes: Christ walking on the water in one, saints — half done already — in the other. Adam and Eve tempted *there*, and cast out *there*. The story of Christ and the Tribute Money, Saint Peter preaching, raising the dead, performing more miracles *here* and *here*. They go back down the ladder and Cassai unrolls the design drawings. 'This is mine,' he says, pinning the long oblong of the Tribute Money to the floor with the pestle at one end, the mortar at the other. 'And this one: Peter is walking down the street, and where his shadow passes, the cripples are healed.'

He isn't proud, exactly, thinks Filippo. More carried away with the excitement of *doing*. Filippo finds to his complete surprise that he understands the young painter completely. He nods and exclaims politely, more and more overwhelmed. The drawings are wonders in themselves. They make his head swim. The lines of buildings flare and recede into distances that seem to make the floor drop away beneath his feet. Peter, mending the broken men propped against the wall of a city street with the two faint smudges of his shadow, is coming straight at him. Filippo squats in the thick plaster dust on the chapel floor, nodding at Cassai's words, thinking: I understand. I see what he sees.

'This is in San Frediano,' he says, pointing at the paper.

'It *could* be,' Cassai agrees. 'There's a stone wall like that near Santo Spirito, yes? But I think I put a bit of the Borgo in there as well.'

'And this bloke, with the eyebrows...' Filippo is bending low, studying the men who have just been healed. 'And the bald one, who's about to stand up. He looks like someone I've drawn. You've given him a broken nose as well. Are you from Florence, then, Ser Cassai?'

'No. From Castel San Giovanni. Near Montevarchi. But I've lived here for a while, off and on.'

'Oh. And the others?'

'Maestro Masolino is from Umbria, but he's lived here for a long time. He worked in Lorenzo Ghiberti's *bottega*.'

'On the Baptistery doors?'

'That's right. He knows a lot of the sculptors. Says he should have been one, actually, but he paints like an angel. My assistant is from here, though: from the Unicorn. Andrea, he's called.'

'And the other one? He really is a plasterer, isn't he?'

Cassai chuckles. 'Ruggerio? He's more than that. A maestro of plastering. Carpenter, of course. Cook, procurer of things for starving artists who don't ask questions... From Grosseto, he is. Though he has a Florentine soul.'

It is Filippo's turn to laugh. He likes the idea of a Florentine soul. And then he remembers where he is, who he is now. 'Holy Mother! I have to go!' he says, standing up hurriedly, dusting the white from his brown habit. 'I should have been in the chapter house all this time!'

'Praying?'

'Reading! Oh, Lord, the prior...'

'Tell him you were contemplating the life of Saint Peter,' says Cassai. 'Isn't that a proper study for a friar?'

'I doubt they'll see it that way,' Filippo says, batting furiously at his robe. Streaks of plaster dust are still clinging to it, and white billows around him like smoke. 'Thank you, though, Ser Cassai! Whatever they do to me, it'll have been worth it.' He grins. 'To think all this is happening here, in our church! I've got to go but... How long will it take to do all this?'

'A year, I expect. Don't worry, young brother. We'll talk again.'

'I hope so!' Filippo feels himself becoming awkward, so he

turns and bolts for the chapter house. The hours pass, the Early Fathers' lives slip in and out of his brain unremarked. All he can think of is Saint Peter walking through Oltrarno, and a bald man with a broken nose who feels the cool of the saint's shadow, feels himself change, his limbs working again, rising of their own accord. To think of this happening on Borgo San Frediano, or Via Squazza, to think of it happening right now... And those faces, he thinks, turning another unread page. I know those faces. I've drawn them. The prior is watching him out of the corner of his eye. Filippo bends his head, runs his finger along the lines of old handwriting. Soon it will be the midday prayer. Perhaps he can slip away again. The Early Fathers are not on the page. They are out there in the sunshine, walking along Via Serragli, waiting to be drawn.

'Fra Filippo.' Filippo jerks, looks up into the prior's lined, unsmiling face. 'A word with you.'

Quaking, Filippo follows Fra Pietro out into the cloister. Sparrows are chirping, squabbling in the box hedges and the carefully shaped orange and lemon trees.

'You have spoken with Ser Cassai the painter,' says the prior.

'I ... I have,' confesses Filippo, wincing.

'Hmm.' To Filippo's surprise, the prior crosses his arms and rests his chin on one up-pointed finger as he walks. 'He tells me you are greatly interested in his work. The Carmelites...' He trails off, taps his chin. 'You are acquainted with Ser Bicci di Lorenzo?'

'Ser Bicci? Yes, Reverend Father,' says Filippo, nervously.

'He needs help. In his *bottega*.'

'Really, Reverend Father? I thought he had an assistant. I heard the painters ... that is ...' Friars do not eavesdrop. He grits his teeth, feeling the ground about to open beneath him.

'Quite right; quite right. But he has gone off to Arezzo and left Maestro Bicci in a predicament. We were talking this morning – Ser Cassai, Ser Fini and I. There was a general agreement that you might benefit from some education in that direction. Under the eye of a recognised master.'

'Me, Reverend Father? Go to work for Ser Bicci? Could I?'

'I am allowed to give you a dispensation, for certain reasons, to leave the cloister. You have a talent, Fra Filippo, which can only come from God. I think I can justify letting you nurture that talent. I do not believe the chapter house is your natural home.'

'But I try, Reverend Father! I want to serve God more than anything...'

'I am sure you do. But the Order might be better served by directing your... *energetic* spirit down a more fitting path. There are other ways to serve God. I do not believe there is any reason why a friar should not paint holy pictures. In fact, who better?'

'But the Rule...' Something is compelling him to talk his way out of this miraculous opportunity. Could it be that it scares him? Surely he can't have changed so much? But when he imagines stepping out into the city, he has the same sensation that Ser Cassai's drawing of Saint Peter had given him: space, waiting for him. No, it is not terrifying. It is a miracle.

'Perhaps you should let me interpret the Rule, Fra Filippo,' says the prior, blinking seriously. 'In any case, Ser Bicci agrees. You will go to his studio tomorrow, directly after Lauds.'

'Wonderful!' breathes Filippo, but the prior is already striding silently away. Filippo knows he should go back to the chapter house, but there has been a *general agreement*. About his spirit. What does it mean? He doesn't know, so he sits on the low wall that runs between the arches of the colonnade and listens to the sparrows bicker in the orange trees, and further away, the voices of Florence rising and falling. Waiting for him to join them.

4

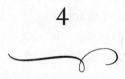

I**T IS SILENT IN THE** *bottega* of Maestro Bicci. The painter has gone out for his afternoon snack. His son, little Neri, is asleep upstairs. The plump *bottega* cat, a magnificent ginger bruiser enjoying its retirement, is curled up on the window ledge. A half-finished altarpiece is drying on its stand: a Madonna and Child in his master's careful, austere style. The faces and hands are done, but there are blank patches waiting to be filled: the robe, which will be in aquamarine that the client has yet to pay for; the architecture of the throne; the background, waiting for its gold leaf. Filippo has left off grinding ochre and is standing quite still, listening to the silence.

It is different from the silence of the convent, which is heavy, deliberate, enforced. The convent exists, so Filippo sometimes thinks, to stifle unnecessary noise. Sounds come at prescribed times: the bells, the shuffle of sandals on the way to prayers, or meals; the closing of cell doors. Here in the workshop, though, the silence is full of potential. He could start grinding again, chasing the deep yellow crumbs around the marble bowl. Neri might wake up and call for his mother. The cat might stretch out its back leg and knock that jar off the ledge. But there is another sound that Filippo decides he would like to hear. Dusting off his ochre-stained hands on the front of his habit, he pulls up its skirts, rummages in his undergarments and comes out with a pair of dice. Glancing towards the door, he squats down, cups his hands, shakes and throws the dice. They skip across the terracotta tiles and hit the wainscoting with a satisfying clatter. The cat's ears flinch, and its back leg stretches, paw splayed, claws out. It touches the earthenware jar, which falls and breaks with a dull *pop*. Filippo checks the dice. He has rolled the lowest score. No surprise there: that'll teach me. Tucking the dice back into his underwear, he gathers up the shards of pottery, offering up a quick prayer to the unfinished Madonna on Her stand and to the real one in Heaven, giving thanks that the jar had been empty and not full of aquamarine. The cat lifts its head and watches him with greenish-yellow eyes as he opens the window and chucks the shards out into the overgrown garden outside. Filippo rubs the animal behind its ragged ears and smiles at the purr that starts up at his touch. He leans out of the window, craning as far as he can, straining to catch a glimpse of the street. The dice, as they always do, have made him think of the friends he has left out there, the street urchins of Oltrarno: Albertino, Il Cucciolo, Federico, Nuzzio, Il Gallettino ... No, the Little Cockerel had died five years ago: The Eight had pulled his body out of the river. And Meo, dead in the reeds. But the others would be out there, enjoying the sun on their backs, enjoying their freedom, throwing dice ... He would love, at this moment, to lose a few pennies to Albertino, just to see him smile. He leans out further. There it is, a narrow, vertical stripe of light and movement framed between the walls of two houses.

Filippo stretches, lifts one foot, feels the ledge dig into his stomach. His stocky torso is cantilevered out precariously over the garden, but he can see shapes, colours moving across the narrow frame. The people of Oltrarno. He has been at their mercy. He has depended on their good hearts, their generosity, their forgiveness. On their slowness of foot, when he has had to get away fast. On their slowness of wit, when he has had to steal. And most of all, he has depended on their grace.

He feels a stab of longing, immediately followed by a pulse of guilt. He hates to be disloyal to the convent, even in his thoughts. Santa Maria del Carmine makes sure his unworthy body is fed and sheltered. The rhythms of the convent are bland but comfortable. And he is serving God every minute of each day. Hasn't he been a credit to the Green Dragon, to the memory of his father?

But still, the Florentine streets and their crowds are his world, even now. With something like yearning, he sees two men in homespun tunics walking fast, heads down. Stonemasons, on their way to the new house being built on Via dei Serragli. An old woman, black robe, white cowl: she is going to the Carmine, to ask the Madonna about her rheumatism. A horse clatters past. The rider is a messenger, heading out to Empoli or Pisa. That man in black is a banker. Those children, running across the frame so quickly that they are no more than a blur: off to swim in the river, or look for pennies in the mud, or hunt feral cats in the orchards below San Miniato al Monte. That girl, who has stopped in the middle of the pavement and is looking up at something... It must be the flock of white doves that has taken to slumming it down here in San Frediano, risking the cats and children for the sake of the leavings in the market. Yes, there they are, rising and turning like snowflakes. But who is the girl, with her hair bound up in a white scarf, wearing a mouse-grey dress that shows the swell of her breasts, the jut of one sharp hip... Does he know her? Had he ever spoken to her, in that other life of his? He had not really thought of girls much, back then, at least not in the way that he does these days, now that he is sworn to celibacy.

Celibacy? He'd barely known what the word meant when he had taken his oath. He knows now, though, and, dear God! he might not have been so quick to swear had he forseen the admittedly sweet torments he endures now. On his short walks to and from Bicci's studio his blood boils and cools, boils and cools every time he walks past a girl, or sees a woman leaning out of a window, her dress slipping just a little. He tries to fight it but still it heats him up, as the sun heats up his tonsured scalp. Out in the streets he had never felt bad when he had given in to temptation, because the temptations were always so small:

a stolen apple here, a filched pie there, coins spilled from a drunkard's pocket. They were what the Holy Mother sent him, to keep him alive. But this is different. This is sin.

A small, sharp piece of the broken jar is digging into the palm of Filippo's hand. The girl stares up into the sky, at the doves which are spiralling towards Heaven. He knows what it feels like, to be caught like that, in the middle of all the noise and the rushing about of a city day. The world is so beautiful. He imagines her staring at white wings against blue sky, how she must be empty of everything but the wonder of it. No, this cannot be sinful, to breathe the air, to watch a beautiful form. But he feels things stirring anyway, the all too familiar heat rising. This is a different sort of rapture. Stop it! He is not lusting, he is ... he is studying. Still watching the girl, he finds the shard with his fingers and begins to scratch her image into the window ledge. She is too far away for her face to be clear, but he can see her in his mind's eye. *Scratch, scratch*: the curve of her neck in silhouette as she looks up at the birds, the cleft of her chin, a ringlet of hair escaping from beneath the scarf ... He leans out further, trying to get a better view, and disturbs the cat, whose rasping purr gets louder. The creature stands, sticks its bottom in Filippo's face, turns and bumps him under the chin with its head. The doves whirl and clap their wings, the girl drops her head as if she has woken from a dream and steps out of the frame, out of sight.

'All right, all right,' Filippo sighs, digging his nails into the thick fur behind the cat's ears and scratching. 'I expect you'd like one of those doves, eh?' The cat bumps him again and, still purring, jumps down into the room. Filippo has a sudden, bright vision of a dove, broken on flagstones, white wings outstretched, crucified, flecked with vivid red, and the cat's sleek, striped head lowered to feast. He looks down at the window ledge. The girl is there, her profile scratched into the stone. He has caught her well, he thinks: the girl he saw in his head, that is. Flattening his palm against the drawing, he feels the warmth of the stone, imagines cupping his hand around the curve of the girl's chin. Ah. Well... Perhaps he could draw her properly, just a quick sketch on some of the maestro's scrap paper? But when he turns back into the room, he sees the Virgin keeping watch from the painting.

'Forgive me, Mother,' he says, not to the painting, exactly, but to the presence he knows is there, in the paint and the wood, and in the air above. He smiles. 'I know you see everything,' he says. 'But I only see a tiny splinter of Creation, and it's all so marvellous! I looked at that girl – you know what I was thinking, and I am sorry. But... If I say that by drawing beauty as I see it, I am honouring you with every drawing, is that all right? You live in everything beautiful. So you must live in that girl.'

The Virgin looks past him. She is very pale. Her face is a long oval, her nose is neat and very straight, and she has long, narrow eyes with heavy lids. Her baby son is nuzzling the side of her face – Filippo thinks of the tomcat bumping his cheek – and gazing at her adoringly, but she is elsewhere, pondering something beyond the squirming needs of children, the appetite of cats, the deeper, more shameful needs of young monks. Maestro Bicci always paints the Virgin that way, Filippo thinks. So distant, as if she's not interested in us. And that isn't true. Filippo knows all about mothers who look right through you, who see you but don't see you. He has not seen his own mamma, Antonia, since he made his profession to the Order. But when he had used to visit her, in her little room on Borgo San Frediano, she had sometimes worn that look, as if she was thinking some unbearably deep thought, though there was nothing in her mind at all. Once she had been a handsome woman, shouting jokes and gossip to the neighbours, and laughing with delight when big Tommaso had stamped into the house at the end of the day, full of news, and wine, and the thought he'd been keeping all day, as he always said, which was to grab his lovely wife like *this*! How she had roared with laughter, and pretended to struggle. But that laugh had never come back. Grief had hollowed her out until she wasn't even mad any longer. For years she has been lying in bed, staring at the wall, at nothing. No, the Virgin shouldn't look like Mamma Antonia. It is almost more than he dares, to imagine painting the Virgin himself, but if he did, he wouldn't do it like that.

Bicci has explained that patrons with ties to the Carmine want their Madonnas to look like the Madonna del Popolo, to look, well, old-fashioned. 'It is called the *maniera greca*,' he had said, 'because when the first friars made their home on Mount Carmel, they worshipped what they found there: the icons of the Greeks. It is the Carmelite way. And that is what they pay me for.' But we are not living in caves, Filippo thinks. We are in this great city, where wonderful new things are made every day. Clothes change. The way women wear their hair, the length of swords ... If hats can change from year to year, why not paintings? He spits on his fingers and erases his little drawing, closes the window. Ser Cassai would not paint Our Lady like that, would he?

'I mean no offence,' he mutters out loud, banging the pestle down onto the ochre, which must be ready when the maestro gets back. 'I'm grateful. I couldn't be more grateful.' It has been almost a year since Filippo has been coming here. He leaves the Carmine after Terce, walks around the corner to Bicci's house in Via del Leone, where he mixes paint, prepares boards with gesso and watches the maestro as he paints. Not that exciting, if he is truthful: there is far more pleasure to be had from the short walk to and from the *bottega* than in the quiet, methodical business of Bicci's work. How can it be called painting, and yet be so different from the frescoes taking shape on the walls of Ser Felice Brancacci's chapel?

Taking shape, but only just. True to Ser Cassai's predictions, the work is still not finished. The artists have paused and left their scaffolds and their drop cloths, and vanished. Maestro Masolino has gone to Hungary, so Bicci says: Hungary? Filippo does not even know where that is. And Ser Cassai is in Arezzo, doing an altarpiece for a merchant there. Bicci disapproves. He has muttered to Filippo about the merchant who has lured the artist away, about the dangers of money, and Filippo has had a hard time stopping himself from reminding him that he, Maestro Bicci, works for money, and has gone off and worked in Arezzo himself, and Stia and, in fact, wherever men have had the coin to pay him. All Bicci and his fellow artists ever talk about, it seems, are their patrons, the ones they have, the ones they have lost and the ones they would like to snag. Filippo loves to hear them talk. It is another world entirely, this world of painters. As far as he can tell, some of them would cut their own mother's throat for the chance to paint an altarpiece. Everything is contracts and promises and the price of ultramarine and gold leaf. When he goes back to the cloister in the evenings and stands in the choir with his brothers, surrounded by gilded saints and Virgins, he finds himself wondering if the other friars have any idea of the business that has produced the images they worship.

He wishes that Ser Cassai would come back to Florence, but to Filippo's way of thinking, the man who has enticed him to Arezzo, whoever he is, has excellent taste. Because already, Felice Brancacci's chapel is a wonder. The lunettes are done, beautiful but austere in Maestro Masolino's reserved style, and the little painter has also done Saint Peter preaching, and Tabitha being raised from the dead. A smaller section has been giving Filippo a great deal of trouble, recently. A few months ago, in one of the narrow panels on the right-hand wall of the chapel, Adam and Eve had appeared, and now Filippo hardly dares to walk past. The original man and woman are there, standing under what looks like a fig tree, round which a green serpent with an all-too-innocent blond human head has coiled itself. Both of them are naked: gloriously, unashamedly naked. Which is all about to change: the serpent looks down on the fig in Eve's hand: he already knows what is going to happen. She doesn't, though; and neither does Adam, who looks like a steady, sensible merchant type, if someone like that would ever stand around with his *ucello* out. Perhaps in one of the taverns on the other side of the bridge, the Buco or the Malvaggia ... It isn't Adam's *ucello* that always grabs Filippo's eyes, though, but Eve. She looks sensible too, from the neck up: calm, her yellow hair plaited responsibly. She doesn't have much in the way of breasts – oh, tortures, for a friar to have such demeaning thoughts! – but lower down ... Tortures, indeed. Filippo does not even dare imagine what might happen if one of his brothers caught him looking up there, at the woman's long, poised body, pale, the golden pink of peach flesh, every line of her body, every angle of her limbs apparently designed to draw his eyes to the centre, to the triangle, the cleft. Couldn't the prior have stopped him painting that? In a church? It is unbearable. As is the ladder propped against the wall, tempting Filippo to climb up, to get a better look. Oh, the horror of it. Eve drifts in and out of his days and haunts his nights. And yet, every day, Filippo gives fervent, unconditional thanks to the little man's skill. And every day, the serpent's neat little head looks down serenely, as if it knows everything. Which, Filippo reminds himself constantly, it does.

If only, he thinks, Saint Peter could walk past him one day in Via del Leone and touch him with his shadow, take away these appalling yet delightful afflictions. In the painting that Ser Cassai has finished, the sun is shining down into the San Frediano street, the bald man rises, the monkey-faced boy is about to feel the miraculous brush of the saint's cool shadow. In the distance, a glimpse of an ancient temple. If he closes his eyes, Filippo can almost hear the tap of feet, the pleas of the stricken. What would Peter think, if he could see Filippo's thoughts? Perhaps it would take more than the touch of a shadow to drive out his visions of the pale woman bending over him, her plait swinging down into his face, straddling his body ...

And yet, nothing is as it seems. The young man who walks behind the saint, pious and unmoved, is none other than the famous Lo Scheggia, Bicci's ex-apprentice who, it turns out, is Ser Cassai's younger brother. From the vague hints that Bicci has given, The Splinter is a man more in need of a miracle than Filippo, self-restraint not being one of the gifts he has received from his Creator. It is all an illusion, Filippo tells himself: the trickery of perspective, the bodies that appear to move in free space, the acolyte who is really a wastrel. The naked woman who has leaned her hip, very gently, against a coil of the serpent's body as it curls around the fig tree is nothing but paint and plaster. Or so he tells himself, over and over again.

The ochre is fine enough, and Filippo can hear Maestro Bicci opening the street door. He stretches and rubs his face, knowing he has left yellow trails across his nose and cheeks. Little Neri has woken up: his feet hammer lightly across the floor above, and his mother laughs. Filippo is thinking of the girl he has drawn. Now that he's given it some thought, he is sure he knows who the girl is: that weaver's daughter from Via del Campuccio. Far too full of herself to talk to the likes of him. And yet she had stared up at the doves as if she had heard the wings of angels... He might draw her again later, on the tablet he keeps in his cell. But not in profile this time. He'll have her turn her face towards him, perhaps the headscarf will come off and spill her ringlets down onto her shoulders. Eve steps into his head but he banishes her. Neri is jumping up and down and screeching just above his head. A dead spider trailing a shroud of old web is dislodged from a beam and falls onto the painting. Filippo goes over and brushes it away. And then he wonders, just as Maestro Bicci comes into the room: how would that girl's face look here, in this altarpiece? Could you give the Madonna a real face, a beautiful one, such as you might see out in the streets, if you were very lucky? He is about to ask the maestro, but Bicci is holding out a package of fig leaves wrapped around some grilled sausages, and so he grins instead, and takes them with his yellow fingers. Because the answer is — he bites into a sausage, nodding gratefully — the answer is that, if he can see Our Lady in a girl walking down Via della Chiesa, then he can paint her that way too.

5

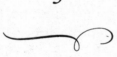

It turns out that little Neri is not well — a fever, some vomiting (which Monna Esmerelda describes in vivid detail) — and so the maestro, who must go to the apothecary, sends Filippo away early.

'I can help with the little one,' Filippo offers. He finds he does not want to leave the comforting domesticity of the Bicci house just yet, not matter how much vomit there might be. But Bicci sighs.

'He's not that unwell,' he says in an undertone. 'Just a little indigestion, I expect. But we lost one, you know, and so my wife gets upset whenever...' He waves his hands, miming a cough, an ache, a flood of something from the mouth. 'And besides, I have to make a list of things she needs from the apothecary, and it's as long as the Easter Mass. You'll distract me.'

'I'll be quiet!'

Bicci shakes his head kindly. 'I know. You're a good lad, Pippo. But actually I'm not feeling too well myself. The sight of all that vomit...' And indeed the maestro has taken on the slight greenish-ivory tint of an old Greek Madonna. 'I need some fresh air. You go, and I'll see you on Friday. Yes?'

'By the grace of God you'll all feel better tomorrow,' Filippo tells him. 'I'll say a prayer for Neri. And for you too, maestro.'

'I don't think we need prayers just yet,' says Bicci, crossing himself. 'But... Yes, for the little one. Just in case.' He opens the street door, ushers Filippo out with a theatrical bow.

'Bless you, maestro.' Filippo pauses on the front step. 'I'm thankful that you let me help you,' he says. 'It is good to ...'

'I know, Pippo,' says Bicci, squeezing his shoulder gently. 'I understand. You're always welcome here.'

Out in the early afternoon sunshine, Filippo sighs with resignation and heads off down the street. But when he gets to the corner of Via dell'Orto, he stops. A right turn will bring him to the Carmine in less than a minute. But he is not expected until Vespers, which is four hours away. Well, he needs to pray for little Neri. He needs to pray in any case, because he has been neglectful. The long hours of the day and night, when a Carmelite friar must sit in silent prayer and contemplation, have been a trial for Filippo recently. His mind is always too full of other things. Every time he settles down and turns himself towards God, a door seems to open, and beyond it, the streets, the river, the Ponte Vecchio with its crowds, the smell of food, the swaying skirts of girls. Something – a cough, perhaps a nudge from a watchful sub-prior – will bring him back, but sooner or later, another door will open. It is not that he wants to shirk his duties as a servant of God. And he has devised strategies to keep himself on the right path. As he prays, he draws in his mind, the words becoming lines, the lines becoming faces, bodies. Our Lady, kneeling to hear the words of the Angel Gabriel. Elijah and Elisha, the Carmelite founders. Saint Agnes, Saint Peter.

He rolls his shoulders, trying to shake himself out of his indecision. He really should get back to the convent. But Via del Leone carries on in front of him, towards the river. Well, he has a little time. No-one will miss him yet. He crosses the street, feeling a stab of guilt, but this is not exactly a temptation that he is yielding to. He hurries along, head down, feeling as if he has made the right choice. At the end of the street he turns west towards the city walls and the honey-coloured bulk of the Porta San Frediano. The gates are open and he can see the countryside beyond. Someone greets him – *Pippo! Go with God!* – and he recognises the man and waves. He used to know everyone around here, but since the plague, and being away in the cloister… People get old, and they change inside and out. They die. But the city doesn't change. This wall, this doorway, the shrine on the corner of Piazza dei Nerli, these are like the lines on the palm of his hand. He breathes: the air has always smelled like this here: onions, piss and pigeons, straw, moss in the deep shadows, hot stone in the sun. He crosses himself beneath the shrine, and silently asks for Our Lady's blessing. A few more strides, and he turns through a pair of old, iron-bound gates, almost chewed to dust by woodworm. In the tiny courtyard beyond, the smell of moss and piss is stronger. He looks up, at the lines of washing that hang criss-crossed in ascending layers, like a flock of great, off-white doves rising up to Heaven. He crosses himself again, climbs a flight of uneven steps and pauses in front of a door. It isn't locked, and squeaks open. He puts his head inside, flinching at the old air full of decaying plaster and black mildew.

'Mamma?'

'Who is it?' A woman's voice, coming from the end of the gloomy corridor in front of him.

'Leonarda! It's Filippo.'

'Really?' There is a scrape of chair legs against bare floorboards, and a patch of light appears at the end of the corridor. A young woman steps through a doorway and holds out her arms to him. Filippo shuts the door behind him and hurries to embrace her.

'My little brother!' She hugs him tight, then pushes him away. 'Madonna, you've grown. I haven't seen you since you made your profession.' She touches the top of his shaved scalp, gingerly.

'We don't go out,' he mutters, feeling overwhelmed and oddly shy.

'But here you are!'

'Well… I've been helping a painter during the week. Maestro Bicci. Do you remember him?'

'No, not at all. So why didn't you come sooner?'

'They let me out after morning prayers. The maestro waits

for me, and lets me go just before Vespers. They would notice if I was late. Even if I stop to take a stone out of my shoe, I get a scolding.'

'And today ...'

'The maestro's son is ill with a stomach ache. So he let me go early.' He shrugs, embarrassed. 'I came straight here.'

'Did you really?'

'Yes, really, Leonarda! To see you and ... How is she?'

His sister's mouth goes thin. 'Come and see her,' she says after a silence in which she seems to be searching him for a sign of ... what? Filippo can only guess: pity? Revulsion? Relief. He holds out his hand to her.

'Take me in, then.'

Leading him, Leonarda pauses before the open door. The light coming through it is weak: courtyard light, filtered through hanging laundry.

'She's bad today,' Leonarda whispers. She puts her arm across his shoulders, but Filippo touches her hand and steps away from her, into the room.

It is a tiny space. A big man could touch both walls with his arms outstretched. They are painted with peeling dark ochre, blotched with waving lines of damp. Here and there the bricks show through where the plaster has fallen away entirely. The only decoration is a crucifix of gilded wood, on which someone has painted a fading image of Christ. I did that years ago, Filippo remembers. I stole the paint from the men repairing the shrine down the street. I got the arms wrong. I got everything wrong. I could do it again, properly ... He is staring at the cross, he knows, because he does not want to look at the woman in the narrow bed that takes up half the room. But that is why he came here.

His mother lies back against a pile of bright-white bolsters, the brightest thing he has seen since coming in from the street. Her dark hair has been brushed out and it falls down to the faded black coverlet that is drawn up to her neck. Her long face, pale as tallow, is framed in black and she looks just as Filippo was afraid she would look: like an ancient Madonna, *ala maniera greca*. She is staring past him with huge, dark eyes, not seeing him at all, or his sister in the doorway, or the decaying walls, and her little mouth is gathered in on itself, as if refusing to smile or pout, or show anything at all.

He kneels at the side of the bed, on the floorboards. 'Mamma?' he says, but she makes no sign of having heard. He puts his hand on the coverlet, and finds that she is almost hollow beneath it, hardly there at all.

'She won't answer you,' his sister says behind him.

'Is she always like this now?'

'She has good days. When she knows who I am. We'll talk, and say our prayers together. She even goes out, sometimes. Last week we went as far as the palazzo in Piazza dei Neri. But afterwards, she always falls back into this. It's all too much. If she sees too many things, too many people...'

'So does anybody come to visit?'

'The *commesse*. You know: Monna Dianora and her friends. They come and sit with her. And bring...' She shuffles her feet uncomfortably. 'A little food, sometimes some clothes.' Filippo can hear the shame in her voice.

'How do you manage?'

'By the grace of God. And the *commesse*.'

Filippo looks around at the tiny room. 'I don't even remember what this used to be.'

'Papa used it as a storeroom. I think the Confraternity kept things in here, for their processions.'

'And what about you? Where do you live?'

'In the other room. It's the kitchen as well,' she says, trying to put some pride into her voice, some defiance. Filippo looks past her. The room across the corridor, as far as he can see, is even smaller than this one, with a crude fireplace, a smoke-blackened wall and a rolled-up mattress under an old pine bench.

'Why, Leonarda?'

'Because it's my duty,' she says, but she isn't angry. 'To stay here. Just as it was your duty to leave us, so we didn't have to feed another mouth.'

'Does she ever talk about me?'

'No,' she says simply.

'That's ... That's good. I've been a bad son.' He leans close to her, noticing how her almost translucent skin holds a mad tracery of fine, threadlike veins. 'Mamma?' he whispers. 'I pray for you every day. It's all I can do. Every day, though, Mamma.' He stands, backs away from the bed. 'I should go back to the convent now. Perhaps I shouldn't have come. I might have upset her.'

'No, you haven't. I'm sorry, Filippo: she doesn't know you're here.' He tries to squeeze past her, but she catches his arm. 'It's better you live at the convent, Pippo. I couldn't bear to see you running out in the streets. I'm not scared for you now.'

'Were you ever?' Filippo does not mean to be angry, but somehow he cannot stop the heat from getting into his words.

'Always.'

He grabs the door latch, throws open the door. A couple of old women stop gossiping in the courtyard and turn their faces up towards him. They must know who he is: the guttersnipe who became a friar, the good-for-nothing son of the man who once owned this building, who had been a good man ... he can almost hear their thoughts. What had Signor Tommaso done, to die young and leave such a disaster? A mad wife, a mad son and a spinster daughter. It wasn't always like this! He wants to shout. There were people laughing, and the brothers of Saint Agnes coming and going ... And respect. But friars don't shout at old women, and besides, if he opens his mouth, he thinks that he will cry.

'I'm sorry, Filippo. Will you come again?' His sister is in the shadow of the corridor. He stops on the stone landing. Somehow, next to the mould-blackened walls of her home, she looks like a being just descended from Heaven. *Leonarda is only twenty*, Filippo realises with a shock, as if it were impossible to be young

56

in this place. Her skin is white, unblemished. She still has the small, delicately upturned nose he remembers, the same mouth, the same pout that could be happy or sad. *But sooner or later, she'll turn into Mamma, old and empty.* He cannot bear to think of his sister's face transformed into the face of some ancient Madonna hidden away in a forgotten chapel that no-one visits.

'I'm going to be a painter, Leonarda,' he blurts out. 'I'll make a lot of money and save you and Mamma. I promise.' Then he turns and almost hurls himself down the steps, taking them two at a time, the hem of his robe clenched in his fist. Ignoring the two old ladies who are staring at him with mouths like the ends of drainpipes, he runs out into the street.

The people of the Green Dragon have seen most things, and not much makes them turn away from their business, but the sight of a young friar, habit flapping, white mantle flowing out behind him, pounding down Borgo San Frediano as though all the imps of the Inferno were chasing him, is worth a look. Some of them recognise young Pippo Lippi. Some laugh, others cross themselves and spit or make horns with their fingers to ward off the evil eye. Filippo doesn't see them. He lets his feet carry him past the end of the long piazza that leads to the Carmine, across Via dei Serragli, all the way to Santo Spirito. He finally stops, panting, when he sees three boys standing on the corner of one of the alleys that lead down to the Arno.

'Albertino!' he calls when he has caught his breath. 'Nuzzio!' He doesn't know who the third boy is: he is short, his face badly scarred by smallpox. The boys scowl, peer at him under the flats of their hands. Then the tallest grins.

'Pippo lo Schizza! What the fuck?'

Filippo walks over and the two boys hug roughly. Albertino grabs a fistful of the Carmelite mantle in his dirty hand, holds it up.

'Look at this!' he says in unfeigned wonder. 'They've washed all your sins away!'

The other two boys gather round. Filippo sees that the scarred one is an acquaintance called Tonio.

'What happened to you?' he asks.

'The pox,' says Albertino. 'We call him Bonafortuna now. He can't speak, though: the pox took that away.' Bonafortuna grins and nods his head. He prods Filippo in the chest and crosses himself.

'I'll pray for you! Of course I will,' says Filippo. 'And what are you doing today, gentlemen?'

'What are we doing? What does it look like? What are *you* doing: that's the question.' Albertino pulls himself up with a bit of a swagger, and Filippo understands he is being told that this is not his patch any more.

'I'm taking a little holiday,' he says.

'From what? Good food, dry bed?' Albertino is beginning to sneer.

'Or is it the buggery?' Nuzzio makes a gargoyle face and pumps his fist back and forth. 'Does it get a bit tiring?'

'It isn't like that,' says Filippo.

'So what is it, then? Showing up here after all these years, just to see if we're still alive?' snaps Albertino.

'Yes. I wanted to see you. As a matter of fact, I wanted a game of dice.'

'*As a matter of fact . . .*' Nuzzio warbles effetely and minces around Bonafortuna, who grins and makes a horrible rasping noise that might be laughter.

'What have you got to bet with? Monks don't have money.' Albertino reaches into his tunic and pulls out a shiny silver *grosso*. The fleur-de-lys of Florence catches the sunlight. Filippo hasn't seen one of these for a long time. Lily on one side Saint John on the other. That would buy a lot of food. Albertino flicks it up in the air and catches it. Flick, catch. Flick, catch. With every toss of the coin, Albertino seems to get more angry. Filippo wonders if he had ever been this angry, when this was his life. He could get angry now. He doesn't really know what he is doing here.

Then he remembers his mother, alive and dead at the same time, and the dark, choking decay of what had once been his home. He needs to get as far away from that place as he can. Isn't this what he has always done? And now he knows what he wants: to see the dice roll, to feel that desperate little spark of excitement as they come to rest. He looks around.

'See that bloke over there?' he says, pointing to a surly young man lounging in a doorway, dressed in the very pinnacle of the year's fashion. His legs, in tight orange hose, are crossed, the better to show off his fine red boots, and a long sword hangs from his belt. He is cooing at every woman who walks by, and kissing the air lasciviously. 'If I win, I get your *grosso*. If I lose, I'll go over and kick his arse as hard as I can.' The three boys turn and consider the young *bravo*, who, seeing a couple of other sword-wearing dandies approach, has pasted an arrogant snarl across his face.

'That's your life against a *grosso*, I'd say,' Nuzzio considers. 'Have your brains gone soft since they locked you up in the convent?'

Two more women walk past, but they are more interested in the four boys – the Carmelite friar in the company of three urchins – than the *bravo*, who is sticking his chest out like a courting pigeon, all to no avail. One of the ladies catches his eye. She looks quite shocked, but she is pretty, so Filippo grins at her. She says something outraged to her companion and they hurry on.

'He's not going to kill a friar,' says Albertino, plainly intrigued. 'But he'll do you some damage. You never were any good in a fight.'

'There you go, then,' says Filippo. 'You're always lucky, Albertino. It's got to be a safe bet, eh?'

'Well...' Albertino rubs the coin between thumb and fingers, caressing the silver lovingly. 'You're on. When he gets to work on you, we'll be taking bets on how long you last.'

Bonafortuna digs inside his breeches and pulls out two dirty bone cubes. 'Best of three?' says Albertino.

'One throw, highest wins,' says Filippo.

Albertino frowns, makes his decision. 'To hell with it. Let's go.' He leads them into the shadows of the alley, and they squat down behind an abandoned handcart. Bonafortuna gestures for the coin, takes it, points at Filippo. 'Saint or lily?'

'Lily,' Filippo says. The boy sends the coin flickering up, catches it, holds it out. The figure of John the Baptist looks up at Filippo. Bonafortuna gives the coin and the dice to Albertino, who glances at Filippo. 'Ready?' he asks.

'Throw,' says Filippo, and rubs his hands together. Albertino clicks the dice between his fingers, raises his fist to his ear, throws. The dice clatter on the flagstones, hit the back wall, spin and settle. The boys all crane in, bumping shoulders. A five and a six.

'Oho!' Albertino crows. 'Eleven to beat! There's going to be a thrashing, all right!'

'Can you give us your nice white cloak?' says Nuzzio. 'Before it gets blood all over it?'

'Maybe,' says Filippo. He gathers up the dice. A warm glow is creeping through him. The flesh, he thinks. You can lull it to sleep, but it's so quick to wake up again. He rubs the dice between his palms, relishing the clatter of bone on bone. In the old days he would have prayed to the Madonna del Popolo, but that doesn't seem right.

'Throw then, *cagniuola*,' says Albertino, his voice cracking with excitement.

So he makes a fist around the dice, knocks the knuckles against his forehead and throws. The dice jump and clatter.

'That'll be two sixes for the boy from the Carmine,' he says, as they spin and come to rest. 'Who's the bitch now, eh?'

'You *bastard*!' shouts Albertino. He is staring at Filippo, his mouth open, all his teeth on show. Then he throws back his head and bellows with laughter. 'You lucky bugger! Here!' He shoves the *grosso* into Filippo's hand. 'What are you going to spend it on?'

'I don't know,' says Filippo truthfully. He hasn't thought about it. 'I should put it in the offering plate, I suppose.'

'You should,' says Albertino seriously. 'And we should go. The whole of the Green Dragon will know there's a friar down here making crazy bets. We don't want you to end up in the nick.'

They leave the alley and Albertino buys them each a meat pie from a hawker, making a show of all the coins he has stashed in his tunic. He so plainly wants Filippo to ask him how he came by them that Filippo almost asks, but then he stops himself. He is not ready to be Albertino's confessor. They wander down to the river, where they sit and watch the swimmers dive off the piers of the Ponte Santa Trinità. Nuzzio and Albertino keep up a constant patter of commentary: that one's a whoremaster, that one a cuckold; the thin one's a notorious bugger, those are his little friends; we robbed that one outside the Fico Tavern; that one pinched Bonafortuna's arse. They throw stones at the crows who hop around at the water's edge, fighting over scraps from the slaughterhouses upstream. No-one asks Filippo anything about the convent. It seems to worry, even scare them. At last Filippo decides it's time to go. It is good, to be sitting here, drenched in profanity and all the dirty minutiae of city men, but then again he isn't quite here. He feels himself hovering just outside the picture in front of him: the sluggish summer river, the splashing men and boys, the strutting black birds. It is his robes, he supposes, and his tonsure, but he does not fit here any more. Strange: he only lives a few minutes' walk from here, but he might be watching the goings-on of Indians or Circassians: it all seems barbarous, somehow, and exciting, but he can't get hold of any of it. It slips past him like an exciting dream. He gets up and brushes off his mantle.

'Goodbye, lads,' he says. 'I must be back for Vespers.'

The three boys don't get up. Instead they reach out and pat his legs amicably.

'Good to see you. You're as mad as ever, Pippo,' says Albertino.

'Yes, still the same Pippo,' adds Nuzzio, but Filippo can tell they don't mean it. As he walks away, he hears Nuzzio call out falteringly behind him: 'Pray for us!'

If he hadn't heard that, he will decide later, he might have gone straight back to the Carmine. But something in his heart rebels. The thought of praying for his friends, to have their lives weighing on his... And should he not pray for all of them? The thieves and the seducers, the swindlers, the boy-chasers, the pandars, all those bodies flailing in the dirty river? He does not want that responsibility! In the shadow of Santo Spirito, he stops and hugs himself tightly, as if to warm his body, though the day is still warm. There is enough on his conscience already. He is a bad monk: even now he is letting the prior down with his behaviour, and all his brother monks, and the memory of his father, and the Confraternity... He can almost hear the whole of the Green Dragon tut-tutting at him, not in surprise, but because *we told you so.*

There must be something of the old Pippo left after all, because a voice inside him says: might as well be hanged for a sheep as for a lamb. He shakes his head, but the voice will not keep quiet. These inner arguments have become quite familiar to him. Friars are supposed to do this: to struggle with the Devil and his temptations. But they aren't supposed to give in. He is not sitting in his dormitory, though, or in the chapter house. He isn't Fra Filippo. He is Pippo Lippi in a borrowed Carmine habit, Pippo who fends for himself. Who makes his own choices.

Instead of turning west, he walks in the other direction, winding through the streets until he reaches the Ponte Vecchio. Half the people he passes stare, the other half look away, but he tells himself he is in disguise, and ignores them. The bridge is crowded – the bridge is always crowded. The air is heavy, salty and laced with iron from the blood and hanging meat in all the butcher shops that line the parapets. Almost across, he pauses in front of a busy shop, where the butcher is hacking steaks from a carcass while his assistant wraps them in chestnut leaves and sells them to an eager line of customers. *BALDI*, says the sign above the front. It used to be *LIPPI*. Filippo can still remember standing in there, by the window, listening to knives hissing through flesh, cleavers splintering bone. He had first drawn a picture in there, a portrait of his father's assistant, whose name he can't even remember. And just there, on the sawdust, among the blood and the bone splinters, his father had fallen down and died.

The assistant sees a young friar staring at him. He raises his hand, whispers something to his master, who does something with his knife, flicks a perfect round of tenderloin onto a leaf. Grinning, the assistant wraps it and holds it out to Filippo.

'For you, young brother! Pray for us!'

Everyone is staring at him. Filippo watches his own hand reach out from beneath the white mantle, take the cold, softly yielding little packet. He stares at it, looks up, at the man, at the butcher, at all the people, the men and women, all gazing at him with hungry, desperate eyes.

'Bless you,' he stammers. 'Bless you all!'

Then he is running again, on aching, blistered feet, back across the bridge. He dives into Oltrarno, wanting the streets to swallow him, to make him nobody again, but the crowds part and let him through. He runs until he is almost at the southernmost gate of the city, until the pain in his feet and ankles forces him to stop. He doubles over, panting, diaphragm knotting up beneath his ribs. The little package of meat is still in his hand, and a little blood has spilled through his fingers. Reluctantly, he peels back the tooth-edged leaves. The flesh glistens, red as a cardinal's robe. The butcher's son can tell it is prime, a couple of days wages for a poor worker. He sniffs the iron perfume of it. His jaw tingles and his dry mouth starts to moisten. Bless us...

He turns back towards the city, shaking his head, trying to get all the faces out of it. How strange that just this morning he had been straining for the smallest glimpse of people through

Maestro Bicci's window ... And then one face detaches itself from the whirling mass: the girl who had been stopped by the sound of doves' wings, who had stood there in the street, looking up, as if she had heard angels passing above Florence.

Back along Borgo San Frediano he goes, slower now, feeling the eyes following him, imagining the whispering, the heads shaking. He has to force himself up the steps to his mother's door. Taking the *grosso* from his habit, he tucks it into the leaves around the piece of meat. When Leonarda opens the door to his knock, he holds the grubby parcel out to her.

'The best *bistecca*, Leonarda. For Mamma.'

His sister takes the meat frowning, presses the leaves with her thumb and holds it up to her nose. Her fingers find the coin.

'Where did you get this, Pippo?' He winces at the suspicion in her voice.

'It's a gift from ... From the *commesse*.'

'Really?'

'Yes. From Saint Agnes herself. I've got to run, Narda.'

When he is standing out in the street again, the late afternoon breeze wafting clean smells through the Porta San Frediano, he finds he can't go back to the Carmine, not yet. Via del Campuccio is not far away. He limps along, and when he turns into the street he sees that the western sky is beginning to flush with pink. He thinks he remembers where di Pressi the weaver lives: quite far down, almost to the Camaldolese convent. There are fewer people here, and perhaps they are used to friars coming and going, because they pay hardly any attention to him. He studies the buildings, trying to drag some recognition up out of his memory. Signor Pressi was something to do with the Confraternity, and Filippo had run an errand for him once before he had entered the cloister, pageant business, fetching something ... But nothing looks familiar. None of the passers-by look friendly to ask – they've always been a little frosty, this side of the Green Dragon. He is almost at the end of the street, when he passes a blank space in the line of buildings, a patch of waste ground where a house once stood. The family that lived there would all have died of the Black Death, and the house, ownerless, would have fallen in on itself, to be scavenged for its stones and wood and tiles until only this patch of rubbish-strewn brown grass remains. The city is still full of these empty places, though the great plague had been seventy years ago. Filippo has spent half his life in them, playing, hiding, sleeping. In this particular hole in the city sits a young woman, cross-legged, leaning against a half-dead oak sapling. There is a baby in her arms and she is suckling it unselfconsciously, staring up at the pigeons strutting along the eaves of the houses across the street. Her breast, which she is steadying between two splayed fingers, is being noisily enjoyed by the child, whose head is an untidy mass of knotted, reddish-brown curls. The woman herself must be the same age as Leonarda, but Filippo recognises the signs of rough living in the chapped skin of her face, in the shadows under her eyes. Filippo wonders if she knows this street, or if she has just wandered here. But perhaps...

'Monna,' he asks, politely showing her he assumes she is married or a widow, 'do you know where Signor Pressi the weaver lives?'

'Pressi?' The woman shifts her bottom on the ground and beams up at him. 'I've never heard of him.'

'I think he has a daughter. Tall, fair... pretty.'

'Well, Florence is full of such as that. But I don't think on this street.'

Filippo sighs and hangs his head. Somehow he knows the woman is right. The girl he had seen from Bicci's studio could have been anyone. Or perhaps he hadn't seen her at all. Just a thing he had wanted to see, brought to life by his idle, unfit mind. Without thinking he kicks at a block of rotten wood and sits down on it, almost shoulder to shoulder with the suckling woman. She seems so calm, so untouched by life. Except, of course, she is anything but that.

'What's his name?' he asks, nodding at the baby.

'It's a her. She's called Lucrezia. Aren't you, precious? Aren't you, sweet one?' The baby gurgles with irritation and scrabbles at the woman's breast with soft, ineffectual hands. 'Oh, hungry, hungry...'

There have been many fires lit on the waste ground. Charcoal is crunching under his feet. He finds a charred piece of twig, looks around for something to draw on. There is nothing, but this is something he must do, he realises. The day, all his follies and stupidities, have led him here. Our Lady has been guiding him all along. So she won't mind if he does this: turn the corner of his white mantle over, pull it tight across his lap, start to run the charcoal across the rough weave, which does not want to take a line, but if he presses hard enough...

The woman has gone back to studying the pigeons. Maybe she is a little soft in the head. Maybe hunger – hers and the child's – has loosened her wits. He draws her face, tilted up, eyes unfocused, mouth a little open, the little girl's fist reaching up for a strand of her hair. He draws the girl's fat cheeks, though he can't show the streaks of milk and dirt. On the rough wool of the mantle her matted hair becomes delicate wisps, her greedy little mouth becomes polite. He cannot catch the desperate suction of her feeding, the angry love in her eyes as she stares up at her mother, but he tries.

It does not take long. When he has done all he can, he sighs and throws down the piece of charcoal. The woman glances over, sees the image on the mantle and gives another soft, warm smile. Filippo isn't sure she has even realised what it is that he's done. His heart comes to life at last. He wants to take her in his arms, to kiss her smile, to wipe the dirt from her baby's cheek. But he is Fra Filippo again, late for Vespers, with a desecrated mantle and blistered feet.

'Will you say a prayer for us, little brother?'

'I'd better go now. I'm late.' He stands up. 'But... Yes, I will say a prayer for you.'

She beams at him again, but then the child finally succeeds

in grabbing her hair and she chuckles and whispers as she prises open the little fist and presses it against her cheek. Filippo backs away, hoping she will look up again but knowing that she will not. So he turns and hurries away down the street, wincing as his sandals chafe the blisters on his feet, hearing the pigeons clap their wings and burble on the eaves. The evening fires are being lit.

Filippo knows what is in store for him. The prior will already have heard that young Fra Filippo has been running wild in the streets. Gone back to his old ways. Who will be surprised? The gossip will have filtered into the convent through the church from delighted or disgusted reporters. He will walk into silence. His brother friars will turn their backs on him. There will be heavy penances: he will eat dry bread on the stone floor of the refectory, he will sing psalms for hours in the chapter house with his hands tied behind his back. He will have to seek forgiveness from every one of his brothers. There will be no visit to Maestro Bicci on Friday, and perhaps he will never be allowed there again. And indeed, when he limps into the Carmine, the eyes of the brothers almost flay the skin from his face, even though he is not − quite − late for prayer. The sub-prior − stern, passionate Fra Mariano − herds him wordlessly to the prior, Fra Pietro di Francesco, in whose scriptorium he stands, enduring the lash of both men's tongues, until Fra Mariano, noticing a further transgression, the dirtying of his pure white mantle, grabs the hem and lifts it.

The two priors fall silent. Without speaking, Fra Mariano unclasps the mantle and lifts it carefully from Filippo's shoulders. He holds it up.

'Is this what you were doing today?' he asks. Fra Mariano, whose sermons draw people from all over Tuscany, has a deep, rich voice. Filippo feels utterly wretched. He might as well be standing naked, waist-deep in ice like Judas in the Ninth Circle of Hell which is reserved for betrayers. But the priors are not looking at him. They are studying the drawing of the young mother from Via del Campuccio. 'Yes,' he answers.

'Go to Vespers,' says the prior. 'Fra Filippo ...' He clicks his tongue. 'You are filthy. Wash your feet. Then join your brothers in prayer.'

Filippo nods. 'Yes, Your Reverence.' He is sure that they are about to say something else, but they are standing silently, their faces like carvings. So he limps out of the room, feeling every step he has taken today, feeling blood between his soles and the leather of his sandals. He needs to pray. He has so many people, suddenly, to pray for.

6

THE MORNING AFTER FILIPPO'S TRANSGRESSIONS, the prior
summons him while the friars are assembling to sing Terce. He
limps through the cloister, the others staring. A couple of them
have doubtless laid bets, he knows, as to what will happen to
him. Whipping is leading the odds, or imprisonment. He has
been shunned at each of the four night services, when he has
risen, stiff and sore, to sing and pray in the dark church. He
has sung with all his might, raising his cracked, tuneless voice
to the looming shadows of the ceiling. At Matins, at Lauds in
the dead hours of the night. And he has prayed, as hard as he
has ever prayed in his life, to the Madonna del Popolo. She is
there, far away in a side chapel, lit only by a single candle, but
he can picture her in his mind anyway. Her lips are not pursed
in amusement, but in disapproval. Her pale face and huge eyes
are looking straight at him, he knows. They have seen the ruin
of his soul. No, worse: they find him pitiful. And still he prays,
eyes squeezed so tight that his head aches. In the thin dawn light
of Prime, the Madonna's face becomes his mother's, framed with
black hair streaked with grey, wide eyes, not blind but seeing
nothing. His throat is so raw by now that he can hardly make a
sound, which is a small mercy, because he is sobbing, not singing.

'I am sending you to the cloister in Pisa,' says the prior. His
lined face is even more expressionless than usual. 'And I would
like you to leave immediately. Happily, Ser Giacomo Nerli's agent
is going in the same direction, and I have made arrangements
for you to ride with him. He should be waiting in the piazza.'

Filippo does not dare to open his mouth. Blinking like an owl in daylight, he watches the prior scribble a letter to his counterpart in Pisa, as he wonders, in growing terror, if he is being banished from Florence for ever. He has been to Pisa. Every year the friars of the Carmine go there to celebrate the Feast of the Annunciation. But only for a couple of days, and he remembers nothing about the city save that it is cold and damp and the bread tastes wrong. Is he being sent away for good? He'd rather be expelled outright. Then at least he would be taking his chances on the streets of Oltrarno. He thinks of Albertino and Nuzzio. Would they welcome him back as one of their own tattered brotherhood, or would he be an outcast from that as well? He stands, shifting from one leg to the other. One of his blisters has started bleeding again.

'What am I to do there, Your Reverence?' he croaks at last. He can barely speak anyway, after last night's singing.

'You will help,' says the prior, simply, holding out the letter. There is the merest ghost of a smile on his lips. 'Go.'

Filippo has owned nothing since the day the boys from the Scala had taken his bag. So there is nothing to do except to bow to the prior and leave. He goes out into the cloister, then into the church. The choir is empty but a few black-swathed women from the *commesse* are walking slowly up the aisle. Filippo puts his head down. He does not want any of them to recognise him, not now. The main door is open and he can see the piazza, but instead he turns away from it and walks quickly around the corner of the transept to Felice Brancacci's chapel. Eve is waiting for him. Her hip seems to be tilted a little more provocatively today, as if she knows the serpent can feel the warmth of her skin against its cold flesh. But her faint smile seems rueful, as though she has already bitten into the fruit and found it sour: not worth the calamity that will surely follow. His flesh stirs obediently under her gaze, and he sighs. Not today, he thinks, and drags his gaze away to the fresco beside the doomed couple. Masolino has painted Saint Peter raising the good woman Tabitha from the dead, but Filippo has decided the figures are too dated, too mannered. The piazza behind is much more interesting, because it looks real. It is Masaccio's work, and Filippo notices what he has not seen before: the street that leads off the square into the distance is the same street that Peter is walking down on the opposite wall, touching the sick with his shadow. Somehow he finds this detail cheering. He crosses the chapel and tries to imagine himself crouching against the wall, trying to catch a stranger's eye with his drawing pad – waiting for the grey *cursus* of the shadow to reach him.

'Pippo Lippi?'

Filippo spins on his heel. The chapel has filled, silently, with the widows, and Monna Dianora is standing beside him, looking up at the wall. 'Monna!' he exclaims, knowing he sounds guilty, but then again, at least she hasn't caught him ogling the naked charms of Eve. 'I'm so pleased to see you!'

'Are you?' Monna Dianora says sceptically.

'I ... Yes! Always!' Filippo is trying to think when he last saw the *commessa*. In the congregation at mass, at the pageant of Saint Agnes; but they have not spoken for years. He has never forgotten that day, though, when she and her sisters had found him, bloody and defeated, limping down Borgo San Frediano. 'You know, Monna, I never thanked you and the other *commesse* for taking pity on me. For bringing me here.'

'Oh, nonsense,' says the woman. 'That was not pity. It was common sense.' She sniffs, looks him over with her sharp, flickering eyes. 'And does it suit you here?'

'Very much,' says Filippo eagerly, though he feels the words sting like vinegar in his mouth. *I can't tell her I've just been banished, can I? That I'm the same little beggar she's always known?*

'You used to make pictures of people, I remember,' the widow says. 'You must find all this to your liking.' She flicks a bony hand at the walls of the chapel.

'It is wonderful,' says Filippo, glad to be able to tell her the truth about something. 'And you, Monna? Do you like it?'

She looks at him, brows lifted, unblinking. 'It is partly because of us, the *commesse*, that Ser Felice has this place decorated,' she says. 'I approve, certainly. My sisters and I would approve far more if it were actually finished. When will that be, do you suppose? Have you any insight, Fra Pippo?'

'I'm afraid not,' he says, wincing. 'Maestro Masolino is in Hungary ...'

'We know,' says the widow briskly. 'And the other one?'

'The rumour is that Maestro Masaccio has gone to Arezzo to make an altarpiece,' he tells her. 'I expect he'll be back any day now. I saw him here a few weeks ago, though we didn't speak together. Perhaps if you asked the prior?'

'Fra Pietro is too busy to be bothered by the silly anxieties of women,' she says, though Filippo is sure she thinks no such thing.

'But it will be finished soon,' he says, though that doesn't seem to be true at all. There are huge gaps on each wall.

'Artists ...' Monna Dianora mutters, shaking her head. Then she smiles and touches Filippo's sleeve. 'I am glad to have seen you, Pippo. I'll tell your mother. You haven't seen her, of course, but I visit every few days.'

'I'm sure she is grateful,' says Filippo, remembering the empty stare of the woman in bed. 'I did see her just ...' He hesitates. '*I'm* grateful, Monna. You know that, don't you?'

'You do not need to be grateful, Pippo. But thank you. Say a prayer for me.'

'For all of you. Well, I must go. And Monna?'

'Yes, Pippo?'

'Tell Mamma that I ... That I pray for her. I do. At least, I try.' He slips clumsily past her and almost runs down the aisle of the church towards the sunlight. Out in the piazza he sees a paunchy, middle-aged man with grey hair escaping from under an almost fashionable black hat standing next to a large brown horse. A boy is holding its reins in one hand, and with the other is gripping the bridle of a mouse-grey mule.

'Are you the friar who's coming with me?' says the man brusquely.

'Could be, if you're going to Pisa,' says Filippo. Out here in the busy piazza, he has already felt his desperate mood begin to release its grip.

'Mount up, then, brother. I'd like to get as far as Montopoli today.' Grunting, he hauls himself into his saddle.

'Thank you, sir, but you know, friars are supposed to walk,' says Filippo.

'Your prior has given you a dispensation,' says the man absently, trying to find the most comfortable spot for his ample arse. 'Well, come on!' he adds. 'My master, Ser Giacomo – his brother is one of you friars: Fra Albizzo. *He* always rides.'

'Well, in that case ...' Filippo climbs inexpertly onto the mule. The young groom gives him the reins, and before he knows it he is trotting through the Porta San Frediano.

Ser de' Nerli's agent is called Berto, and proves to be a garrulous companion, which is fortunate, because Filippo's spirits plunge as soon as Florence drops out of sight behind them. Berto doesn't notice that his young charge is sinking further and further into gloom with every mile that passes, and chatters on and on about matters pertaining to the immortal soul – *his* immortal soul, to be exact. Filippo jogs along, the mule's narrow back cutting into his tender parts, wishing the man would shut up, but trying to be as polite as he can. By the time they have reached Montopoli, an easy day's ride, he has the uneasy feeling that he may have given Berto the impression that quite a few of the man's sins have been absolved. The agent suffers from temptations of the flesh, most of them to do with the male brothels near the fish market in Florence, and from guilt over certain loans he has made to various brothers-in-law. Filippo privately doubts that even His Holiness in Rome could absolve the man for the latter, so venal are his rates of interest. But he doesn't say that out loud. Instead, he mostly agrees, nods, agrees some more, gives the sort of indulgent chuckle that, from his observations, priests seem to make when they don't have anything better to say. At least, between the jouncing of the saddle and the man's gabbling, Filippo's mind is distracted from whatever he is riding towards, and from his guilt over yesterday's escapades.

They reach Pisa at lunchtime the next day, and Berto delivers Filippo to the door of the Carmine convent, a small, brick-built church with a small, elegant cloister built on one side. It stands in the middle of gardens in the Chinzica quarter on the south side of the Arno. The quarter is less built up than the denser quarters across the river – there are gardens, vineyards and orchards, the houses thickest towards the riverbank, and though there are plenty of houses around it, the cloister feels isolated to Filippo the street urchin. The prior, Fra Antonio, greets him with a certain amount of confusion, but the letter from Fra Pietro, which he reads twice, with much lifting of eyebrows, seems to explain matters to his satisfaction. Nothing is explained to Filippo, however. He is simply shown to an empty cell and left there. There isn't much he needs to know, he thinks. The Order is the same wherever the cloister happens to be. In an hour he will go into the church for None. The Pisan cloister is very small: only sixteen friars, less than half the size of the Carmine at home: he will have met all his fellow brothers by Vespers. The mattress is hard and unforgiving to his bruised arse. He winces, wondering if the food here will be better or worse than at home. He sits and listens to the silence.

In the days that follow, Filippo tries to obey his prior's command and be as helpful as he can. He strives to be invisible when he is not being useful. But is that right? Is it what Fra Pietro wants him to do? Are any of his Pisan brothers helped? He does not know. At first he tries to make himself indispensable, but there is nothing really to do apart from pray. So he prays, and sings, and is diligent when the opportunity presents itself, though no-one seems to notice.

Do they actually know who I am? he wonders, often. Do they know why I'm here? Do they know that I'm being punished? Am I, in fact, being punished? His behaviour that day in Florence is never mentioned by the prior Fra Antonio, by the sub-prior Fra Bartolomeo; by anyone. After a week has passed he wakes up for Lauds at the dead hour of three in the morning and, as he slips on his sandals, he realises that he must have got away with it. No, no, he thinks. The Madonna heard my prayers. She looked after a boy from the Green Dragon, as she always does. You just have to ask properly.

It is one thing to escape being disciplined by the Order. Filippo is suffering, though. Sometimes he cannot bear the homesickness that overcomes him at sunset, standing in the choir singing Vespers. Although he is confined to this tiny cloister, which could really be anywhere, the air smells different. The wind sounds strange, and brings briny, marshy smells to his nose. The voices of the congregation are uncouth. Whenever he sits in contemplation, his mind sets him down in San Frediano, tempts him with the smells of good Florentine food, with the play of light on familiar walls. Worse, it leads him into the Brancacci Chapel and tilts his chin up to regard Eve. He tries to think of his sister, of her mournful life in that mouldy apartment. He tries to pray for his mother. He thinks of Saint Peter's shadow.

But every image he summons melts and changes into Eve, or the girl who had watched the doves, or Cati Serragli. There had been a serving girl at the inn in Montopoli where he had passed the night next to Berto, who had brought him the bowl of cabbage soup he had insisted on (though Berto had tried to tempt him with a pheasant), a sultry, fierce-eyed girl with thick chestnut hair, pouting lips and the hint of a double chin, and breasts that danced beneath her tunic. She had caught him staring at her and widened those eyes in feigned outrage and Filippo had felt the air thicken with unspoken thoughts – his, but hers as well. But then the landlord had shouted to her from the kitchen and she had vanished in a flounce of linen and he had gone back to Berto's endless confessions.

There is only one way he can think of to banish these faces that haunt him. So he finds some letters that are being thrown out of the library – just ancient accounting lists, nothing of a sacred nature, he is careful to check – and, every morning, at an hour when he can slip off into a corner and pretend to be deep in contemplation, he begins to draw.

At first his hand falters. It wants to work, but Filippo's confidence is shaky. He draws the first things that come into his mind: the swimmers from the Arno. At first he scribbles out one figure after another. He throws the vellum away, but fishes it out of the pile where it waits to be burned, and starts again. He draws Prior Pietro, frowning. He draws Bonafortuna's pox-ravaged face. He draws a man about to dive from the bridge. He draws a baby waving fat fists at the sky. Sparrows, pigeons, cats: whatever comes before his eyes, he draws. But no girls, no women: not even a study for a Virgin. He doesn't dare let his imagination drift into thoughts of the flesh. Instead, he uses the Rule to keep himself in check. If his skill is a gift from Heaven, as everyone has always said, he will use it to honour Our Lady. He won't let his soul, dirty and disordered like the streets of the Green Dragon, corrupt her gift. For a precious slice of time each day, he feels his hand tune itself to his eyes, so that they begin to dance together. He hides his work inside his bedding, and makes sure that it remains a secret.

★

Summer slips away, and the autumn of 1426 begins to ebb. Cold winds blow off the sea and rattle the shutters of the city. One day towards the end of October, Filippo is sitting in his cell, as deep in contemplation as he ever gets, when a friar puts his head around the door. The prior is asking for him. Filippo follows the man, but the prior is not in his study but in the church, where he is standing, talking to a young man in a deep red tunic, a man with wiry black hair and a long nose.

'Maestro Masaccio!' Filippo says before he can stop himself. The prior, a thin, rather stooped man with a gentle face and kind eyes – Filippo has drawn him many times by now – shakes his head in mild reproval, and beckons him over.

'Fra Filippo Lippi. You know Tommaso di Ser Cassai, do you? Of course you do.'

'Yes, Reverend Father! The maestro here has been painting a chapel at our church in Florence. But ... I thought you were in Arezzo, maestro!'

'Why would I be in Arezzo?' says Masaccio. 'I've been here. And in Florence. And back here.'

'The *commesse* of Saint Agnes are furious with you!' Filippo tells him. 'They want the chapel finished. Monna Dianora ...' He glances at the prior, lifts his hands in embarrassment. 'Sorry, Reverend Father! I shouldn't gossip.'

'I've done a bit more in the chapel since you've ... since you saw it last,' says Masaccio. 'Which is why you haven't seen *me* before this. My plans are all over the place. You were meant to ...'

'Meant to what?' says Filippo, puzzled.

'To help me,' says Masaccio, as though it is the most obvious thing in the world.

To help. Filippo hears Fra Pietro's words, remembers the prior's fleeting smile as he'd spoken them. 'Forgive me, maestro, Reverend Father, but I'm lost,' he says. 'Help with what?'

'With my altarpiece,' says Masaccio. 'But we must have passed on the road, or near as damn it – your pardon, Reverend Father,' he adds. 'I had to go back to Florence, got stuck working in the chapel ... Meanwhile, Ser Giuliano degli Scarsi has been going mad here in Pisa, waiting for his altarpiece to be finished. I'm shockingly behind on both, now.'

'When is the altarpiece due?' asks the prior.

'December 26th,' says Masaccio, heavily. 'As you know, prior, as it was you who drew up the contract.'

The prior inclines his head. 'Indeed,' he says quietly. 'So it appears we are potentially in some difficulty.'

'*We*, prior? *I* am in some difficulty,' says Masaccio.

'I can assure you that Ser Giuliano is breathing down my neck just as hotly as he is down yours,' says the prior, chuckling. 'More hotly, in fact. I would be *so* grateful to you, my son, if you could just finish the damned thing and set us all free.'

Filippo looks at the prior in amazement. But Masaccio sighs and drags his fingers through his hair. 'The Virgin is done,' he says. 'And the Crucifixion.'

'All excellent,' the prior agrees.

'The predella is finished, all except the death of Saint Peter, and that's almost done. The main saints ... they're all done to your satisfaction, yes, prior?'

'Indeed. Fine work.'

'Which leaves the pilasters.'

'And those are underway?'

'In a manner of speaking. I think you'd better come and see, Fra Antonio.' Masaccio drops his arms morosely to his sides.

'If you wish. There is a little time before the midday prayer. Fra Filippo will come with us.' Without saying another word, the prior strides towards the door, Masaccio following him gloomily. Filippo pauses. I don't have a clue what's going on, he thinks to himself. The morning has taken on the odd angles of a dream.

'Are you coming, Fra Filippo?' the prior calls from the door. Filippo looks around the empty church, feeling almost furtive, then hurries after him.

They walk briskly to the river and across the old bridge. Masaccio takes the lead, and the two Carmelites follow him through a crooked maze of streets, each one a little more disreputable than the last, until he stops in front of what looks like a disused warehouse. Filippo can see the river beyond a cluster of sagging houses. Broken barrel staves are piled against the wall, and there are shattered roof tiles and potsherds on the grass-grown cobbles of the street. Masaccio rattles a lock and stands aside to let the prior enter. Filippo follows. Inside, the building is less ramshackle, in fact the walls have been freshly whitewashed and the remains of a fire are glowing in the hearth, beneath a hanging iron pot. But everything is in chaos. Every flat surface has something piled on it, or spilled across it: pigments, eggshells, empty jars and pots, piles of wood shavings, nails, dirty plates, brushes, palette knives. Near the window, a stand put together from fresh pine lumber is supporting what looks like a very large, ornate door. The prior is already examining it, his large Adam's apple bobbing, his slightly hooked nose hovering above the surface like the beak of an eagle searching for the tastiest piece of entrail in the beast he has just caught and split apart.

'I warned you,' Masaccio says. He is poking the fire and looking with distaste at whatever is in the pot.

'You did, my son. Well ... Fra Filippo. Do come over here, won't you?'

Fillipo goes over to him obediently, and is about to ask what the prior requires of him; but all at once there is nothing to think about except the Madonna at the centre of the great panel, because she is a real woman, a being of flesh, filled with a life he recognises. And at the same time, not despite of, but because of that, she is Our Lady.

She is not very old, with a face somewhere on the border of plain and pretty, the face of a younger daughter, Filippo thinks, a face he has seen so often in church, sitting on the outskirts of large families. A girl you might glimpse through a window in the good parts of town, bent over her sewing while her older sisters laugh and gossip around her. She looks tired, too, as though the naked little boy in the crook of her arm, limbs dusted with gold, upright and confident and stuffing his tiny mouth with a fistful of the grapes his mother holds in her hand, as though the Son is not meek and mild at all, but has kept her up all night. Perhaps she is thinking of another ordeal, infinitely worse, that she will endure, which is happening above her: Jesus, stoical on the cross, looking down calmly on Mary Magdalene, who howls in grief below him, arms thrust out in the ecstasy of despair, her yellow hair incandescent against the scarlet of her robe. An older Virgin stands to the side, hands clenched in prayer, mouth set: feeling the nails in herself, feeling the thorns in her brow. I bore Him: only for this?

It is Filippo's eyes that are hungry now, darting from panel to panel, feasting on the pink of Saint Paul's robe, the sadness on the face of Saint Andrew, the way – he blinks, refusing to believe what he is seeing. At the Madonna's feet sit two angels, each playing a lute. The neck of the lute on the right seems to stick right out of the panel, the one on the left recedes into some magical space created in the vertical plane, a space which does not exist, and yet the angels are turning their ears to catch notes that are sounding in it, that Filippo himself can almost hear.

But it is the narrow panel at the bottom of the altarpiece, in the centre, that sends him, crossing himself and bowing, right up to the altar, to lean close, to lean into the painting. Mary sits on a gilded wooden chair, bowing politely and slightly worriedly as a group of richly dressed men approach her, while their servants deal with their restless horses. But here the magical space falls back behind the Magi, whose faces reveal that they are going through the motions of a diplomatic necessity and would sooner be elsewhere, back to a low, dove-coloured skyline that gives way to a far distant line of mountains, dark blue under a cloudy sky. The Wise Men might be discussing interest rates outside the Signoria, except for the bearded old gentleman who kneels and leans forward, stiffly, to kiss the foot of the infant Jesus. From between the heads of two horses, the red, sweating face of a servant appears, trying to catch Filippo's eye, trying to share a joke: oi, you! Over here!

'It is a small setback,' the prior is saying.

'Rather more than that, Reverend Father. I am on the rack!

Florence turning one wheel, Pisa the other! If Ser Giuliano won't pay me ...'

'Oh, he'll pay you, my son. But not until you've put this right.'

'What could possibly be wrong, Ser Tommaso?' Filippo is aghast.

'This. He came here to give his final approval and to pay me. Well, he has not given it. His approval is withheld, pending.'

'Oh. What? Really? Come off it!' Filippo is genuinely amazed. 'Hasn't given his approval? Why not?'

'Because of this.' Masaccio steps up to the altar and stabs a finger at the right-hand side of the frame, at one of the narrow panels that flank the Madonna. In each of them is a saint about as tall as a man's forearm, some from the Gospels, some of them wearing the brown and white robes of Carmelites. It is to one of these that Masaccio is pointing.

'Saint Albert of Trapani,' he snaps.

Filippo looks closer. 'Blessed Albert,' he agrees. 'Looks all right to me.'

'Well ...' Masaccio drops his voice. 'Honestly? I don't believe you. Look again, Fra Filippo. With the eyes you use when you draw.'

'I am going to visit a lay member who lives just around the corner,' says the prior. 'Fra Filippo, I expect to see you back in the cloister before Vespers.'

'Yes, Reverend Father.' The door opens and closes. Filippo frowns, bends close to the altarpiece. He has not really paid much attention to these outlying figures, who pale in comparison to the Crucifixion, the Adoration and the luminous Madonna. The saint in question is a Carmelite monk with a tonsure, looking ... Filippo makes himself forget the Virgin, the magnificent saints who flank her, the Crucifixion. Be honest. He clicks his tongue: it is true. The Carmelite is not well painted. He is, in fact, shockingly bad. A couple of the other small saints lack the quality of the main figures but this one ... Stiff and flat, with a face as lacking expression as a child's doll. Filippo takes a deep breath.

'It isn't great,' he admits.

'No. It's *horrifying*. I should point out that I didn't paint that. Don't look so surprised, Fra Filippo. I didn't have time for so many little pieces. So I paid a couple of acquaintances to do them. And they did a good job. All except this one. I mean, for God's sake! You can't trust anybody.'

'A friend ought to have tried a bit harder than that,' Filippo agrees.

'Friend? Ah. Well, he *is* a friend. He also happens to be my little brother Giovanni Lo Scheggia.'

Filippo whistles. 'That's bad,' he says.

'And Giovanni's a painter! You wouldn't know it from that, would you? He makes a decent living from wedding chests. Anyway, it won't do. Much as I'd rather bite off my own finger than admit old Scarsi is right, he is, damn it. Actually, it isn't his fault. The man has no taste at all, no eye. Unfortunately he is aware of his failings, which is rare enough, I suppose ... Anyway, he has given all the decision-making to your Prior Antonio, and the prior has excellent taste. The prior pointed Saint Albert out to Ser Giuliano, and now he won't pay me.' He sighs. 'He's right, though. I wouldn't pay for that either.'

'So now you have to stay and re-do Saint Albert,' says Filippo.

'No, I have to get back to Florence. The frescoes there have to be finished: everybody is breathing down my neck. And I need the money, doubly so now that ...' He stabs his finger again at the offending panel. 'So I made a proposition. Another painter. A far better one. Re-do the saint, pay the bill, we're all happy.'

'Who have you asked? Another acquaintance?'

'Fra Filippo, you need to be a bit quicker on the uptake if you're going to work for me. I haven't asked yet, but now I'm asking. Can you paint me a decent Saint Albert?'

'Me? Ser Tommaso – Ser Masaccio – no! I can't! And anyway, Prior Antonio would never agree!'

'He already has. He suggested you.'

'You're playing a trick on me, maestro. This is a *beffa*, isn't it!'

'No joking here. This is your job if you want it, young brother. Three saints, by December 26th.'

Filippo rubs his scalp. 'What makes you think I can do it?' he says at last.

'Well, can you?'

'I've done some bits and pieces for Maestro Bicci – in paint, I mean. Some heads in a crowd, hands, boots. But nothing complete. Certainly nothing important, like this!'

'I appreciate that a friar must be modest, but we don't have time. I know you're capable, brother, because when I was in Florence last month, Prior Pietro showed me something. A defaced cloak.'

'Oh, no.' Filippo pinches the bridge of his nose. 'That was terrible. A terrible thing to do, I mean. I'm ashamed. Fra Pietro should have given it to the laundress.'

'You must be joking! It is a beautiful drawing. I felt it ...' Masaccio thumps his chest with the flat of his hand. 'I could barely have done better. If you can produce something like that, three little saints won't give you any trouble. And I'll pay you.'

'Really?' Filippo is genuinely surprised.

'I pay my assistants, you know! I'm a decent master!'

'I'm sure you are. But I'm a friar. We can't accept money,' Filippo says, hoping the regret isn't obvious in his voice.

'I admire your scruples. And obviously I'd like to keep the money for myself. But no: I need an artist. Artists must be paid.'

'The prior—'

'He'll be pleased as long as this is finished. When he said that Ser Giuliano is on his back, he meant it. He's a rich man, Ser Giuliano, and he wants the best – for his reputation, and for the sake of his soul. Keeping him happy is good for the Carmine, so the prior will do whatever he needs to.' Masaccio grimaces. 'Which is lovely for Ser Giuliano, but not so lovely for me. Not that I was trying to fob my patron off with rubbish – I honestly had no idea that Scheggia would let me down like this – but it means that Fra Antonio will be paying special attention. Everything will have to be perfect.'

'Well, why don't you do the saints yourself?' says Filippo. 'Three small panels. It shouldn't take that long, surely?' He is torn. The idea of being allowed to do nothing but make pictures is almost too wonderful to bear, but then again he has taken vows, he wants nothing more than to follow the Rule... 'But just out of interest,' he finds himself asking, 'how much would you pay me?'

'Aha. So you do have the soul of an artist, Fra Filippo! I will pay you ...' Masaccio screws up his eyes and kicks at the floor like a man with a bad toothache. 'To hell with it. I will give you a florin for each picture.'

'Three florins!'

'Christ! Take it or leave it, friar! I was going to pay Scheggia seventy lire each, and that's generous. But I need this piece to be finished. I need to get back to Florence. I need everyone ... Madonna!' He raises his fists, shakes them furiously. 'Why is everything so bloody difficult?'

'No, no, maestro: honestly? Three whole florins?' Filippo has never touched a gold coin in his life. He imagines holding one up in front of Albertino ... No, not Albertino. Mamma and Leonarda.

'I'll try, maestro,' he says. 'Though I'm afraid I might let you down as well.'

'You won't,' says Masaccio. 'I'll tell you truthfully, brother: I've never seen anything quite like what you drew on that cloak. I mean I have, but in here.' He taps his head. 'Can I ask you something?' Filippo nods. 'Is that how you see the Virgin?'

'The Virgin?' Filippo looks at him in surprise. 'It wasn't the Virgin. It was just a poor woman sitting in the street with her little girl. I drew her because ... Because that is what I do. What I've always done.' And then he sees. 'You thought ... The prior thought I had drawn the Madonna!'

'You had, Fra Filippo. You had.'

'Not on purpose! But if that is how it looked … I was thinking about my mother, and about a painting Bicci was working on that day. And then I came across this poor girl, who was so beautiful. So good, maestro, even though the world had just spat her out. She didn't mind, and it broke my heart. I saw something, and I just drew it.'

'I know what you saw,' says Masaccio quietly.

Filippo goes over to the altarpiece. 'What I saw in that girl I can see in your Virgin here. You've made her a real person. I've always wondered why no-one has ever tried to do that. What it would look like.'

'And what does it look like?'

'She's tired.' Filippo hesitates. 'It isn't easy, being a mother. To one greedy little boy, let alone to the whole world. And she's just beginning to understand.'

'Really.' Masaccio rubs his chin thoughtfully. 'Understand what?'

'The weight of the world. Such a terrible burden. A terrible future: what has to happen to her little one. She isn't afraid, but she's resigned to it.'

'Isn't that the nature of our world?' Masaccio hooks the nearest chair with his foot, pulls it to him and sits down heavily. 'What good is it if we don't see the Virgin as one of us? And Christ, and the saints? Everyone has heard the scriptures. They've seen the stories painted in church. But don't you think that those stories don't involve us?'

'What do you mean?'

'We look at them, but they don't touch us. We don't see ourselves there. All those stories are for us, but they aren't about us.'

'I know you paint real people,' says Filippo. 'Like Saint Peter and the beggars. I don't recognise them, exactly, but I've probably seen them.'

Masaccio nods. 'I expect you have.'

'And the street where Peter is walking. It's just round the corner from Santo Spirito.'

'Well, have you ever been to Jerusalem?' Filippo grins, shakes his head. 'No. But you've walked down that street more times than you can count. And that's the place where you want a miracle to happen, isn't it? Where you might have a chance to be part of it?'

'When I used to sit like that, with my stomach empty and nothing in my pockets, I sometimes thought: it's going to happen. It has to. You hear people say those things, all the time. The Lord will bless me. The Holy Mother will reach out her hand.' He sighs. 'It never happens, though. I shouldn't say that, should I? Now that I'm a friar.'

'Having seen the Virgin that you drew on your cloak, I don't believe you,' Masaccio says. Then he stands up and cracks his knuckles. 'Now: have you decided?'

'I think, maestro, that I'll try and have a go at one of those miracles.'

7

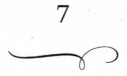

FILIPPO MISSES NONE. HE HEARS the city's bells striking three of the clock, but he is listening to Masaccio explain the secrets of mixing paint, the subtleties of shading, and many other things, more knowledge in a scant two hours than he has learned from Bicci di Lorenzo in almost a year. This has not been Bicci's fault, he realises, but his own: he had seen his time in the painter's studio as an escape from the cloister, when really it had been a school. If only he had paid attention, as he is doing now! But Masaccio seems satisfied. 'I'm going to be here until the end of the week,' he tells Filippo. 'Prior Antonio has another contract for me to sign with Ser Giuliano ... Another one! Madonna! And then I should get the twenty-five florins I'm owed. Then I've got to slip back to Florence. And here's the thing, brother. The contract I'm signing: it's me promising Ser Giuliano that I won't work on any other painting until I've finished his. But in Florence, there's Ser Felice fretting about his chapel – and your old prior is none too pleased with me either. I've got to be away for at least two weeks, more likely three – and I need a month. If Ser Giuliano happens to come around here—'

'Will he?' Filippo says, uncertainly.

'He's a bloody notary. Of course he'll come to make sure his contract is being followed to the exact damnable letter. Or perhaps he won't ...' Masaccio bites his thumbnail. 'No, he won't, most likely. But if he does, for God's sake, brother: tell him I'm in the market, or off buying paint from my man in Lucca, or ...

that I'm locked in the jakes. Anything! Something tells me you'll be able to convince him.'

'I have an honest face,' says Filippo.

Masaccio chuckles. 'Really? I hadn't noticed. Do you play cards, Fra Filippo?'

'I play – *used* to play at dice. Everybody plays at dice,' he adds hurriedly.

'Your honest face tells me that when you play, perhaps you go a little bit further than most people. Forgive my guess ... But I would say that is how you go through life.'

'I wouldn't know,' mumbles Filippo. He feels as if the artist's sharp eyes are carving him up. It is not unpleasant, exactly, but he is used to keeping things hidden.

'I think I'm right. That's the painter's way, young brother: take life in your fists. Shake it. Squeeze the juice out of it. And when the patron comes knocking ...' He makes a fist and throws invisible dice.

'All on one throw?'

'Always!' Masaccio slaps Filippo's knee. Then he winces. 'Do you think I'll go to hell for saying such things to a Carmelite?'

Filippo shakes his head ruefully. 'I wish I could say yes to that, maestro. But I'm a pretty poor excuse for a friar. I don't think I have the power of damnation. You're safe. That's just me, though.' He grins. 'I can't speak for all of us. I wouldn't, for example, try it with Prior Pietro.'

It is getting dark by the time they leave the studio. 'I should take you back to the cloister,' says Masaccio. 'But ... Would you like to take a quick stroll?'

'If I can be back by Vespers,' Filippo says.

'We're not going far,' says Masaccio. 'And I thought you might like to meet someone else from Florence.'

'I would!' Filippo says, though Masaccio is already walking away. I should go back, thinks Filippo. But if I'm with the maestro, it should be all right.

They cross the busy street that leads to the bridge in one direction, and to the Carmine in the other, and through narrower streets filled with the smell of kale leaves frying in lard. Masaccio stops and knocks on a door in a tall building that has been built out from a fortified tower. He knocks again, then opens it and calls: 'Eh! It's me!'

There is an echoed salutation from deep inside. They head towards it through a somewhat damp corridor. At the back of the house, a half-open door leads to a small, high-ceilinged room, a part of the ancient tower, Filippo decides. The space is cramped but two large doors are wide open, revealing a courtyard with a marble well in its centre. For a moment, Filippo thinks that a company of fat, naked people are lolling about on the flagstones of the yard, but no, they are rough blocks of white stone. In front of the door is a heavy easel, more of a scaffold of thick timbers, and on it, a rectangle of marble. Something crunches under Filippo's sandals. He looks down, and finds that the floor is strewn with white marble chippings.

'Tommaso! Masaccio! Dear one!' A very Florentine voice, and then a man appears from behind a drop cloth that is hanging from the ceiling. He is around forty, thinks Filippo, with a long-nosed angular face, the bottom of which is adorned with a neatly forked, greying beard. The man's head is wrapped in a cloth that may once have been black but is thick with whitish dust. 'Old fellow!' The man grabs Masaccio and kisses him hard on both cheeks. Then his large, twinkling eyes come to rest on Filippo.

'What have we here? A Carmelite, no less?' He plants his feet apart and props his fists on his hips, studying Filippo curiously.

'This is Fra Filippo Lippi of San Frediano,' says Masaccio.

'Is he your new confessor?' By his manner, Donatello seems to find this thought quite amusing.

'No, though I ought to have one. He's my new assistant.'

'Indeed? Are you a painter, then, Fra Filippo of San Frediano?'

'Maestro Masaccio seems to think he can make me into one,' says Filippo. The man looks very familiar, but he can't quite …

'This is Donato Bardi, Pippo,' Masaccio says.

'Now I know you! You're Donatello!' Filippo exclaims. 'I've seen you in Santa Maria, sir! You were helping Maestro Brunelleschi with the Saint Agnes pageant.'

'Aha: and there was a young friar there a couple of years ago, who quite astonished my friend with a drawing he'd made of a clumsy assistant. Would that be you?'

'I have no idea, sir.' Filippo blinks. He doesn't remember the drawing, only the angels he'd repainted. 'Can I tell you, though, that I think your statue of Saint George on Orsanmichele is wonderful? People love it. I know, because I used to sit under it sometimes, and when I did I always got a bit more money.'

'A begging friar?' Donatello raises his eyebrows. 'How very traditional.'

'No, I was an actual beggar,' says Filippo reluctantly, wishing he had kept his mouth under control.

'Fra Filippo made his own way in the world before he joined the cloister,' Masaccio explains. 'Drawing for pennies. I expect he's had more commissions than you or I will ever get.'

'So this is the one who's going to get you out of the mess your brother landed you in?' Donatello brushes dust from his gown of rough homespun cloth, and retrieves a clay bottle from behind a piece of marble. He takes a drink, gasps appreciatively and passes the bottle to Masaccio, who tips it back, gulps and hands it to Filippo. It is good wine, or at least better than the thin, weak stuff they get at the cloister.

'That's my hope,' Masaccio says. 'I'm going back to Florence for a couple of weeks. Will you keep an eye on Filippo for me? Make sure he has everything he needs. Advice, and so on.'

'Of course, of course.' The bottle is passed again, and Donatello lifts a drop cloth here, parts a curtain there, takes them out into the yard, explains to Filippo that he and a colleague are making a large tomb for a cardinal in Naples – *'Naples, for God's sake!'*

He twitches back a sheet and for a moment Filippo thinks he is looking at a cadaver: a hollow-faced old man wearing a mitre, shrunken inside his vestments. It is stone, though: 'He isn't even dead yet,' says Donatello. 'In reality.'

'I can't imagine paying someone to imagine what I'm going to look like when I'm dead,' says Filippo, crossing himself. 'What an odd sort of vanity.'

'Have you ever drawn a corpse, brother?' asks Masaccio, suddenly.

Filippo wonders if Masaccio is a bit drunk. It is a strange question, and stirs a strange memory. 'Yes. Once. A drowned slave woman my friends and I found under the Ponte Santa Trinita. She didn't even look dead, really.' He shakes his head, remembering other faces he could not have drawn: the plague dead, lined up in Borgo San Frediano, their feet always bare and strangely large; the old man he had found in the doorway of the church there, sitting quite straight, as if he'd dozed off. The faces of the starved, the diseased, the suicides. The woman murdered by her husband and dragged out into the street. She had looked dead. 'I've only ever wanted to draw the living. Their faces change. You have to be quick to catch what you want. The dead . . . There's nothing worth drawing.'

'A good answer, Fra Filippo,' Donatello says. 'I shall be interested to see how you get on. Are you in one of your moods, Masaccio?'

'No, no. Almost. I have to do a tomb as well.'

'Another job? Shouldn't you finish at least one of the ones you have now?' Donatello draws the sheet up over the face of the stone corpse.

'Fine advice from you, dear man,' says Masaccio.

'Where is it, this tomb?' asks Filippo.

'Back in Florence, in Santa Maria Novella,' says Masaccio.

'Painted tombs? A dangerous precedent,' says Donatello, with mock gravity.

'I intend it to be a sculpture in paint,' Masaccio says. 'And if it starts a fashion that puts you chisellers out of business, well, you taught me most of what I know.'

'I should get back to the convent, gentlemen,' says Filippo. He feels left out of the two artists' sparring, good-natured though it is. And he doesn't want to miss Vespers. 'I think I can find my way.'

But Masaccio won't hear of it, and after another dusty embrace from the sculptor, he leads Filippo back through the lanes to the Carmine, which is nearer than Filippo had thought.

8

Maestro Antonio Biagio the carpenter pops out the first panel – as if it was the spoke of a wheel to be mended, Filippo thinks, fascinated at these new ways to see things he has always thought of as too sacred even to touch – and Filippo takes it in his hands, still feeling an overwhelming sense of reverence even though, now, the panel is no more than an extremely bad painting of a monk. Another panel comes free, and another. Filippo wraps them in a clean cloth he has brought with him, says goodbye to the carpenter and walks back, deep in thought, to the cloister.

He carries the panels to the convent's tiny studium, which has been set aside for him. There is a long table where the convent's brightest friars study the lives of the Carmelite saints and huge, peeling books of canon law. Filippo himself has never been asked to join the studium, so it is with a certain smugness – not a suitable emotion for a friar, but he can't avoid it – that he spreads a sheet of sailcloth over the table, sets up the folding stand of polished wood that has been brought from Masaccio's studio, lays out the pots of pigments and minerals, the pestle and mortar, the myrrh-like crystals of rabbit skin glue, the brushes.

How to begin? The two blank panels are the obvious choice, but somehow that seems too easy. He picks up the image of Saint Albert. A skinned hare in a Carmelite's robes, he thinks. Well then: all on one throw. The convent's novices are crowded in the doorway, gawping at him. He shoos them away and latches the door against interruption. He knows what he has to do next but it would be better if no-one else sees.

If the painting were even a little better, thinks Filippo, I don't think I could do this. As it is, laying the board down on its back and attacking it with a sharp palette knife is by far the most terrifying thing he has done in his life and he has to pace back and forth across the room three, four, five times before he can steady himself enough to begin. His hand is shaking as he picks up the knife and picks, reluctantly, at the bottom left corner, where there is no figure, only ground. The fresh paint comes off before he has even thought about it. He scrapes some more, then more again... The face of the saint regards him blankly. Filippo decides he has to act. He kneels, says a quick prayer to Saint Albert of Trapani, and scrapes off the painted head. With that, the spell is broken. The board is soon scraped clean of paint, and by the afternoon Filippo has given it a new coat of rabbit skin glue, which he has cooked up in the refectory under the horrified gaze of the cook, a layman like all the people who attend to the daily needs of the convent, who is appalled by this young friar with the sleeves of his habit rolled up, dissolving odd-smelling substances in his pots. Filippo offers to teach him, but he raises his hands in superstitious horror and goes back to his carrots.

The board is sized with gesso before the first evening prayer. The prior comes in to inspect, looks at the white surface and leaves without saying a word. At the evening meal, Filippo finds himself eating alone, and during the night services he feels the other friars watching him, but he doesn't mind. He has changed. Of course people will notice. That night he expects to dream of Saint Albert, but instead he dreams he is swimming in the Arno, which is thick and warm. As he passes under the Ponte Vecchio he looks up and waves at his father, who is leaning out of the back window of his shop.

Filippo doesn't even remember to break his fast. He goes straight to the studium and begins to draw. The figure seems to grow of its own accord: easy, really, because it is nothing

94

more than the shapeless robe and mantle of the Carmelites, onto which he must attach a head and a pair of plausible hands. He draws, looking down at himself, at his arms beneath his robe. Someone comes to fetch him for Prime, and after he has sung and prayed he goes back to the studium. Saint Albert is waiting for him, headless. Filippo closes his eyes, takes a deep breath, picks up his drawing stylus, and gives the saint the head of Ser Tommaso di Lippo, butcher of the parish of San Frediano. His father. There isn't much of a memory left inside Filippo's head with which to bring him to life, but there is just enough. He can remember a tall man with a round head, round, hooded eyes, a heavy mouth, who would put his hands on his thighs and bend down to his son's level. Filippo remembers kissing his cheek, rough stubble against his lips. No more than that. But it is enough.

★

'Will it do, Maestro Antonio?' Filippo is watching the prior and gnawing on a thumbnail that tastes a little of rabbit skin glue. Fra Antonio clasps his hands behind his back and leans in towards the panel. Filippo, so nervous that he feels like sprinting for the privy, can see the prior blinking, narrowing his eyes. It has taken him almost three weeks to make the Saint Albert. His first composition had not satisfied him: it had been too similar, in his eyes, to Scheggia's. So he had redrawn it until he was certain that he had made it his own. He had messed up some early batches of paint, but then he had made himself remember what he had learned in Bicci's studio, forced himself to recognise that he *had* been paying attention. Fortunately, the panel is mostly taken up by the saint's white Carmelite cloak, which Filippo had decided to drape down to hide his feet. The modelling of the cloak's folds had been a useful place to experiment, and his confidence had grown, slowly at first and then in a great rush. It had taken him two days to paint the saint's left hand, no bigger than Filippo's thumbnail, and it still isn't right. The right hand, though, had taken no time at all and looks perfectly natural. He isn't entirely happy with Albert's ear but the face... the face is right.

At long last, the prior straightens up. 'Well, well. Fra Filippo,' he says. 'I am more than satisfied. I think this little panel is quite marvellous. Not only does your brushwork far surpass what was there before – not a difficult task, it has to be said. No, this is good. Genuinely good. You have given our beloved saint... Hmm. You have shown us his honesty.'

'Thank you, Reverend Father!'

'And now Pope Gregory and Saint Ambrose. How is Ser Tommaso, by the way? We have not seen him here in some days.'

'He... Well, I'm not surprised, Reverend Father. He is working all hours of the day and most of the night. Never have I seen a man more dedicated to his craft.'

'Is that so.' Is Filippo imagining it, or have the prior's eyebrows twitched? 'Well, press on, my son. And, Fra Filippo...'

'Reverend Father?'

'We need the studium. If you would be agreeable, I give you permission to work in Ser Tommaso's *bottega*.'

It is slightly alarming, to be alone in Masaccio's empty house. The prior has given him the large key, and lent him one of the novices to carry the paintings, but Filippo tells the boy, who is pathetically excited at the idea of going out into the city, that he isn't needed. The last thing he wants is a set of prying eyes carrying tales back to Fra Antonio, about there being no sign of Ser Tommaso. When he lets himself in for the first time he locks the door behind him and leans against it, gazing at the chaos the artist has left behind him. Messy Tom, indeed. Filippo takes a deep breath, and another. Then his nervous gaze settles on the Madonna, still weary, still beautiful. He puts down his bundle of panels and, very carefully, bends down and sets a tumbled chair back on to its legs. Years of monastic order makes the studio almost terrifying to him, but he takes off his cloak and sets to work. He shoves the mismatched, dusty furniture against one wall, leaving only the worktable, which he drags into the middle of the room.

He finds that he has forgotten how to do the simplest domestic things, such as lighting a fire, which is a necessity in the damp cold of late November in Pisa. Then there is the silence. Not the carefully managed silence of the cloister or the friendly quiet of Bicci's studio. This is *his* silence. He controls it. He finds it, in a sense, a responsibility he isn't quite prepared for.

Fortunately he has plenty to occupy him. Two panels to complete inside a month. On that first day alone, he had taken out his finished saint and with fingers so nervous that he had almost fumbled it, held it against its empty slot in the altarpiece's frame. It looks almost decent. In fact it looks perfectly ... adequate. It doesn't quite mesh with the finished saints in the opposite pilaster: Augustine, Jerome and a bearded Carmelite. So for the rest of that day he fusses with washes and glazes, tidying up the modelling on Albert's cloak, finally correcting the unsatisfactory ear, attending to rough spots in the gold background. When he holds the panel up again, in soft candlelight this time, he thinks he can accept that it belongs there.

Filippo decides to leave Saint Gregory for last: the papal tiara worries him. So he launches himself at Ambrose. It is much easier to work here: he isn't plagued by curious friars and novices. He doesn't have to stop working for prayers, although at first he finds this profoundly unsettling. Best of all, he has Masaccio's finished saints for inspiration, and though he tries not to copy the painter's technique too slavishly, he understands that he is being taught, even though his master is not here. Ambrose takes shape quickly. The saint's stern, bearded face he models on an old man he had used to see every day in Florence, sweeping the steps of San Frediano, and his bishop's mitre is lifted from Donatello's dead cardinal. He gives Ambrose an ornate crozier, which is enjoyably complicated, and when it is done he feels ready for Gregory.

The prior has given him all sorts of special dispensations. Permission to work is the most earth-shaking one, because Carmelites do not work beyond the simple chores required to keep the cloister tidy. He is excused the three daytime prayers. He can walk about in the streets. If Filippo were not so busy, he knows he would be fretting about all the possibilities that have suddenly appeared in front of him, all the temptations that, he understands all too well, would keep opening, and opening, never to be satisfied no matter how many he embraces. Isn't this enough, though? It is. He is being tested — what for, he doesn't know, but he knows he has shaken the dice, flung them. One throw. Something hangs in the balance. What is he playing for? What, exactly, is at stake? He doesn't know. But, now he thinks about it, that has never mattered to him. He works, sleeps, works, and by the first day of Advent, which this year falls on the third day of December, he has the three panels finished.

★

'You have far surpassed my expectations, Fra Filippo,' says the prior when he comes to inspect. He has enquired after Masaccio, and Filippo has used the excuse of the frame-maker in Lucca. 'I suspect that Ser Tommaso, who is a clever man as well as a fine painter, knew exactly what he was about when he chose you.'

'You are very kind, Reverend Father.'

'A gift from God is not to be ignored, my son. This: this is a proper use of such a gift. And now ... Well, Christmastide is coming, and then I suppose you must leave us. You would like to see Florence again, I think.'

'I've grown to like it here in Pisa,' says Filippo. 'Though yes, Reverend Father. I'd like to go home. But it is your decision, not mine.'

'We'll discuss it after Christmastide, then.'

9

THE ALTARPIECE SECURELY LOCKED UP in the studio, Filippo prepares to surrender to the unembroidered rhythms of the cloister once again. The habit of the Order is so ingrained in him by now that the day after he has put the last touches to Pope Gregory's panel, he is sitting in his cell, thinking about the season of Advent which has now begun, and which will have the cloister preparing for the great feasts and celebrations to come. Most of all he is thinking of Florence, of walking through the Porta San Frediano and into his own world. He has hardly given any more thought at all to the work he has just completed. So he is surprised when a puzzled novice appears with a message from a Ser Donato di Niccolo di Betto Bardi, who is waiting in the church. Who? he thinks, before he remembers. 'Maestro Donatello! In the church?' Sure enough, there is the fork-bearded sculptor, examining the carvings on an old altar.

'Fra Filippo from San Frediano!' he booms when he sees Filippo.

'Ser Donatello,' says Filippo, bowing. 'How is your tomb?'

'My tomb? Ha! Excellent question from a friar. It's almost finished. Fortunately, because its owner is soon to have need of it. The poor old cardinal has taken sick, I'm afraid. Still, his timing couldn't be better. If he holds out for another few months, he can have his last bed ready for him, so to speak. And speaking of readiness, how is your commission?'

'My ... You mean the panels? They are all done,' Filippo says proudly.

'Good. Excellent. Would you ...' He pats his tunic, frowning. 'Could you spare me a few minutes? I have something for you, but I've left it at my house.'

Filippo considers. Fra Antonio hasn't revoked my dispensation, he decides. 'Certainly,' he says, and follows the sculptor through the lanes to his tower-house. Donatello has to rustle around in his studio for several minutes before he finds a letter, which is sitting in plain sight under a mallet.

'From Masaccio in Florence,' says Donatello. He smooths it, scans with a rough finger, finds a passage. 'Here we are.

As for the altarpiece for Messer Scarsi, I have the Julian, Nicholas, Peter and Baptist ready here in Florence, though it has almost cost me my health... Nonsense. Ahem: *Ask Fra Lippi if he has finished the three saints for the pilaster. If he has, and God willing they are done, please ask him further if he is prepared and able to do another piece for me. It is the left-side panel of the predella, which is to be Saint Julian murdering his mother and father, and Saint Nicholas dowering the three daughters. I have prepared a drawing* – Here it is!' Donatello waves another piece of vellum, shoves it at Filippo – '*and Fra Filippo should be able to follow it. Tell the honest friar that I will pay him another florin and twenty lire, and if he haggles...*

'I will not read this part. But, young man, I advise you to hold out for two florins. Etcetera, etcetera. The predella panel must be done before December 26th, and again ... Ah: *embrace young Filippo for me, and convey to him that he has pulled my feet out of the fire.* Well, that's the gist of it. Can you do as he asks, Fra Filippo? He says that he's sent word to your prior, *suddenly called away,* tum te tum ... Does the prior think he's been here this entire time?'

Filippo is studying the design, beautifully drawn in Masaccio's bold, unhesitating hand. He looks up, realising that, of course, Fra Antonio has known very well what has been happening.

The sardonic looks, the careful avoidance of any discussion that might touch on the artist's whereabouts. 'No,' he says. 'He knows exactly what's been going on. The maestro should be worried about the patron, not Fra Antonio.' He goes back to the drawing. On the left, a figure stands over two others asleep in bed, a sword raised above them. At the right, the poor man and his three girls, asleep in their tiny cell of a room, and in the centre, the saint peering in at them through a little window, ready to make bags of gold appear. 'Is this the size of it?' he asks. Donatello nods. 'Then ... Do you think two florins is out of the question? No, no,' he adds, as the sculptor begins to laugh. 'A florin and a half. Of course I'll do it. Does the maestro say when he'll be back?' Why haven't I thought about this before? he wonders and shrugs.

'Before Christmastide,' Donatello is saying, but Filippo is already planning. The other two predella panels are fitted: the Adoration of the Magi, which Filippo has been studying every day; and the martyrdoms of Peter and the Baptist. He knows how this one needs to look. Small figures, though, in poses ... He has never tried anything like this. 'I'll start this afternoon,' he says.

The predella turns out to be more difficult than he expects. Masaccio's design is to scale and perfect in all respects, and Filippo knows very well that he should just prick it out onto the prepared board, but something forces him to copy it out, freehand, onto the gesso. That does not go smoothly. He cannot manage to convey the tension, the balance in Masaccio's figures. His own look childish in comparison, so he redraws them, and redraws them. Though they improve each time, they never approach the perfection of the originals. He tries to put human feeling into the little faces, and perhaps he succeeds, although almost all the figures are sleeping. Does the snoring mother have an inkling of her destiny, of the sword, wavering over her head? The sleeping family are uneasy. They know all too well that the dawn will bring nothing good, but of course they are wrong.

The only face he can make his own is that of the woman telling Saint Nicholas about the miserable girls. All in all, he is not best pleased with the finished panel.

★

He is waiting for the last brush strokes to dry one afternoon – it is the feast of Saint John of the Cross, the 14th of December – when there is a tap on the door. Filippo jumps up and throws it open, expecting it to be Masaccio, but instead he finds a pink-faced, carefully dressed man of about his own height, who seems a little taken aback to find a young friar in a paint-stained tunic answering his knock. Filippo is equally surprised, but one look at the man's clothes is all he needs to guess the identity of his visitor. The man is wearing clothes of excruciating ordinariness, but cut from the most expensive black cloth from Flanders. He has a long, sharp nose, a protuberant upper lip and keen but unimaginative eyes. No-one has ever looked more like a notary than this shiny, bland man. He is, of course, one of the two bored-looking men watching the Magi present their gifts to the Holy Infant in the centre panel of the predella.

'Ser Giuliano degli Scarsi?' he croaks, his heart plummeting.

'Yes. And who might I be addressing, Fra …'

'Fra Filippo Lippi.' Filippo stammers, unwillingly. 'Can I help you, sir?'

'I've come about the altarpiece,' the man says bluntly.

'Of course.' Filippo has planted himself squarely in the doorway but Giuliano degli Scarsi is trying hard to look past him. Filippo calculates. If he manages to get rid of him now, he will only come back. And at some point…

'Could you fetch Maestro Tommaso, please?' the man asks. He is being perfectly polite, and he plainly has some reverence for Filippo's habit, but there is a bland implacability to his voice that tells Filippo all he needs to know.

'Ser Tommaso isn't here at the moment,' he says. 'Though …'

I expect you would like to inspect the paintings.' Scarsi nods, curtly. Taking a deep breath, Filippo bows, and steps aside.

'You are ...?' Scarsi steps past him, looking around the room with a faint look of alarm. Although Filippo has kept the place tidy after a fashion, this has been achieved by simply shoving everything against the far wall, where it all lurks like the miserable aftermath of a flood.

'I am Maestro Tommaso's assistant,' says Filippo. 'I live at the cloister of Santa Maria, but with the prior's approval I do a little work for the maestro.'

The notary walks over to the altarpiece. He hesitates, then strikes a mannered pose, one black-clad leg set in front of the other, one hand on hip, the other held against his chest. Filippo can see his eyes moving over the painting, but there doesn't seem to be any emotion at work in his face at all.

'The missing panels,' he says at last.

'In fact, they are the reason for my master's absence,' says Filippo brightly, his mind turning like a mill-wheel. He must throw the dice. What else can he do? 'They are so very beautiful, so exquisitely imbued with the light of the Holy Spirit, that someone has asked to see them. A ... A private viewing, so to speak.'

'Is that usual?' asks the notary suspiciously.

'No. But it is certainly allowed, and very much, ah, to be desired,' Filippo says. 'Especially when the request comes from such an important personage.'

'Personage?'

'Yes, indeed. The, in fact, the ... His Holiness.' Oh, for God's sake, thinks Filippo. Now what?

'The Holy Father?' Scarsi's fleshy mouth is hanging open, though whether in credulity or disbelief, Filippo does not dare guess.

'Well, perhaps it's a secret,' Filippo tells him. The pope? he is thinking. What am I doing? Couldn't I just have said the archbishop? Or that the maestro's slipped out for a drink? Meanwhile, his tongue is running on. He doesn't seem able to stop it. To his surprise, Filippo has found his feet. 'His Holiness, as you know, has a good friend in Messer Giovanni de' Medici, and is at this moment paying him a visit in Florence. Word reached the Holy Father about the wonderful painting Ser Tommaso has made here in Pisa, and ...' He flourishes his hands at the altarpiece. 'Being a pious and a serious-minded man, Ser Tommaso feared to travel with the image of Our Lady. So instead he took the four saints, from here and here.'

'The pope?' Scarsi is frowning, but Filippo hears something eager in his voice.

'I expect a man of your standing has met the Holy Father as well,' he says. This is no different from flattering a man on the street into buying a sketch.

'No, no: I have not had that privilege.' The frown vanishes and the pink blandness returns. 'Extraordinary. An ...'

'An enormous honour. For us humble painters, of course, but how much more for the man who caused these images to be made!'

'Quite extraordinary. I had no inkling. And when will Ser Tommaso return with ... with ... We have a contract, you understand. In the circumstances, of course, but ...'

'I expect him daily,' says Filippo. 'Please. Sit and contemplate. Shall I send for some food – perhaps some wine?'

'No, there is no need,' says Scarsi hurriedly. He is already moving towards the door, away from the tidal debris of the studio. 'I simply wanted to make sure, brother, that everything is in order. Plainly it is, and my thanks for the news.'

I've done it! thinks Filippo, amazed to find himself disappointed that the man is leaving. Yes, he has done it. Too well, though? 'Signor, this is a big, big secret,' he says quickly. 'If you could only speak of it to Ser Tommaso when he returns, and no-one else? It is supposed to be between him, Messer de' Medici and His Holiness only. The holy father's private affairs ... I hope you understand?'

'Of course. Private affairs.' The notary shakes his head, blinking. 'Extraordinary! You will tell Ser Tommaso to call on me, of course, as soon as he returns?'

'The very instant,' says Filippo. 'God bless you,' he adds, but Scarsi has already turned away up the street. Filippo leans in the doorway, watching the stiff black figure until he is out of sight. Then he runs back into the studio and relieves himself urgently in the tiny, stinking jakes. I should have said you were locked in here with the flux, maestro, he thinks. And left him here, banging on the door. Where in the Devil's name are you, anyway? He begins to laugh, braced with one arm against the wall, leaning over the reeking hole in the floor, laughs until tears run down into the neck of his habit.

He is dying to tell somebody about this short but intense adventure, but who? Staggering back into the studio, he sees the pale Madonna, and winces. No wonder she looks so weary of the world. None of his fellow brothers at the convent can ever know what he has done, though he suspects that the prior's reaction might surprise him. Still, he is not about to test that theory.

His hands are shaking slightly as he makes sure the embers of the fire are safe. He makes a prostration before the altarpiece, but the Virgin looks so upset that he can bear it no longer. 'I'm sorry, Holy Mother! But what could I do?' he says, straightening up. 'Messer Scarsi wants your beautiful picture for his altar. Maestro Tommaso needs money, so he can paint more pictures to honour you. And here am I in the middle!' The Virgin does not seem mollified, so Filippo makes another prostration and leaves the studio. It is one of those sharp December days when the sky is blue and full of little drifting clouds, and the cold has, for once, taken the damp out of the air. He takes a deep breath. If he was in Florence, in the old days... He would steal some wine and go down to the river, where someone would have a fire going. But he doesn't know anybody in Pisa, except the friars, and with the best will in the world, they aren't his friends.

The painter's smock he is wearing conceals his brown habit. He lets himself back into the studio, finds an old black cap, a simple truncated cone of felt, which he had found during his tidying and which he has used to keep his scalp warm. He pulls it on. Habit and tonsure hidden, he looks like any old painter's assistant. Back outside, he turns right, away from the cloister, and begins to stroll, nervously at first, but then as he relaxes his gait settles into its old, street-honed roll. He soon finds himself beside the Arno. It is starting to flood, and he stares at the brown, muscled water slipping past. This is not the familiar river of home, and no-one is on its banks. He sighs, and walks downstream to the bridge. The few men he passes do not give him a second look.

As a friar, Filippo has never grown used to the looks he gets from lay people. The habit and cloak, and especially the tonsure, always provoke some sort of reaction. Usually it comes in the form of pious reflex: an automatic genuflection, the sign of the cross, or simply a down-turning of the eyes. At first this was bearable to him, even pleasant. He was used to disdain and suspicion. To be dazzled with smiles and friendly waves had made him feel reborn, that the profession he had made to the Order really had transformed him into a completely different creature. But it had soon become a little strange, then irritating, then oppressive. And then there had been the people for whom the sight of a churchman had the opposite effect. Funny, he thinks as he strolls along, feeling almost invisible, I was always one of those. I always spat when I saw a priest, or made the horns behind my back, in case the evil eye should fall on me. And then he had gone over to the other side. In a way, he doesn't mind when he sees people spit, or avert their eyes. He understands it. Could he have become a *jettatore* himself, someone who can throw the *mal'occhio*? He's never tried, though he has to admit that it might come in handy, now and then.

He is getting cold, and the nervous excitement of duping poor Ser Giuliano has almost worn off. He has decided to go back to the convent when he sees a landmark he recognises: the crumbling turret of Maestro Donatello's tower-house.

The door is unlocked, and he hesitates, then pushes it open and calls out, as Masaccio had done. There is no reply, but he thinks he hears the tap of steel against stone from the far end of the house, so he shuts the door and walks softly down the corridor. He isn't really sure what he is doing here. Perhaps he just wants to hear a Florentine voice. And Maestro Donatello, he feels certain, will appreciate his story. But the man who turns to see who has opened the door of the workroom is not Donatello.

'Who are you?' says the man, distractedly, lowering a chisel and a heavy mallet. Filippo recognises the accent of north Florence, but not the square, bearded face set on a thick neck, the wide shoulders, the sturdy legs.

'I'm looking for Maestro Donatello,' says Filippo.

'Not here. Who are you?' The question is not rude, but matter-of-fact.

'Fra Filippo Lippi, from the Carmine.'

'The friar who's been painting for Masaccio?'

'That's me.'

'Well, well.' The man lays down his tools. Filippo sees that he has been working on the capital of a column, a flowering of leaves and curlicues. 'Have you done it, then? Saved his bacon?'

'My bit is finished,' says Filippo. 'I expect Ser Tommaso has done the last panels in Florence.'

The man laughs, loud and deep. 'I wouldn't bet on it,' he says. 'No, no!' he adds, and Filippo realises he must be looking horrified. 'Don't worry, Fra Filippo! I'm sure Masaccio will pull it all together at the last minute. He always does. *Almost* always. Where are you from, anyway? At home?'

'Borgo San Frediano,' says Filippo proudly.

'Borgo San Frediano,' the man repeats. Filippo grins. It feels good to hear the name of his street spoken in the proper accent. 'I'm from Via Guelfa myself, near Sant' Apollonia.'

'I could tell you were a northerner,' says Filippo. He sticks out his hand. 'Pleased to meet you.' The man's hand is hard and finger-numbingly strong.

'Michelozzo. Donato's partner for this job. I'm sorry that Donatello isn't here. He's gone to Colonnata, to the quarry. I expect he'll be back tomorrow.'

'I'll come back, then. I just wanted to tell him ...' He shakes his head. 'Never mind.'

'What, then?' Michelozzo is staring at him quizzically.

'Nothing to do with Maestro Donatello,' Filippo assures him. 'Just a story. I thought it would make him laugh. But I should be getting back to the cloister.'

'I'm intrigued. Tell me instead.' He points to a stub of marble. 'Sit.'

'I'd better get going, maestro ...'

'Bollocks. Have a drink and tell me your story.' Michelozzo retrieves a familiar clay bottle from next to the sculpted corpse, holds it out to Filippo, who hesitates. Oh, why not? he thinks. I need it. So he tips it back, lets the cheap but decent liquid fur his mouth and turn it sour, feels it slip down his throat, warm his insides.

'Thanks,' he says, sighing as the warmth takes hold. He takes another swig and hands the bottle to Michelozzo, who has rolled a piece of column over for his own seat. 'Well, I think I've saved Ser Tommaso's – Masaccio's skin, but I've lied to a notary, involved the pope and done it all in front of the Virgin Mary.' As soon as the words are out, he feels a huge sense of relief and before he knows it he is laughing so hard that he almost topples off his marble stool.

'Then I can't let you leave until you've told me the whole thing,' says Michelozzo, taking a pull on the bottle and handing it back to Filippo. And so Filippo tells him the story, spinning it out a little, making himself a little more ridiculous, a touch more scheming, although it had just happened. He had been preparing a carefully selected and prepared assortment of lies against the event of Masaccio's patron turning up, but none of them had been as audacious, or as implausible as the one that had actually burst out of his mouth. Telling it again, he is more and more certain that some dreadful fate has been set in motion for him. He's done it now, for good and all. But he takes another drink, and then another, and the feeling of doom begins to lift. Michelozzo lets him talk, smiling and nodding and passing the bottle.

'It's good to hear another proper voice,' he says. 'I hear Donato all the time, so I've got used to him. But listening to you, it's just like walking over the Porta Santa Trinita and getting robbed in Santo Spirito market. I expect you miss it? Are you here in Pisa for ever?'

'Christ, I hope not,' says Filippo, and crosses himself a little unsteadily. 'I think they're sending me home after Christmastide, but after the prior hears what that notary has to say, they'll probably burn me at the stake.' He stretches and burps happily. 'Still, if they do, it was worth it.'

'I wouldn't worry too much. Donato and I know Fra Antonio quite well.'

'He's a dry one, to be sure,' mutters Filippo.

'Not as dry as you think. He's sharp as a razor and to hear him talk about painting, you'd think he had his own *bottega*. It was Fra Antonio who got Masaccio the commission from degli Scarsi.'

'Is that so?'

'He saw the frescoes in your church back in Florence. Don't forget, he could have recommended Masolino. He's the famous one, but ... I'm very fond of Masolino. We worked together for a few months in Maestro Ghiberti's shop when I was very young, very green. But you can tell, now, that he's learning from Masaccio, not the other way around. I mean, if you've got the eye, you can see it.'

'Fra Antonio has the eye?'

'Oh, yes. And, young friar, if he got you the job of saving Masaccio from ruin, you can be assured that his eye's on you.'

'That's what I'm afraid of!' Filippo takes another drink. 'Now tell me about yourself, sir.'

Michelozzo turns out to be about ten years older than Filippo, the son of a poor tailor, who had apprenticed him to the city's mint where he had cut dies for coins. From there he had moved to Ghiberti's studio, picking up all manner of complicated mathematical knowledge, which Filippo's increasingly furry brain cannot fathom at all. He had already planned and built a church out in the countryside before letting Donatello talk him into helping with this tomb.

The conversation turns inevitably to home, to the people and things they might have in common, to smells, sounds, legends, gossip... Michelozzo finds some more wine, and a basket of stale honey cakes. Night comes unnoticed. Filippo is surprised to see that it is quite dark out in the courtyard; the marble pieces look even more like fat, pallid bodies. The bells of Santa Maria start to ring, and he is shocked to count nine chimes. He has missed Vespers and Compline.

'The prior is going to have me excommunicated!' he says, finding it is harder to stand up than usual.

'Then don't go back,' says Michelozzo. 'You can sleep here, in Donato's bed.'

'But the prior...'

'I'll send a message round to him. We'll say that you've almost finished the... what part was it?'

'Predella panel.'

'And that, like a brave captain, you have kept your post to the end. I've insisted that you sleep there, and you'll be back in time for Prime. After the lie you told today, this is like a flea on the back of an elephant.'

'There is that,' chuckles Filippo. He is tired, after all, and the panel is done, and he is in a workshop... Justification is such hard work, and the bottle they are on now is still half full...

★

When Michelozzo shakes him awake, it is still dark, and he appears to have gone to sleep with a piece of salt cod in his mouth. This proves to be his tongue, which refuses to work while the sculptor, who seems more or less unscathed by the excesses of last night, drags him out into the courtyard and shoves his head into a bucket of well water. The frigid liquid sears his freshly tonsured scalp like molten bronze, and he howls. Michelozzo ducks him again and he comes up, spluttering. Ragged memories of last night start to assemble themselves. Michelozzo had taken his note to the convent while Filippo had watched from a doorway. Then they had gone to Masaccio's *bottega* to look for more wine. They had found none, but Michelozzo had lit a candle and spent a long time in front of the altarpiece. 'Worth a lie,' he had said at last. 'Worth a lot more than that.'

'Only a few minutes to Prime,' the sculptor is bellowing cheerfully into Filippo's ear. 'Drink this!' Filippo takes the cup, which is filled with warm, frothy goat's milk fresh from the teat. It is the last thing he wants but it seems to have some medicinal effect because his knees stop shaking.

'My God,' he gasps.

'He won't be your God much longer if you don't get going,' says Michelozzo. He makes him drink another cup of milk, then marches him, like a jailer hauling a prisoner to the gallows, outside and down the street to Santa Maria. Filippo wants to slip in but the sculptor takes hold of his arm and walks him through the church to the cloister, where they find Fra Antonio in the refectory, talking with the cook. Filippo grits his teeth, ready for whatever justice has in store for him.

'Good morning, Fra Filippo,' says the prior. 'I gather you have finished Ser Giuliano's predella.'

'Y-yes, I have, Reverend Father.'

'Everything seemed present and accounted for when Ser Giuliano made his inspection.'

'I hope so,' says Filippo, smiling as innocently as he can.

'All except for the saints which are at this moment being enjoyed by His Holiness.' Fra Antonio narrows his eyes. His gaze feels worse on Filippo's skin than the freezing well water. 'What a blessing. Ser Giuliano, who is a proud fellow but extremely God-fearing...' The prior's eyes are probing Filippo's soul like a surgeon about to lance a boil. 'Ser Giuliano knows he must not breathe a word to anybody, but he is quite delighted. As, I'm sure, we all are. Is that not true, Ser Michelozzo?'

'Delighted, and, I would say, astounded,' says the sculptor, who is eyeing a heel of bread on one of the tables. 'But then, our friend Masaccio is an astoundingly talented painter. As, I'm bound to say, is young Fra Filippo here.'

'Hmm. We can only hope that His Holiness is finished admiring the panels before the Feast of Stephen, which is eleven days away.'

'Without a doubt,' says Filippo hurriedly.

'The loyalty of assistants...' Fra Antonio folds his hands. 'You will be late for Prime, Fra Filippo.'

'The poor young man was quite worn out,' says Michelozzo. 'But he would have got up for Dawn Prayer had I not insisted that he go back to sleep. Even so, he recited...'

The prior holds up a hand, wearily. 'Let us not overwork the composition, my son.'

Michelozzo shrugs. 'I defer to you, Reverend Father.' His hand edges towards the bread.

'Take it. You must be hungry after your exertions on Fra Filippo's behalf,' says the prior, in level tones. Michelozzo grins and stuffs the bread into his tunic. 'I must prepare for the service. Fra Filippo, you will show me your work afterwards.'

Filippo and the prior walk to Masaccio's studio in complete silence – silent, that is, except for the rumbling of Filippo's belly, which has received nothing except red wine and goat's milk since yesterday evening. He fumbles the key into the lock and lets the door swing open to let Fra Antonio inside. The prior stalks over to the easel, bends in the same sharp way that Filippo had seen the first time he had come here. He peers, then prises the panel loose with a finger and takes it over to the window.

'It is plainly not as good as Ser Tommaso's work,' he says at last. 'The figures lack the last degree of ease. They are arranged …' He clicks his tongue. 'And yet you have not done at all badly, my son. These scenes do not have the life of your saints, with which I can find no easy fault; and put alongside Ser Tommaso's martyrdoms, to say nothing of this Adoration, of course, they lack finesse. But I understand that it is your fortune to have your first work placed next to that of a truly gifted master, and that comparisons must needs be harsh. Note that I did not say *misfortune*, though. I said fortune, because you have acquitted yourself. You have paid back Ser Tommaso's trust in you. That is lucky for him.'

'Thank you, Reverend …'

The prior stops him with an upheld finger. 'And it is lucky for you, Fra Filippo Lippi. Do you understand?'

'I understand very well, Reverend Father,' Filippo says quietly.

'Good.' Fra Antonio puts the panel back in its place, and paces over to the hearth, eyes narrowed. 'Ser Giuliano di Colino di Pietro degli Scarsi. He came here yesterday, and talked, as he put it, to a dirty little friar. Who told him … You know what you told him. Ser Giuliano is a man of some weight here in Pisa. He is one of the leaders of this quarter. He may be haughty. He may lack imagination. God has not blessed him with the ability to see art for what it is, only for what it is worth. He deals with money, Fra Filippo, and in that he is very expert indeed. Money is power here on Earth. You of all people are aware of that. You do not play games with men of power. You do not tell them lies, not if you are nothing but a dirty little friar.'

'No, Reverend Father. That is true. I do not deserve to be forgiven.'

'I am not forgiving you.' The prior pushes a piece of charcoal into the cold hearth with the toe of his sandal. 'But – your fortune again – at the time that you told this infamous tale to Ser Giuliano, you were still in the employ of Ser Tommaso Cassai. You were his paid assistant – paid? Yes?' The prior gives Filippo a look that turns the goats milk to cheese in his guts. He swallows and nods. 'His assistant in his studio. No doubt Ser Tommaso gave you strict instructions to fob his unlucky patron off with whatever excuse came to hand, should he come knocking?' Filippo nods again. He is sure he's going to be sick. 'I know nothing of business. But I do know that an apprentice, an assistant, is paid to be loyal to his master. Loyalty above all else. Masaccio should thank the Lord that he found himself such a loyal servant, because if Ser Giuliano had for one moment thought that his painter was off working for someone else, a Ser Felice Brancacci, for instance, he would have cancelled his contract on the instant, started legal proceedings to get back the money he had already paid, and then he would most certainly have turned his displeasure towards the one who had suggested such a dishonest rogue as the painter for his altarpiece. So I have good reason to thank that quick-witted apprentice as well.'

Fra Antonio has been pacing as he speaks, and he has come to rest in front of the altarpiece. He stares at the image of the Madonna, who seems, to Filippo, to look particularly downcast this morning, although her fat little son seems to be stuffing his face with more than usual energy. The prior stares and stares, as if asking for guidance. Finally he turns to Filippo, who has been supplicating the Virgin with his own desperate request: that something – apoplexy, earthquake, a lightning bolt – strike him dead before he has to face what is coming next.

'I have come to know an honest and talented apprentice, but here in front of me is a dishonest, unworthy friar. My dilemma is that I do not know which of these is you, Filippo Lippi.'

Filippo swallows painfully. He is still standing here. Lightning has not struck. The terracotta tiles of the floor have not parted and sent him careening down into Hell. He has to say something. But what? Excuses and prayers flick through his mind. He sees the exhausted Virgin out of the corner of his eye, knows very well what she would say. Sometimes — *sometimes* — you have to tell the truth. 'I'm sorry, Reverend Father,' he says at last, 'but I don't know either.'

There is a long, chilly silence. Filippo can hear a rat scuffling in an upstairs room. He can smell the sweetly sulphurous aroma of drying egg tempera paint in the air, his own boozy sweat wafting up from his robe.

'I doubt you could have said better,' says Fra Antonia, at last. He sighs, and smiles tightly. 'My guess is that this answers my question.' He taps the side of the altarpiece. 'You are doomed to be both, my son.'

Filippo just gapes at his prior. Is this a reprieve, or a sentence? He remembers Michelozzo's words from the night before: Fra Antonio has the eye of a painter, and you can be sure his eye is on you. 'What is going to happen to me?' he says. 'Do I have to leave the Order now?'

'No, no.' Fra Antonio suddenly looks tired. He runs his fingers along the thin border of hair that fringes his scalp. 'Friars can paint, you know. Perhaps they *should* paint. Why should it be laymen who make our sacred images? I sometimes wish...' Filippo sees deep unhappiness flicker across his eyes. 'No. You can do both. Be a painter and a friar. It is not the easy path to take. Our Order gives us a life that is not difficult. We are greatly blessed by it, by the Rule. The ways it offers give a man a sheltered passage through life — serving God along the way, of course. But there are places, very few, where those ways diverge and show paths that are far more difficult to tread. I believe that you have come upon one of those places. You will have to make a choice, Filippo.'

'Between the Order, and... this?'

The prior comes over to Filippo. 'No. Much harder than that.' His hands are on Filippo's shoulders, and he is searching his face with the same care as he had examined the painting. 'Between being a good man, and a sinful one.' He grimaces, shakes his head. 'Not even that. If you create beauty, many things come along with it. Praise, money, flattery. And the reverse, don't forget: criticism, jealousy, rejection. All these things, if not guarded against, will make your soul, not bad, but... *mediocre*. Grimy, like your robe. Serviceable, but not delighting the Lord. You will be able to delight the eyes of men, Filippo, with your work; but what does that matter, if you do not please the sight of the Lord?'

'How can I choose?' Filippo almost shouts. 'I used to be a beggar! I drew pictures of men and women and made them look handsome, or pretty, or young, so they would pay me! My soul is already stained!'

'An unworthy man could not have made those paintings,' says the prior. 'I understand you, Filippo. I know all about your past. Do you think you are the first boy who went from the streets to the cloister? Do you really believe that there can be no goodness in men and women who live in poverty? We are all beggars, after all, we friars.'

'No, no. There is grace in everyone. The poor... the poor especially.' Filippo hesitates. 'That doesn't mean I think that Ser Giuliano degli Scarsi deserved...'

'We won't speak of that now. When I was in Florence last, Fra Pietro showed me the robe you drew on. The Madonna as a woman living in the gutter. I don't think the choice is as hard as you think, my son.'

'Reverend Father, I am the most unworthy friar. I try to understand the teachings, but dogs will turn into cats before I become a theologian. What I can say is the Carmine saved my life. I don't know what would have happened to me if I had kept on living in my old way. I expect The Eight would have pulled my body out of the river long ago. I'd be in a pit under quicklime, and no-one would have cried over me. How can I go to the good widows of the *commesse*, or to Fra Pietro, and tell them I've gone back to my old ways? They would think I'd betrayed their trust! The only way I can thank them is to be Fra Filippo the Carmelite, not Pippo Lippi the scribbler!'

'You surprise me, my son. Again. But would it be a betrayal of their trust if you used the great gift the Lord has given you, to serve the Carmelites? If they knelt before a wonderful altarpiece which had been painted by you? I don't think so.'

'Then what must I do?'

'I'm sending you back to Florence. You will probably pass our dear Masaccio on the road.' The prior reaches into his habit and produces a grubby letter. 'He is on his way: he may be here tomorrow.'

'You knew he wasn't in Pisa?' Filippo is aghast.

'I'm afraid so. As the guarantor of this whole affair, I've made it my business to know the whereabouts of our erratic young friend.'

'I don't think Masaccio means to cause people trouble,' says Filippo. 'I think he wants to please people, and ...' He hunches his shoulders, apologising on his master's behalf. 'He needs money. Everyone needs money, Reverend Father. Except friars. At least he didn't go to Hungary.'

'That would have been more difficult,' Fra Antonio agrees. 'We will go back to the cloister now. You will make a full confession, and do penance for being unkempt at morning prayers.'

'Just ... just that?'

'You saved me from the wrath of Ser Giuliano. I can't very well punish you, can I, my son? Do you see how life outside our walls is tangled? Once you put your foot outside, everything becomes ambiguous. But a man may ride a boat down a sewer and as long as his craft is sound and he pilots with care, he will stay clean.'

'I've never been good in boats,' Filippo says.

'Well, I daresay the hem of one's robe may trail in the stink from time to time,' says the prior. 'The trick, Filippo Lippi, is not to capsize.'

10

No mule for Filippo on his way back to Florence. As he walks out of the city gate, wrapped in his cloak and with Masaccio's black cap on his head, mud is already squelching between his toes. It had rained in the night, and though the sky is clearing, it is cold and the grey line in the distance, hovering above the distant mountains, says that he will be soaked before nightfall. But he is happy. Except for a little sack slung over his shoulder he has nothing again: all the strange, unlooked-for responsibilities, the homesickness, the guilt, all that is behind him. He is going home. The prior — if Filippo understood their conversation in Masaccio's studio properly — has given him a strange sort of absolution. And he is owed four and a half florins — Masaccio had not, after all, haggled very seriously — into the bargain.

The rain does come down, and he has only reached Cascina. But he pushes on, and by sundown he is within sight of Montopoli. He is soaked and frozen, but although by rights he should be miserable, he is feeling strangely virtuous. This, perhaps, is the penance the prior should have given him. As he trudges into the town he is even hoping that tomorrow's weather will be even more vile. That way, he can positively bathe in virtuous suffering.

He still has two of the five *grossi* that Masaccio had given him for expenses, twisted into his underwear. He knows that the local priest will put him up — all he has to do is knock at the door. But as he sloshes up the main street towards the bell tower, he remembers the inn where he had stayed with Fra Albizzo's agent. There had been a huge fireplace, and decent food. He also remembers that, when he had come through Montopoli with his Florentine brothers, the priest's lodgings had been sparse, and his elderly cook had provided soup more watery than the stuff that is presently streaming down his neck and back. In the end, the prospect of a fire clinches it. And as things transpire, when he walks into the inn and stands on the threshold in a spreading puddle, the innkeeper's wife appears at once, begins to coo and fuss, and insists on giving him supper and a bed for the night. Her youngest brother lives in the Dominican priory at Fiesole, she tells him as she takes his sodden cloak, gives him a clean tunic of homespun to wear and a heavy blanket, and lets him slip behind a door to take off his habit and change into his dry things. Then she bustles him into the dining room, which is almost empty, sets a chair for him before the fire, which is roaring, and brings him a plate of bread and cheese, and a jug of ale.

When the serving girl walks into the room with a wooden bowl full of the cabbage soup he has insisted upon, he tells himself firmly that he had forgotten all about her. And perhaps he had – his mind, in any case. His body remembers her immediately. And then his mind catches up. She is wearing the same slightly foxed linen dress, tied at the waist with a scarf of once-bright Turkish silk. Her hair is done up in the same fanciful yet precise style, an arrangement of coiled plaits held in place with a twist of scavenged damask. She is his age, more or less, and walks with deliberate, studied grace. She bends to put the soup down on the stool in front of him and he has to avert his eyes quickly, because the neckline of her tunic is loose and she is not wearing a shift beneath it. But not so quickly that he misses a glimpse of curved white breast and one dark, jutting nipple. After she has straightened, he grins, blushing, and finds she is looking at him quite boldly.

'You were here in the summer, weren't you, brother?'

'I was, yes,' he says, feeling a pleasant surge of heat.

'Thought so. I recognised you.'

'I expect we all look the same, don't we?' Filippo has tried to learn that airy yet concerned tone that the priors and priests use, the one which says: I care very deeply about you, but please don't come any closer. Perhaps, though, he hasn't quite mastered it. And besides, he doesn't want to keep her away: he should, but he doesn't. Not at all. 'Filippo,' he adds. '*Fra* Filippo.'

'I can't tell most of them apart. Friars, monks ... Not you, though. Brother Filippo.'

'Ah.' The heat from the fire is lapping up and down one side of his body, but the other side is quite cold. He remembers the prior's words about the boat drifting down the sewer, and tries half-heartedly to put all of his feelings into the cold side. 'The soup smells delicious. I am very fortunate. God bless you, my sister.'

'Thank you very much, brother.' The girl drops a pert curtsey and walks away, in her strangely regal way. She didn't mean that at all, Filippo thinks. Or she meant something else ... The soup smells too good to resist, though, and as he spoons the rich broth into his mouth, he gratefully allows his hunger to dislodge the girl from his thoughts.

When he has finished, he leans back contentedly and looks around the room. There are a few other men eating and drinking: farmers, mostly, and a couple of travellers with mud-spattered legs. The girl bustles here and there. Without thinking, Filippo rummages in his sack, pulls out a square of old vellum. His one stick of charcoal has been crushed to atoms, though, so he finds a charred twig in the hearth and begins to draw. He sketches the travellers, quickly, just one look and a flourish of charcoal. He draws the landlady's comfortable figure, a stack of soft circles. Then the charcoal describes a strong black curve. He glances up: the serving girl is walking past with a tray, her eyes on the far end of the room. His hand makes another line: the thick mass of her hair, coiled and tied. The slight weight of her jaw, her full mouth, black brows, wide, shadowed eyes. Then she is standing in front of him.

'I'm sorry…?' Filippo blinks, focusing.

'I asked if you enjoyed your soup.'

'Delicious.'

'What are you doing?' She frowns, which does something even more delightful to her face. Filippo gazes at her for a moment, head to one side, looks at his drawing. It's good: I would have got a coin or two for this in the old days, he thinks, then holds up the sheet of vellum for her to see.

It had always delighted him to see his customers' reactions when he showed them their sketches. A laugh, a grin, occasionally a frown, even a curse. The girl does none of those things. Her head goes back, her brows go up. She stares at the paper, then at Filippo, her lips pursed so that the freckles on her upper lip gather together. She has lines at the corners of her mouth, Filippo thinks. I missed them. Then someone calls from across the room. The girl makes a little hiss of annoyance. She thrusts the vellum at Filippo.

He shakes his head, studying her face. 'Take it,' he says. 'A gift.' She narrows her eyes, flicks the vellum at him and sweeps away in a rustle of linen. The vellum, pillowed on warm air, drifts out of his reach and glides into the fire.

Filippo is left chuckling to himself ruefully. But when he gets up to use the privy, he almost bumps into her in the narrow passageway that leads to the back of the inn. He flattens himself against the wall to slip past her but he could swear that she sticks out her backside so that his hip brushes against it. There is an instant of friction, of yielding, rebounding. At the door he looks back and she laughs, perhaps thinking she has shocked him, but he isn't shocked and when she sees that, she turns quickly and hurries into the kitchen. After that, she keeps her eyes down in the dining room, pouting. He likes the subtle heaviness of her face, her brown, almond-shaped eyes. He wishes she would look at him again.

The landlady doesn't want him staying up late. She is worried that he has caught a chill, that he hasn't eaten enough, that he's eaten too much. What luck, she tells him, that they are almost empty – 'Not for you, Monna!' he protests, but she brushes his concern away with a wave of her hand – because the poor young friar can have a room and a bed all to himself. The fire is made up. 'Get to bed, brother. The longer you sleep, the more dry your clothes will be in the morning.' He can't protest too much: his eyes are already drooping and the hot soup in his stomach is very pleasant, so he follows her upstairs to a room at the back of the inn. His robe and cloak are there, drying in front of the hearth. She bustles around, stabbing at the fire with a poker, slapping the bed and drawing back the covers to show the sheet, which is not at all clean, pulling out the piss-pot from beneath it and flourishing it as though it were a sultan's treasure. The dark-haired girl glides past the open door with an armful of linen. She glances in at the two of them, her eyes catch his and then she is gone. He listens to her feet padding down the corridor as the landlady chatters on, smiling and rocking on his heels until she runs out of things to fuss over and leaves him alone. When the door is closed, he sits down on the hard straw mattress and looks around him. In the flickering light of the fire and the candle stub she has left him, he feels the same sense of unnerving space as he had in Masaccio's studio: he has never had a bedroom this big all to himself. Not the grandest room in the house: it seems to double as a store for old furniture, as there are crooked chairs stacked against the wall, table boards, a small chest on which are stacked battered old ledgers from which foxed pages are spilling. The air smells of wood smoke and drying wool. Rain is sluicing off the roof tiles and spattering against the buckled, leaded glass in the tiny window. He snuffs out the rush light and gets into bed, finding that the sheets are cold but dry. He pulls the bedclothes around him tightly, and he is at the blissful point where warmth triumphs over chill when he falls asleep.

But his training is too strong to let him rest. He finds himself awake again, lying in darkness, painfully aware of the empty space all around him. A bell is tolling: he swings out of bed and is halfway across the floor before he realises that he is not in the cloister, that the bell is clanging out midnight over Montopoli. He stands, his eyes picking out a faint ribbon of light beneath the door, the fainter blue glow of the sky beyond the window. A door slams downstairs, another one creaks nearby. The landlady's voice issues some perfunctory command, then the serving girl wishes her mistress goodnight. A door-latch clicks and a lock is set. Footsteps pad away from him along the corridor. He stands there, remembering dark hair clinging to damp skin, firm flesh beneath rough fabric. An image drifts out of the darkness, so familiar by now that he knows every crease, every curve: Masolino's Eve, his night-time companion. The bell has stopped ringing. He is wide awake, alone. He is free. The thought ripples through him like joyful fever. And then he hears the soft pad of feet coming back down the corridor. He hesitates, but only for a moment. The door creaks softly as he opens it and peers out.

A light is bobbing towards him. As it comes closer the serving girl's face seems to form out of the glow of the candle flame. Filippo is beyond the weak circle of light it casts. He watches as it sweeps towards him, his blood racing. Then it is lapping across his robe, and she sees him standing there.

She stops, blinks. She's tired, Filippo thinks. She's annoyed. I'll make some excuse. I'll...

'Can't sleep, Fra Filippo?' She does not sound annoyed after all. Lowered to a whisper, her voice is dark and sweetly rough.

'I'm not as tired as I thought I was,' he whispers back. She cocks her head.

'Can I fetch you something?'

'No, I don't...' He swallows.

'Don't need anything?' One dark eyebrow arches. 'You sure?'

'Well...' He glances up and down the corridor, but they are alone. 'I'm sure about something.'

'And what might that be, friar?'

Wordlessly, he steps back into the room and nudges the door a little further open. He takes another step backwards, then another. The pool of candlelight laps to the door jamb, pauses, then floods inside.

The girl's feet are bare and she presses a gritty sole over his own bare toes. She is wearing a nightdress of some coarse country weave and nothing else. When she presses against him, her heat seeps through the scratchy cloth of his garments. Her lips are on his, her tongue darts and flicks against his teeth. Her dress smells of wood smoke and candle smoke and cooking, but when he lifts it over her head and throws it into the dark behind them, her scent is sharp, like pepper, like newly ground pigment. He takes her hand and pulls her over to the bed, and she helps him wrestle out of the heavy, clinging folds of his clothes.

Filippo lies back, feeling the cool linen against his skin. Even in the dim light of the candle he feels more naked than he has ever felt before. The habit is such a scratchy, sweaty burden, and now he is free of it ... The girl lifts a leg. Her toes brush his hip. 'I thought I was right about you, Fra Filippo. Now I can see I was ...' The raspy skin of her sole glides across his thigh, her toes wriggle. Filippo gasps.

'Turns out we were both right,' he says hoarsely, and reaches for her.

She slips into bed beside him, giggling almost silently. Then their hands reach, touch, search. Her skin is hot and salty and she is hungry, but so is he. At first their mouths are busy, lips crushed against lips, tongues brushing teeth, teeth grazing skin, but when his hand slips between her legs she stuffs a thick hank of her hair between her teeth to keep from crying out. And then they must both stifle the sounds they want to make, his face in the pillow, hers in a fistful of sheet. He wants all of her: her heat, her scent, her softness, the mounds and furrows he is mapping with his hands. But most of all he wants to see her face, which she keeps hiding from him: all he has is glimpses of her eyes, wide in surprise or shut tight. He remembers Masolino's Eve, the hours, days he has spent fretting over her; but the girl in his arms is nothing like cool, pale Eve. A piece of wood in the fire falls into the embers and catches, and for a time they move with the dancing of the flame. After they finally burn themselves out, it is still leaping.

'Am I your first?' she whispers, when they have both found their breath. They are facing each other, nose to nose, her thigh thrown across his waist.

'Was it very obvious?'

She grins, and her hand slips down between them and grips him softly. 'No. I just guessed. After all, you've been locked away in a cloister.'

'Not locked,' Filippo starts to protest, but then he laughs. She puts the knuckle of her middle finger into his mouth, *shushes* him. 'I mean, we're free to leave. It's our vows that keep us, not lock and key.'

'Ah, your vows ... I think I'd trust in a padlock,' she says, and runs the finger, moist with his spit, down his cheek. 'Less easily broken.'

'Hard to break. Very hard,' Filippo says. 'But you are a master – a mistress of locks. I'm undone.'

'Is it very bad?' The thought of his broken vows seems to excite her. Is that why ... No matter. Her hand is moving. He moves along with it.

'Bad? It's terrible! Though ...' He watches the shadows dance on the ceiling, feels the weight of her thigh on his belly. He runs his hand along her leg, cups it over the curve of her bottom. 'You know, I don't think that God is bothered what people do, as long as they're making each other happy. I think something would have happened by now, if I'd made God angry.'

The girl – he doesn't even know her name – crosses herself, which makes her heavy breasts quiver, and suddenly all thoughts of God's anger – even of the prior's – are driven from Filippo's head.

'Don't let me fall asleep,' she murmurs, later. Her hair is sticking to her flushed forehead and she still has hold of him down there. 'I should be in my own bed by now. Monna Anna likes me up at first cock-crow.' She gives him a gentle kiss. 'And that's only a little while away.'

Filippo props himself on an elbow. 'Do you need to go now?'

'No ... Do you want me to?'

'I want you to stay.'

'Hmm. Can you do it again?'

'My lady!' Filippo, to his surprise, is quite ready, but she clicks her tongue affectionately at his *ucello* and shakes her head. 'Not that. What you did earlier. With the charcoal and paper.'

'You mean draw you? Now?'

She shrugs, a bad actor after all. 'If you want to.'

He watches her breathing gently, hair tangled, eyelids heavy. He feels wide awake. He slips out of bed, feeling her eyes on his back, and rummages in his bag. There is one more piece of vellum. He finds a stub of charcoal in the hearth and goes back to the bed.

She makes to rise but he stops her. 'Don't do anything,' he says, and settles down to draw her. He works fast, as though she had paused for him on Borgo San Frediano, but he does not draw to flatter, as he might have done in the old days. He doesn't need to. She is quite lovely. When he is done he flicks the charcoal back into the hearth and blows the dust from the vellum. It is rough, a sprawl of limbs, one foot quite detailed, because he has decided he likes her plump toes, the other a blur; a hand under her bottom, the other lost behind her head; the patch of black curls below her belly. Breasts hidden by the sheet. The slightly heavy sensuality of her face, the full bow of her lips; her small nose, with a little rise at the end; the high sweep of her brows; her shadowy eyes. Brown like chestnut honey, he thinks. If only I had paint. If only I could capture the taste of her skin, her rich, pigment scent ...

'Here,' he says, and turns the drawing around. She hesitates, then takes it almost reluctantly.

'Who is this?' she says, softly, huskily.

'It's you.'

She is silent for a long time. The fire pops and ticks. Then she gets out of bed, picks up her nightdress and pulls it on quickly, almost modestly. She picks up the drawing, stares at it again. Her chest rises and falls. Then she folds it quickly, creases it with a thumbnail and before Filippo can say anything, tears it into two unequal pieces. The larger one she crumples into a tight ball and throws into the fire, where it smoulders for a moment before bursting into dirty orange flames.

'Oi!' Filippo manages to stifle his cry of surprise. But she has turned, and holds up the smaller piece of vellum for him to see. Her face, her hair curling out in tendrils, the line of her neck. She has torn the drawing just above her breasts.

'It's really me, isn't it?' she says.

'It was all you. That and the rest of it. Your beauty.' He says it because it is the truth, not out of reproach, and to his relief she smiles.

'You drew my *fica*.'

'Artists do that nowadays,' he says airily, thinking of Masolino's Virgin. 'You should see the paintings in Florence. And the statues. *Ficci* everywhere. And *uccelli*. Anyway, your *fica's* lovely.'

'Stop it! You're a friar!' She realises what she has said and stifles a laugh with her hand. 'I couldn't keep it. What if someone had found...' She studies the sketch again, lips pursed. 'It's something in your eyes, isn't it?' Filippo shrugs, suddenly embarrassed. 'Well, it was your eyes that had me. In the dining room—'

'When I drew you?'

'When you looked at me. Men look at me all the time. They look, but they don't see. You caught me then. And in the hallway. And the time before: in the summer. I remembered you. A little friar, with eyes that were doing something to me.'

'Not just that, though?' he asks, worried.

'No.' She comes over, squats down beside him. 'Not just.' She puts her hand gently on his mouth. 'I'm going to market in Cascina tomorrow ... today. Early. I won't see you again. Goodbye, Filippo.'

'I don't know your name!'

'Then you won't be able to pray for me, will you?' She grins, and before he realises she has gone he is looking at the closed door.

II

Fɪʟɪᴘᴘᴏ ᴛʀɪᴇꜱ ᴛᴏ ꜱʟɪᴘ ᴏᴜᴛ of the inn just as the sun is rising. It is silent downstairs, and he is praying – even though he knows it is not what he should be asking God – that the girl will be there. But she is nowhere to be seen, and he guesses she has already left for market. As he is padding towards the door, the landlady appears from the kitchen. Filippo grits his teeth, but the expression on her face is concern, not fury.

'You cannot think of walking without breaking your fast!' she says, but Filippo holds up his hand. The Rule of the Carmelites is different from – her brother is a Dominican, yes? Different from the Rule of Saint Benedict. He must be abroad as soon as he is awake, he insists, and no food until after midday prayers. And look: by God's grace, the sun is shining! But she will not let him go until he has knelt with her next to the cold hearth while they say the Catechism together. Finally he makes his escape. As he walks briskly down the hill towards the gate that opens towards Florence, he feels as if he has left some part of himself behind, something he no longer needs. The cobblestones feel as soft and springy beneath his feet as a new Turkey rug. The girl's smell is rising off him like the finest perfume. His only worry is the state of his bed, which he hopes will not give the girl away to her mistress.

By mid-morning he has reached Empoli and the sun is on his back. Empoli is a bigger place than Montopoli and the sight of people out and about their business makes Filippo think of home, of how near he is but, on foot, still two days away. Then he remembers the three *grossi*. It isn't too hard to find a livery stable, and he rents a mule. There are no Carmelites around, so what does it matter whose feet carry him to Florence? Besides, he rode here, so he can ride back. Astride his little mount, he trots along in the thin December sunshine. The sky is full of rooks and gulls. He feels light, as if he has taken off a rusty suit of armour. The girl is there, in the air in front of him, on his lips, on his fingers. He has arrived somewhere: it is a place where he belongs.

He decides it would be courting fate to ride into Florence through the Porta San Frediano, so near to the Carmine. So he takes a ferry across the Arno at Montelupo Fiorentina and comes by muddy lanes and little villages to the Porta al Prato. Once he has passed through, his senses, dulled by the road and by his almost sleepless night, begin to come alive. He can see the campaniles of the Carmine, of San Frediano and Santo Spirito across the Arno. There ahead of him is the skyline of Florence he knows so well. His heart lifts and tears prick the corners of his eyes.

The livery stable where he has to deliver the mule is near Ognissanti. He hands it over and goes out into the street. Time to go back to the Carmine. Time to go home.

He begins to stroll, taking it slowly, letting his feet trace out the map he carries in his head and in the bones and muscles of his body. A left and another left will bring him to Borgo Ognissanti, which will lead him to the Ponte alla Carraia. From there, five minutes and he will be at the Carmine. But because he has a spring in his step and the sun is still shining, he decides to take a longer path. He drinks in the familiarity of it all: the towers, the crenulations, coats of arms carved and painted everywhere: the concentric circles of the Albizzi, the golden balls, the famous *palle* of the Medici; the stags' heads of the Soderini, the Peruzzi pears. Another short cut presents itself but he ignores it. And then, another left instead of a right and he is on the outskirts of the Mercato, the great warren of alleys surrounding the squares of the market itself. He walks past the Chiassolino, and the men who are lounging outside the dingy male brothel give him arch stares and even a whistle. A little further on is the Malvaggia, less of a brothel – though there are girls upstairs – and more of a tavern. He hasn't been in these parts since he used to beg here with Albertino and his mates. The sound of voices loud with wine billows out of the door. His throat is dry after his ride. A glass of wine, just one … No friar, though, has ever set foot inside the Malvaggia, and no friar ever will. He walks on, feeling a little thwarted. But there, set up in a doorway, is an old woman selling a pile of old clothes she has strewn haphazardly across the steps. Filippo hesitates, for a moment. Then he reaches into his habit and pulls out his money. He jingles the coins in his fist.

'I want that pair of hose, Monna,' he says, pointing to a couple of leggings made out of dingy brown serge. 'That tunic.' He prods a stained, rust-coloured rag. 'And that cloak.' He hands over his smallest coin, the woman eyeing him suspiciously.

'What do you want 'em for?' she demands. 'You're a friar.'

'Not really,' says Filippo, treating her to a wink. 'I'm in fancy dress.' The old lady frowns, then a thought, evidently a richly disturbing one, strikes her. With a glance towards the men lolling outside the Chiassolino, she thrusts the bundle of rags at him, crossing herself and muttering imprecations under her breath. Filippo thanks her with a bow.

He changes out of his Carmelite robes in an empty shed on the deserted ground behind Santa Maria Novella, tying habit and cloak into a parcel with his rope belt. He slings it over his shoulder, straightens Masaccio's cap on his head, and strolls back to the Mercato. Apart from his short hair, hardly any of which shows under the hat and which marks him out as ridiculously out of fashion, he could pass as any down-at-heel layman.

He doesn't go into the Malvaggia, but to the Fico, a slightly more salubrious tavern on the main square of the market, near the column of Abundance. One glass, he tells himself. What can it hurt? Of all the vows I've broken today, it'll be the least important. His appearance earns him some glares from the clientele, most of whom are young, fashionable gentlemen, but there are a couple of rougher types there as well, stonemasons and carpenters and even a dyer with bright scarlet hands. Filippo doesn't care about the looks he is getting. He isn't himself, after all. He is playing a part. He drinks a glass and is about to pay and leave, but the landlord is already filling his glass again and it would be embarrassing to turn it down, not to mention he'd have to pay ... To Hell with it. He sips the wine, which is good, dense red stuff from down south near Monte Amiata.

After the third glass, the girl from Montopoli walks into his mind abruptly, with a flounce and a flick of her lovely backside. The pleasure of being back in the city has kept the girl at bay, but now here she is. He lifts his hand to his face surreptitiously: she is still on his fingers, a lovely ghost beneath the smells of mule mane and rein leather. After that, he needs another glass. His thoughts are beginning to thicken, swirling moodily around the memory of last night, the girl standing in the middle like Abundance on her column. The whole world is turning around her. Sometime into the next glass, he happens to glance down and see that he is the only man in the tavern wearing sandals, and that his feet are still filthy with road mud. Some part of him is still a friar, then: his vows still intact from the thighs down, like a ... like a ... His mind conjures the image of a satyr, goat below, man above. Horned man. Man above, friar below. Beast above; what, exactly, lower down? He bursts out laughing, stops himself, stares around at the other drinkers. Their faces, slightly blurry, seem to be human, and no-one seems to have noticed that they have a monster in their company. Not one of them knows who I am, he thinks. None of them know about my vows. They don't know about the paintings. About the girl. Christ ... He pushes his hands up under his hat, feels the rough stubble on his scalp. Who am I? Filippo Lippi, son of Tommaso di Lippi, of Borgo San Frediano. That's what it will say on my gravestone. What, then, is all this other stuff? These vows, these obligations? I just want to be the man on my grave. Just a man. A good man.

He contemplates another drink but he decides it is time to move on. It is easy enough to get to the door, though he is sure that twenty, thirty men are staring at his feet. It is night outside, cold, with sharp little stars arranged accusingly overhead. His bundle – his vows – slung over his back, he begins to walk, a little unsteadily, as though his legs have been carved out of wood by an apprentice carpenter: out into the square, over to the column, its base hung with rusty chains where petty criminals are chained. He could have ended up here if he hadn't gone into the cloister, with men shying rotten apples and pomegranates at his head. But he'd thrown things with the best of them. What sport it had been. What laughs… He rattles a chain: it is heavy and bitterly cold. Not much fun to be sitting here, trapped in front of all those leering, laughing faces.

He wanders across Via Calzaiuoli and through the narrow streets to Piazza Signoria, which still holds small knots of people standing around, gossiping, discussing wool prices, the Flanders trade. He moves on towards the river. This is still his city, he thinks. It will always be his. He wishes the girl was here, so that he could point out the sights to her. Has she ever been to Florence? he wonders. He could go and fetch her here. With those three and a half florins he could dress her in fine wool, buy gold thread to weave in her hair.

He is walking through the thin night-time crowds, men on their way from one bar to another, to the gaming tables, to brothels, to girls or boys. Faces come at him, loom and then pass: happy, angry, stupid. Blessed, some of them? All of them? He could draw that one: wine has made the man's nose pillow outwards like a fungus, but his eyes are wise. This one with the crooked teeth and the long earlobes. Him with the beautiful blond curls spilling out from his red hat, with blue eyes and innocent mouth, no doubt off to throw dice. The slave woman with the Circassian face, grey streaks in her hair. The black-robed lawyer with the disappointed face. No free women, of course: they won't be on these streets at night. He knows where to find other women, though. He might even know some of them, in the alleys near the Malvaggia, the Buco, the Bertuccie. Faces from years ago. They will have aged: Giovanna, Nanna, Mea, Piera. What would they say if he turned up, looking like this? He laughs out loud, but then ... Two streets away. Or down by the river, under the bridges. He could. That's where he came from. And those women would understand a creature like him: half man, half friar, a beast with his vows wrapped up and slung across his shoulder.

Or he could just leave altogether. The world beyond the city walls is a trackless ocean of faces to study, to draw. It would take a thousand lifetimes, he muses, to count all the taverns you could find there. And in how many of those taverns might there be a lovely serving girl? To draw, to listen for in the night, to discover. He imagines himself on a map radiating out in all directions: first he is a giant, then as the perspective rises he grows smaller and smaller, and Florence does too, until city and friar are no more visible than a single grain of sand on the riverbank. I could just go, he thinks. With money in my pocket, and my skills ... I'll find a new master. Or I'll be my own master. I'll cross the river and keep walking.

He finds himself in the lanes between the Signoria and the Ponte Vecchio: dark, narrow alleys lit by the odd flickering torch. There are more torches ahead, and the rise and fall of voices. He wanders on, and sees – of course! – it is the Taverna Il Buco, drinking place, meeting place, most notorious of all sodomitical brothels in Florence. Tucked away in this skein of alleyways, it is fairly safe from the attentions of The Eight, and its landlord, Antonio Guardi – getting on in age now – has for years been providing Florence with gossip, scandal and ribald amusement. Poems have been written about old Guardi. In his time, Filippo has overheard many a conversation about nights spent in the Buco's upstairs rooms: this is Florence, after all. Filippo has never fancied other men, though he sees no harm in sodomy, and as everyone knows, the night police only pick on sodomites so they can fine them and send the coins jingling into the city coffers.

As he walks past, the hum of male voices from inside sounds warm and companionable. Not for him, this place, though he wishes he could go in and pass the time, join in the laughter, without having to consider the other... He hunches his shoulders and walks on past the men, most of them young, who are leaning against the wall, talking to each other in loud, knowing voices or looking up and down the street for company or the police. No-one pays him much attention, though, and he has almost reached the corner of the alley when one of the young men happens to turn his head at the sound of his footsteps. The man's face lights up at the prospect of trade, then falls when he sees the shabby figure going by, and Filippo recognises him at once.

'Albertino?'

'Who's that talking to me?' Albertino mutters, disdainfully. Filippo goes closer.

'It's me! Pippo!'

Albertino looks him up and down, lip curled. Filippo sees that he is wearing a set of more than decent clothes – not new, but cut from expensive wool and altered to fit tightly. 'I don't think you've got enough to buy what you're after,' he says disdainfully.

'What are you doing, Albertino?'

'Whose business...' Then Albertino recognises him. 'Dear oh dear! Pippo lo Schizza! What in Christ's name has happened to you?' he hoots. 'You look like some sort of *bricklayer*. Like you've bricked yourself up by mistake, and had to fight your way out. Couldn't take the cloister, eh?'

'No, I'm...' On my way back there, he almost says, but is that really true? 'I've just got back from Pisa. These are just my travelling clothes,' he says lamely. To prove it, he takes off his cap to show his shaved head.

'Ri–i–i–ght.' Albertino leans back and puts a foot against the wall, sticks his knee out. Filippo sees that he is quite drunk, and also that a purposeful-looking dagger hangs from his belt.

'So this is what you're doing now?' Filippo asks.

'Sometimes.'

'Nice clothes.'

'Aren't they? They were a present.'

'I expect you were grateful.' Filippo means it as a joke. He wants to make Albertino smile, to see an old friend relax, become the boy he remembers, but instead Albertino narrows his eyes.

'All my friends are grateful. So they should be. I'm worth all the money they give me.' He laughs coldly. 'Money for nothing. You should try it … Except who would go with you? Short and bandy. Big ears. Though I expect the tonsure would be bait for some. Takes all sorts.'

'Do what you want!' says Filippo, determined not to take offence. 'But for money, Albertino?'

'Don't come all pious with me, *Fra* Filippo. How d'you think I got that coin you tricked out of me that day? Nuzzio too. We've moved on from the riverbank.'

'Good. Sometimes, though, I miss it,' says Filippo.

'You *can*, living all safe and fat in your cloister. Well, it doesn't make you better than me, Pippo Lippi. The only difference between me and a friar like you is that I get paid for bending over!'

'I wish you good fortune, Albertino,' says Filippo gently. 'Do what you want. What you must.'

'Don't judge me!' Albertino's hand has slipped down to his waist, near the pommel of his dagger.

'I wouldn't dare. I'm not bothered what you do. But … You should come to church. Eh? Once in a while. To balance things out.'

'You must be fucking joking.'

'Why so angry, Albertino?' Filippo raises his hands, palms out. 'We're the same, aren't we? Still alive, in spite of the odds?'

'But I'm not soft as birdshit,' says Albertino. 'Unlike Pippo, lucky little bastard who had it all given to him. Have you forgotten little Meo, that day by the river? I went to get some blood in return for his, and I thought Pippo Lippi was behind me. But he wasn't, was he? Managed to get himself *saved*. By the fucking *commesse*. Well, I take what I need. And I'll take from anyone. Got anything on *you*, little Pippo?' Albertino pushes himself away from the wall. His fist has closed around the handle of his dagger.

'You used to have a good heart,' says Filippo. He swallows down his fear, his anger. Sadness.

'No, I didn't. Nor did you. There's no such thing as good hearts.'

'No?' Filippo looks his old friend in the eyes, but all he finds is the glint of savage enjoyment. 'Then I'll be off. Knife me if you want, brother. You'll find a *grosso* in my belt.' He turns and walks away, heart pounding, but there are no footsteps behind him. He has reached the corner when Albertino calls out, high and mocking: 'Pray for me, brother! Pray for me!'

Out of sight of the Buco, Filippo slumps against a wall, breathing hard. He keeps seeing Albertino's face, flushed with pleasure at his fear, and the bitter singsong is still ringing in his ears. He hadn't been afraid, he thinks: not of his friend's knife, anyway. It is Albertino's words that twist inside him now, because he had been right, in a way, hadn't he? They were the same. What would Filippo have done, if the dice had not landed in his favour? If Monna Dianora hadn't taken him by the hand? She could have chosen Albertino instead. I take what I want, he'd said. Yes, and why shouldn't he, poor bastard?

Something makes Filippo look up. He is standing beneath a painted shrine to the Virgin, jutting out from the corner where two narrow streets come together. He looks up at the old, worm-eaten wood, the raddled face of Our Lady still kindly despite the years and the insects. She needs a new coat of paint, someone to get up on a ladder and make her young again.

'I'm going to leave the Order, Mother,' he tells her. 'I'm going to go off and do...' He rubs his eyes. What is he going to do? Convince the world that he is a great painter? Or sell his arse like Albertino? Which, the Virgin's pock-marked face seems to be asking him, is more likely? 'I've already broken my vows. I've lied. I've slept with a girl and I'm going to do it again. I can't be a friar after that, can I?'

The Virgin stares patiently at the opposite wall, as she must have been doing for a hundred, two hundred years. This is all beneath me, she seems to be saying. What matters is that you are asking. 'So what should I do, Mother?' Filippo insists. The Virgin just stares. 'Well, I've made up my mind,' says Filippo. 'I'll always serve you, Mother. Whatever happens. I'll always show everybody how beautiful you are. Even though I'm not beautiful myself. But that doesn't matter, eh? It doesn't matter.' He pushes off from the wall and sets off south on slightly shaky legs. I'll spend the night in one of the gardens by the Porta Romana, he decides. As soon as they open the gates I'll be away.

The thought is exciting. His blood, thickened by his encounter with Albertino, quickens again, begins to pulse. The sound of drunken laughter comes from nearby: his ears prick up. He knows where it is coming from. The Taverna Baldracca is just around the corner. The money in his belt will buy him a comfortable night there, and no mistake. He and his friends had loitered outside on hot summer evenings and watched the women call to the passing men, shake their breasts, lift up their shifts... The boys had talked of grand stealing expeditions to raise enough money for a few minutes with one of those terrifying, wonderful creatures, but they never had. Or Filippo hadn't. But now...

'Fra Filippo?'

He whips around guiltily, to find Masaccio walking towards him from the direction of the Piazza della Signoria.

'Maestro!' he stammers. 'I...'

'What's all this?' Masaccio waves his hand at Filippo's clothes.

Filippo sees that the man's fingers are heavily stained with blue and brown. For some reason he finds the sight incredibly moving.

'I'm lost,' he says, and raises his own hands helplessly. It is, he discovers, the truth.

'In Florence? I doubt it. Did you just get back?' Filippo nods. 'And are friars allowed to take off their habits for travel?' It is an honest question, Filippo understands.

'Yes,' he says.

'And you're on your way back to the cloister?'

'That's right.' Ribald laughter is coming in waves from the Baldracca. Filippo sucks in his breath through clenched teeth.

'Fra Filippo? Have you been drinking?'

'A bit,' he confesses. 'Do you fancy a glass at the Baldracca, maestro? My treat.'

'The Baldracca? Christ, man! Would I let a friar buy me a drink in a brothel?'

'Why not?' says Filippo, and starts to laugh. Once the laughter has taken hold of his diaphragm he finds he can't stop, until he feels Masaccio's hands on his shoulders. The painter gives him a shake.

'I really am lost, maestro,' he croaks, feeling hot tears on his face.

'No you aren't,' says Masaccio, firmly. 'Don't worry. Come with me.' Filippo allows himself to be led out into a busier street where the crowd envelops them. He follows Masaccio, not looking at the faces, not listening to voices, until he realises they are crossing the Ponte Vecchio. On the other side, the air of home gathers round him. The sound of his feet on the cobbles ... No cobbles anywhere in the world sound like they do. No cabbage boiled anywhere else in Creation could smell as it does here, wafting out from these windows with the perfume of grilling meat, and frying onions sweetened by the sharp December air. This street will lead him to the Carmine. He assumes that is where Masaccio is leading him, but instead the painter turns left into Via de' Bardi. They walk deep into the Scala neighbourhood: almost a foreign country to him. They turn into Via San Niccolo.

'My lodgings,' says Masaccio, stopping in front of an old but freshly plastered house. He unlocks the door. Filippo is exhausted, and the warmth of all the wine he has drunk has faded, leaving him chilled to the bone. He allows himself to be propped against the wall in the little vestibule, which he can see, by the light of Masaccio's rush lamp, is hung with old, threadbare tapestries on which distorted knights on fat-legged horses fight one another. The painter takes him by the arm and leads him gently through a door into a comfortable room with a fire blazing in the hearth, a couple of chairs, a table piled high with papers, books, jars of brushes, jars of pigment...

'Messy Tom,' says Filippo. His teeth have started to chatter.

'At your service.' Masaccio sits Filippo down firmly in one of the chairs, which he has drawn up to the edge of the hearth, takes off his mud-caked sandals and drops what Filippo takes to be a large dead animal into his lap, but which proves to be a moth-eaten old bearskin. He pulls it up to his chin and draws up his feet. Masaccio is squatting by the fire, which is eagerly devouring a pile of dry olive wood, heating a poker in the coals. When it is glowing he thrusts it into a clay jug. There is a loud hissing, and rich fumes curl up. He pours dark, steaming liquid into a cup and puts it into Filippo's hands.

'You've had a bit too much already,' he mutters, 'But this is hot. There's pepper in it, and nutmeg. Drink it down, and tell me what in God's name you've been up to!'

'I finished the predella,' says Filippo, trying to keep his shaking hands steady. Hot, spicy wine burns its way down his throat, dangerous but pleasant. 'Prior Antonio likes it. Everything...'

'Everything what, brother?' Masaccio looks worried.

'It's all right. Ser Giuliano is happy. He's more than happy, maestro.' Filippo takes a swig of the hot wine. It seems to shoot through every artery in his body, every vein. His limbs begin to loosen, and when he starts to speak again, his tongue is loosened as well. It all comes tumbling out: his frightful lie to Ser Giuliano, his carousing with Michelozzo, his night with the girl in Montopoli, the mule, his disguise, his run-in with Albertino, all the wine...

'Madonna...The pope? And Messer Medici?' Masaccio roars with laughter. 'Christ, the lies *I'll* have to tell now! Couldn't you just have told him I was in the privy? Fra Filippo, you have exceeded all my expectations. So what vows haven't you broken? Any of them?'

'I didn't get buggered upstairs at the Buco.' Filippo grins. 'But I suppose celibacy covers that, and I've broken...'

'Ah, yes: Simona, the temptress of Montopoli.'

'You know her?' Filippo lurches forward, shedding the bearskin. 'Wait! You haven't...'

'No, no, no.' Masaccio clucks soothingly, tucking the bearskin back around Filippo's body. 'Not for want of trying – I'll say that. You lucky man.' He pours himself some wine, but when Filippo holds out his cup he wags a finger at him. 'Enough for you.'

'Now you see: I can't ever go back to the Carmine,' says Filippo, his happiness vanishing. 'I've failed the prior. I've failed my brothers. I suppose I've failed everybody.'

'But you haven't failed me,' says Masaccio gently.

'I expect I have. You'll have to dig your way out of that dunghill of a lie I told for you.'

'You are an idiot, Fra Filippo. You have saved me! My reputation, my purse... what else is there? You have no idea of my gratitude. I knew you could do it. Listen: Fra Antonio sent me a letter by someone who made better time on the road than you. I don't have it to hand, but he says something like *Fra Filippo has made the crime of Saint Julian and the miracle of Saint Nicholas equal in wonder. Most acceptable... Great promise...* A lot of that. You have impressed Maestro Antonio, which isn't at all easy. He is a true maestro.'

'If he knew what I've done,' mumbles Filippo into the damp hem of the bearskin.

'Do not underestimate the prior, brother. He sees the world as clearly as he sees Heaven. There are a few sly little hints in the letter. If I know anything about Fra Antonio, it is that he understands compromise. And I'm quite certain that if he had to choose between a bad friar who is also a great painter, and a bad painter with perfect vows and devotions, he'd choose the first.'

'Do you mean that?'

'Completely. Both he and Prior Pietro have said, more than once, that they wish the Brancacci commission could have been done by an artist within the Carmelite Order, like – they always say this – like Fra Giovanni the Dominican, in Fiesole. Fra Antonio has always done business with artists. He knows what we are like.'

'We?'

'Painters! You are a painter, brother. Haven't you got that into your head yet? Don't you want to paint?'

'It's the only thing I *do* want.'

'Just go and talk to your prior. He and Fra Antonio are great friends. And they both have a very considerable love of art. You will be surprised, I promise you.'

'But how can I?'

'Oh, for God's sake!' Masaccio picks up the poker and starts to lash at the fire so that the flames leap up. 'Are you the first friar to get plastered? Madonna! The first one to lie with a woman? Do you not listen to the stories, Fra Filippo? All the tales of what you lot get up to in your cells? You of all people! Stop feeling sorry for yourself. You surprise me, actually. I didn't take you for the self-pitying sort. Drinking and fornicating, yes. But self-pity? That's a proper sin, in my book.'

'Easy for you to say.' But Filippo finds himself grinning. 'I wasn't feeling sorry for myself, maestro. I was just... Well, I was afraid. But if you're right about the priors...'

'I am.' Masaccio sticks the poker back in the jug, and the steam billows out. He pours out two cups and gives Filippo one. 'You might as well have another. Tomorrow we'll get you tidied up and you can turn up at the Carmine as though ... well, as though you'd walked all the way from Pisa. Which is what you'll tell the prior.'

Filippo sips at the wine. 'We could be drinking at the Baldracca now if you'd taken me up on my offer,' he mutters, contentedly.

'Were you really going there?'

'I don't know. I don't think so. I thought I was on my way to Naples.'

'That's a long way to go. Just to get away from the Carmine?'

'That. And so I wouldn't have to think about letting my mother down.'

'Ah. You have a mother,' says Masaccio, stretching out his legs in front of the fire.

'She lives in a dunghill of an apartment with my sister. She's not right in the head, and all she does is stare at the wall all day long. If they threw me out of the Order, she wouldn't even know it, but my sister, Leonarda ...' He shakes his head. 'She works so hard, and she has nothing. Her life is no bigger than those foul little rooms. And yet she's proud of me. Of this.' He raps his knuckles on the stubble of his tonsure.

'Is that how you ended up living on the streets? Because your mother became ill?'

Filippo nods. 'After my father died. It was so unexpected, I suppose – he just fell down dead in his shop. And when my mother heard, she fell down too, right in front of me. I was six years old. We all expected her to get up again, because she was healthy and full of life, and people lose their husbands and their wives all the time. And she did get up, but she wasn't right after that. Papa had left his affairs in a state, because ... You don't expect to die like that, do you? There were debts, and taxes to be paid, and Mamma listened to bad advice. Really, she wasn't listening at all – it took me years to work that out. We had a nice big house on Borgo San Frediano, near the gate, and she started selling it off, bit by bit. And all the time, she was getting worse. I'd find her sitting, staring at the wall. Or she couldn't get out of bed. My uncle, Filippo Lapaccia... he tried to help.'

'Took all your papa's money for himself?' Masaccio is listening intently.

'No, no. He was an honest man. Dull as a roof-tile, but honest. He just did what the creditors wanted. They were the swindlers, not him. What was left had to go, to raise some money to keep Mamma alive, because by then she couldn't do anything. So far there's been just enough for her and for Leonarda. That's why I left. There just wasn't enough for three of us. I couldn't bear to see my sister getting thin because she was giving me her food. I was supposed to live with Uncle Filippo and Aunt Maria, but then Uncle died of the plague and Aunt... She's peppery. Much, much younger than her husband. She got married again fast as you like, to a merchant who travels a lot. She has young children. No time to think about my mamma – not that I blame her. It isn't her business any more. No time for me, that's for sure. I'd spend a week there from time to time, but she's handy with a stick. I was safer out on the streets.'

'So you'd like to do something for your mamma.'

'There's nothing I want more. But what can I do? Pray? Doesn't seem to help. It was stupid of me to become a friar. I should have set out to make money.'

'Like your friend Albertino, you mean?'

Filippo laughs bitterly. 'You're right. That's where people like me end up. At the Buco, or worse. On the gibbet, or in the river. Albertino was right: I'm safe in the cloister. But I'm helpless. I don't know what's worse.'

'Maybe not as helpless as you think. And now you need to get to bed. Tomorrow we'll go to the bath house, get you shaved and shorn and fit for the cloister.'

Filippo allows Masaccio to pull him to his feet. He is dimly aware of climbing a steep staircase, and collapsing onto a hard bed that nonetheless smells sweetly of fresh straw. He lies there as Masaccio dumps blankets on top of him.

'Maestro?' he says, as Masaccio is leaving the room. 'Why are you doing this? Why do you care?'

'Because you're my assistant,' says Masaccio.

'Not any more.'

'Oh, yes. I haven't released you, have I? You're one of us. A painter. And because loyalty is the most important thing that there is in this filthy world.'

12

'Saints' blood!' Masaccio winces as Filippo walks into the room. The fire is lit. Masaccio is sitting at the table, sketching on a roll of paper that is pinned flat with a stone hand at one end – so realistic that Filippo's stomach lurches for a moment until he sees it is just ancient marble – and at the other, a cast-iron twist that had once been the end of a crozier on an archbishop's statue. 'Good morning, Lazarus. Or have you in fact completely risen from the dead? I can't tell.'

Filippo crosses himself. 'Don't say things like that, maestro!' he protests.

'Eat,' says Masaccio, gesturing towards a bowl of curds and a large raisin bun that is teetering on the edge of the table. Then his head goes down and he begins to draw again, a stick of red chalk balanced delicately between his fingers. Filippo takes the curds and the bread and sits by the fire, eating and looking around the room. Propped against one wall are two large panels each painted with two saints: the missing parts of Ser Giuliano's altarpiece. When he has finished eating, he goes and peers over Masaccio's shoulder. He sees a collection of figures, an orderly crowd: heads above robes above feet.

'What's this?' he asks.

'A possible job,' says Masaccio. 'Big commission.'

'It's all about money, isn't it?' says Filippo. 'Everything. The whole world.'

'Is that bad?'

'Funny question to ask a friar,' Filippo observes.

'The answer is yes, in any case, for good or for ill. Work is work. There's no time to sit still. For instance, I'm going back to Pisa as soon as I've finished this one panel in the Brancacci Chapel. A week – ten days at the outside. Ser Giuliano is due to accept his altarpiece on the Feast of Stephen, and I'll get paid.'

'Will you take me with you?' says Filippo hopefully.

'No need. I'll be back before the beginning of the new year. I have to pay the rent. How much do you think this place costs me?'

Filippo looks around, shrugs. 'I have no idea. I don't know anything about that sort of thing.'

'One florin a year, and that's expensive for this end of Oltrarno. But it's funny you should say that about friars and money. Do you know Fra Albizzo de' Nerli? You must. He's one of you Carmelites.'

Filippo nods. 'Only by sight. He's far too grand to even look at me, though.'

'He owns a few houses around the Carmine. Well, he's a Nerli. You'd know all about them, living at that end of the Borgo.'

'Rich as King Midas,' agrees Filippo.

'Fra Albizzo offered to rent me a house in the Piazza del Carmine,' says Masaccio. 'A nice place, sunny. With furniture, and for the same as I'm paying here. One florin a year. I turned him down, most politely, because I've become fond of Monna Piera. She's a good landlady and she tolerates my comings and goings, and the Messy Tom side of me. But everyone's at it, Fra Filippo. Priests, friars, popes ...'

'The whole world, eh? Tell me about this commission, then.'

'I'll tell you about it later. Eat some more and then we'll go out.'

A little later, they are walking together down Via de' Bardi. Filippo is wearing some clothes of Masaccio's: a dark, blood-red tunic, brown hose, short serge cloak. Masaccio has already led him down to the edge of the Arno and made him throw the clothes he had bought yesterday into the fast-flowing brown water. He had watched the rough bundle twist and turn in the current, open like a dingy, ragged bloom and come apart.

'You could have sold them,' he had protested.

'For what? A *denaro*? Not worth the effort,' Masaccio had told him seriously. 'Think like a pauper, be a pauper.'

There is a bathhouse off the Costa San Giorgio, near the city wall. It looks disreputable from the outside but once they have gone in, Filippo sees that it is just a neighbourhood place, where a few old men are soaking and gossiping in the steam. Masaccio pays for a bath, a scrub and a shave for Filippo, who imagines that the scalding, herb-scented water is leeching away at least some of the stains he has been acquiring lately. The barber scrapes his razor across the top of his head, and the sensation, which had been so shocking when he had first been tonsured, is comforting. 'Dispensation,' he murmurs, when the barber, an old man with deep, almost carved lines swooping across his face, looks askance at his layman's clothes. 'Special dispensation.'

Filippo stares into the small looking glass the barber holds up for him. He hasn't seen himself properly in years: there are no looking glasses in the cloister. He has glimpsed his reflection in the distorting curves of polished silver chalices and in puddles of rainwater, but here in front of him is a face such as one might see across a refectory table or in the street.

'Is that me?' he says, amazed.

'Who else would it be?'

He is looking at an almost round head, an elongated sphere, domed like a cannonball above, and gleaming from the passage of the razor. His chin is round as well, dimpled. He had no idea his mouth was so wide. There is a hunger implied in the fleshy, almost feminine curve of his lips which he finds disturbing. He looks into his own eyes. They are heavy-lidded, dark ink-brown, close-set but large, watching him, watching themselves. The irises dart, gathering, betraying an appetite, a need for satiation. This face is thinking, how will I draw you? How will you draw me?

The straight jut of his nose surprises him. The sides swoop up and curve inward, accentuating its thrust. It makes his face look like a fleshy ship, as if God has given him a prow. Something to lead with, to search with. And then his ears, large and whorled, which stick out at the top but fold back so that the lobes touch the flesh at the top of his jaw. Am I a ship or a dog? A butcher's dog, a big cur, sharp-eyed, greedy and stubborn. An honest face? Hardly. But Filippo sees something which he had not expected: along with the hunger, the appetite, there is determination.

'Made up your mind yet?' says the barber. 'Is it you or isn't it?'

'Well, if it isn't, I wish this fellow all the luck in the world, because he looks as if he needs it.'

The barber gives him another world-weary look. 'Say a prayer for me, brother. If you really are a friar. Your friend!' He calls over to Masaccio. 'I've finished with him. Is he quite right in the head?'

'I doubt it,' says Masaccio, taking out his purse.

'Ah, well, those convents,' mutters the barber. 'It isn't quite healthy, if you ask me. Pray for me anyway,' he adds, hastily, as Filippo takes a last glance at himself and puts on his cloak. Masaccio pulls the faded black cap over his shining scalp and they go out into the clear, icy day.

Masaccio does not lead them back to his house, where Filippo has been expecting to change back into his Carmelite habit. Instead they cross the Ponte Vecchio. Filippo almost points out his father's old shop but the memory of last night is still too sharp, so he keeps quiet as they pass the crowd lining up for the day's meat. They walk past the bankers outside Orsanmichele, swaddled in thick fur cloaks and hats, and dive into the narrow streets to the south of the Mercato. Passing the Chiassolino, Filippo looks around for the old rag seller. There she is, squatting behind her piles of clothing, but she doesn't recognise him. They walk on until they reach the wide piazza in front of Santa Maria Novella. Masaccio jogs briskly up the steps and Filippo follows.

He has not been inside the church for years. Before the cloister, he had used to come here, to stare at the great wooden crucifix painted by Giotto, three times life size, that hangs in the sacristy. He assumes that Masaccio is taking him there: it would be an appropriate thing to meditate on, given his current state of mind. Then he remembers him saying something about a tomb in Santa Maria Novella. And indeed, the maestro has stopped halfway down the left-hand wall of the aisle.

'This was why I couldn't finish Ser Giuliano's altarpiece,' he says.

Under a curved, coffered ceiling that recedes into a shadowy crypt, God is holding up the cross on which his son is hanging, lifeless, bloodless. A man stands on one side of the cross, looking up. On the other side, a woman...

'Last night, you talked about suffering,' Masaccio says. 'From your own experience. When I saw the Virgin you drew on your cloak, I knew that whoever had made that picture had an understanding. Of how we suffer. Anyway, I wanted you to see what I have been doing.'

Filippo can't find any words. The old woman, the Virgin who has faced, at last, the future she already has seen in the Pisa altarpiece, has come to rest in the stillness of disaster. There is no point in despairing now. She looks past Filippo with grey eyes. She is getting old now, no longer the young, exhausted mother. This boy will not wake her up in the night again. The horror is over; grief will come. For now, her drawn face is calm, her mouth is set in a stern line. Her open hand offers the corpse of her son. This is for you. Is this what you wanted? Do you have it, now?

I've never known suffering like that, he is about to say, but then he looks again. Below the Virgin, below the two donors who kneel on either side of the niche, a skeleton lies on a marble plinth, jaw fallen onto its breastbone. *What you are, I once was. What I am, you will be* is inscribed on the plinth. It is hard, at first, for him to believe that this tomb is just paint and flat plaster. The brown bones seem to give off a damp, mouldy smell. Everything in the painting above – the beams of the cross, which even God is straining to hold up; Christ's limp body; the Virgin's blue-black robe – seems to be slipping inexorably downward towards the dusty brown grave. But God lifts, Mary stands, Saint John prays. The tension between rise and fall, the lightness of grace and the dreadful weight of the world... He understands.

The perspective, which Masaccio has mastered, creates a magic space, a place which doesn't exist and yet is right there in front of him. The space inside his head, in a way; the thought makes him look again at the skeleton, the skull with its loose jaw. He thinks of his father, and the familiar sadness wells up inside him. But there is the Virgin, stern and patient, pointing. He did this for you. We all share the burden.

'She is beautiful,' he murmurs.

'I thought you would like her.' Masaccio is standing by his side. 'It was partly you who gave me the inspiration. What you said about Ser Giuliano's Madonna. And the woman on the cloak.'

'You shouldn't say things like that, maestro,' Filippo says. 'I'm nothing. I could look at this for a hundred years and never be able to copy an inch of it.'

'Nonsense. What I said last night about self-pity...'

'I don't remember all of last night,' Filippo admits sheepishly.

'I said I despise self-pity. Well, I hate false modesty as well. Wake up, Fra Filippo. Stir yourself. You can be an unhappy friar and chase your tail your whole life, a little bit of sin here, a lot of guilt there. Or you can be a painter. A great one. You know that perfectly well. You can't keep hiding behind your robe while you fish for compliments. Do you want to do this, or not?' He jabs his finger at the fresco. Then he grabs Filippo by the arm and marches him to the sacristy, points up at Giotto's vast crucifix suspended from the ceiling. 'Do you want to do this? Yes, or no. Tell me in front of Maestro Giotto.'

'Yes,' Filippo whispers. Then louder: 'Yes, I do.'

'Of course you do. So: you're my proper assistant, starting from this moment. I'll have a contract drawn up. I'll be your sponsor with the Guild.' He holds up a finger. 'Don't say a word. You've made up your mind now: it's done. We'll go to the cloister and talk to the prior. Agreed?'

'Agreed. All right, maestro. Agreed!'

Filippo decides he ought to go back to the Carmine on his own, to at least try and pretend that he has just walked in from Pisa. He changes into his Carmelite robes at Masaccio's lodgings. Masaccio heads off to the Carmine – there is a panel to finish in Ser Felice's chapel, and he is in enough trouble over it already, he sighs.

'I'll be there, working,' he says. 'After I've had a word with the prior. But we haven't seen each other since Pisa: agreed, brother? Can you play the part?'

'I'm sure I'll manage,' says Filippo.

'I'm sure you will. With your gifts of persuasion, brother, it will go beautifully. I'll see you there.'

Filippo walks up the hill to the Porta San Giorgio and trudges all the way around the city walls to the Porta San Frediano, trying to make it into a penance, but enjoying the crisp sunshine far too much for that. By the time he reaches the cloister he is authentically tired. He hesitates for a moment before crossing the threshold, then steels himself and goes inside.

He finds Fra Girolamo the sub-prior, who welcomes him back so warmly that Filippo almost gives him a brotherly hug, though such things are not done in the cloister. Fra Girolamo takes him to see the prior in the studium.

'Welcome back, Fra Filippo,' says Fra Pietro, steepling his fingers in his familiar way. 'I trust you had an uneventful journey?'

'I was blessed with good weather,' says Filippo. 'Except for the first day. I ...' He pauses, decides. One throw. 'I enjoyed the walking, Reverend Father. But of course it is good to be home.'

'Now ...' The prior puts his finger on a letter, one of many scattered in some sort of order across his table. 'Glowing reports from Fra Antonio. I sent you to Pisa so that you might be of help, and it seems you have done far more than anybody expected. Excellent. Quite excellent. I will look forward to seeing this altarpiece of Maestro Tomasso's – and of yours, I must add. Fra Antonio tells me in his letter that it is quite without equal.'

'Thank you, Reverend Father!'

'*A Saint Albert of blessed gravity and simplicity of demeanour, a face of surpassing honesty.* Well, well.' The prior looks up. 'I am delighted, Fra Filippo. It seems the gift we saw in you, and hoped to nurture, is coming into fruit. Come with me. I have something to show you.' He leads Filippo out of the study. They pass through the cloister, where a couple of older friars see Filippo and smile in surprised greeting, and into the church.

Santa Maria on a cold Thursday afternoon in December should be almost silent. But as soon as Filippo has followed the prior through the door, he hears voices. Men's voices, not pitched to the reverential hush of priests or worshippers, but unabashed, bantering back and forth, laughing. There is a scrape of wood against stone, more laughter, a loud command. One of the voices sounds familiar. He follows the prior towards the altar, then into the right arm of the transept. Filippo gasps. Dazzling light and vivid colours are blazing out of the chapel built into the end wall. And there, halfway up a ladder, is Masaccio.

'Maestro!' Filippo calls, then covers his mouth, wincing. But Fra Pietro merely shakes his head in mild admonition.

'Good day to you, Reverend Father! And Fra Filippo – welcome back to Florence! I thank you a hundred times! Did it all go well? Are the panels ...'

'Finished, maestro. *A Saint Albert of blessed gravity and simplicity of demeanour,*' Filippo quotes. He tries not to look at Masaccio.

'I knew it!' Masaccio exclaims. 'Did I not tell you, Reverend Father? An eye like that, a hand of that grace ...'

'You did. I am glad I thought to show you ...' Fra Pietro turns to Filippo. 'The cloak you drew on,' he explains.

'I never asked your forgiveness for that, Reverend Father,' Filippo says, quite sincerely. 'I didn't have time. But you were right to punish me.'

'I am sorry you thought you were being punished, Fra Filippo,' the prior says. 'I sent you away to learn. Do you think you have learned anything?'

'Time will tell!' says Masaccio brightly. Filippo almost collapses with gratitude. 'I would say, and I am just a painter, mind you, that everything Fra Filippo has learned, he has taught himself. Should we all be fortunate enough to have such an excellent teacher! Now, come and look at the new figures.'

'I have seen none of this,' says Filippo, when they are standing inside the chapel.

'That's right. Well, look here.'

Filippo is already looking. He sees a stormy sky, mountains, green water lapping against a sandy beach, where a man is crouched, dipping his hands in the shallows. In front of a colonnaded building... A crowd of ghosts. A cluster of disembodied heads, hovering above forms that seem to be appearing out of light, or fading into it. Hands float in space. There are cloaks with emptiness where a head should be. Some are just bare outlines of brightness.

'It is Christ telling Peter to find a coin in the mouth of a fish, to pay Caesar,' Masaccio is explaining.

'Go thou to the sea, and cast an hook, and take up the fish that first cometh up,' says the prior, nodding. 'Somewhat obscure as a subject for a fresco, perhaps, but Ser Felice chose it, and it is proving to be quite... dramatic.'

'Christ is finished, obviously,' Masaccio says to Filippo, who nods. The Saviour, young, bearded, sternly patient, as though He is explaining something very simple for the hundredth time, points towards the water. Two worried, bearded men stand behind Him, and a head, with a straight, Greek nose and mop of yellow ringlets hangs, bodiless, to the side.

'And the others? Who are they?' he asks, after a silence.

'Haven't decided yet. What do you think?'

'Me? I have no idea, maestro!'

'Well, find an idea. As my assistant, you are required to use your brains.' Masaccio cocks his head towards the prior. 'With your permission, of course, prior?'

'I was under the impression that Fra Filippo was already your assistant.' Filippo and Masaccio both give the prior a sharp look, but there is no sign of anything out of the ordinary in his face. 'Yes, Ser Tommaso, of course, as we discussed. The financial aspect ... Again, as we discussed, Fra Filippo's wages are of course forfeit, as he holds Orders, but I am sure he would wish them to be made as a donation to the Carmine. My son?'

Filippo sighs with disappointment, manages to disguise the sigh as a cough, rubs his face theatrically. Four and a half florins, gone like that. It stings. But I didn't really expect to keep all that money, did I? he tells himself. 'As you suggest, Reverend Father,' he says brightly. Easy come, easy go ... Filippo looks from one man to the other. Who cares about the money? Something far more important is happening here. 'Can a friar be a painter? Fra Antonio spoke to me about this, but it didn't make sense at the time. That is, am I really allowed?'

'*Frate dipintore*. Friar painters. Yes, there are some,' says the prior. 'It is permitted. I think it should be encouraged. Fra Antonio feels very strongly about that. I agree with him.'

'That excellent Dominican at Fiesole – Fra Giovanni,' says Masaccio. 'And Don Lorenzo in Siena, God rest his soul. I would have liked to have met him.'

'So yes, you can be a friar and a painter. *You*, Fra Filippo. This has fallen to you, of all the friars in this convent, of all the Carmelites in Italy.' The prior's voice is stern. For a moment, Filippo has the odd notion that it is coming, not from the mouth of Fra Piero, but from one of the empty, luminous outlines on the wall behind him. 'It is a vocation that has come to you from God,' he continues. 'And it is God whom you will serve with your gift. God, and the Order of Mount Carmel. If you accept this gift, and this burden.'

'It is a burden, most definitely,' Masaccio puts in. He is glaring at Filippo in an attitude of profound solemnity, but his paint-smeared tunic, stiff with plaster, the plaster spiking his hair, and the plain fact that he is trying not to laugh ruins the effect.

'If you accept,' says Fra Piero patiently, 'there are great responsibilities. It will put you apart from your brothers...'

'It shouldn't have to,' protests Filippo.

'But it will. You will be serving God outside the strictures of our Rule. You will be working with laymen. You will have one foot in the world outside our walls. You will feel its pull.'

'I understand,' says Filippo. 'Reverend Father, I understand that better than most. You took me in, sir. You knew me before: who I was. *What* I was, and what I would have become.' He has been play-acting up until now, but now he is quite in earnest. 'The Order saved my life. And I want to be a good servant. I didn't know how I could do that. I've never been a good friar. I would only have become worse. But now you've saved me again.'

'Listen, my young lad,' Masaccio says gravely. 'It's beyond my abilities to save your soul! Reverend Father, I'm afraid I shall leave that up to you.'

'Agreed. So you will have Fra Filippo as your assistant? Will you sign a contract with me, to that effect?'

'I will,' says the painter. 'I'll teach him all he needs to know to join the Guild. The rest he knows already.'

'Agreed, Fra Filippo?'

Filippo is nodding his head, about to speak, when Masaccio holds up an orange-stained hand. 'Make sure you know what you're getting in to, young brother. I won't lie to you. It will be dull: extraordinarily tedious. You'll work from sun-up to sun-down, no thanks for what you get right, curses when you make mistakes. None of the work will be yours. You won't be able to claim a single eyelash. Understood?'

'I do.'

'That is ...' Masaccio turns to the prior. 'Can I swear at him if he's still one of your friars, Reverend Father?' he asks, quite seriously. 'I don't think I can teach him otherwise.'

'He will be *your* assistant,' says the prior, with a lift of his chin that says, do what you like. 'But I expect you to teach him good, not bad. I want him to learn your art – here I must speak frankly, my son – and not your life. Fra Filippo will remain in the cloister. Do not make his burden any heavier than it is.'

'He won't, Reverend Father. And yes,' Filippo says for the second time that day, 'I agree!'

13

MASACCIO WORKS AT A PACE that seems impossible to Filippo. The only painter he has ever seen at work is the slow, thoughtful Bicci di Lorenzo, who seems to spend as much time in pious meditation as he does in painting his panels. Masaccio stands on his ladder, in constant motion: brush sweeping, dabbing, picking. As he paints he concentrates, and as he concentrates, his body bends and contorts, as though wracked by cramps. Sometimes muttering to himself, sometimes humming tunelessly, he draws the heads of Christ's disciples out of the wet plaster.

'I can only do one a day,' he explains to Filippo the next day, after a morning in which Filippo has ground pigment and watched the master at work. 'See that outline I'm painting inside? That's the day's fresh plaster, the *giornata*. The paint goes into that and binds to it.' He clenches his fists. 'Now, it takes me about two-thirds of a day's work, usually – if it isn't an important subject, of course – to do a head. But I can't start another, do you see? Because if I leave off, the *giornata* will go off, we'd have to take it off and put on fresh stuff, and there'd be a line, like this.' He divides his face unevenly with a finger and grimaces. 'So then I'll do some hands or feet, or something small ... a dog, something like that.'

'Is there going to be a dog?' says Filippo, intrigued.

'No. No dogs! I don't think the prior would approve, let alone Ser Felice. So, do you see, then? We must work fast, fast, fast. For the plaster ... And for the money. Don't forget the money.'

'How could I? As your assistant, I'm getting a wage, but it all goes to the Order, I suppose?'

Masaccio grunts. 'I'm working that out with the prior,' he mumbles. Filippo shakes his head, ruefully.

'So ... Look here. Christ's hand, yes?' Masaccio changes the subject. 'And these hands belong to John – this is him, the blonde one – these to Luke. We'll put in the cloaks tomorrow afternoon: Andrea and I, and you can do this bit here: the hem of John's robe.'

'A hem, maestro?' Filippo has been expecting more.

'What, should I give you God in His glory to do? You'll begin your apprenticeship by kissing the hem of that robe with due humility, Fra Filippo.' He is chuckling, but Filippo understands. Here in the curtained-off chapel, in the lamplight, in the air that is sharp with the tang of pigment minerals, there is a covenant to be made. He is joining another order. 'And by the by,' Masaccio adds, as if completing Filippo's thought, 'must I call you *Fra*? It seems ...' He cups his hands and gestures: heavy.

'Outside the cloister, people called me Pippo,' says Filippo. 'That, I suppose, is what I call myself.'

'Pippo. Were you small, then?'

'I was. I've grown big on the convent's good food.' He snorts: 'Not so good, perhaps, but abundant, and regular.'

'You are eyeing my lunch,' Masaccio observes.

'I know. What's in there: sausage? Cold beef?'

'And a veal torte,' the painter adds. 'You are welcome to a share. We are all brothers here.'

'The Rule forbids us to eat meat,' says Filippo sadly.

'My God! Always?'

'"Unless it is to be taken as a remedy for illness or bodily weakness",' Filippo quotes.

'Bodily weakness? Well, you are worn out by your ride from Pisa, it is quite plain.'

'Well, no ...'

'You are. You looked peaky yesterday, and no better today.

Worse, in fact. Andrea, doesn't Fra Filippo – I beg your pardon: Pippo – doesn't Pippo look ill?'

'On his last legs,' Masaccio's younger apprentice agrees. 'He needs something stronger than lettuce, I reckon.'

'There you are. As your maestro I am everything: priest, *condottiere*, and doctor. My medical training tells me you are in urgent need of a remedy. Shall we prescribe a slice of pie?' Masaccio cuts a piece and hands it to Filippo, who takes it almost reverently. The last time he tasted meat had been the empanada that Albertino had bought him, after they had thrown the dice. He bends his head, sniffs. The aromas of bay leaf, pepper and cinnamon tickle his nose. The crust is the colour of Saint John's curly hair, and the meat...

'Don't eat it in one bite!' Masaccio says, alarmed. 'I don't want to have to explain to your prior how you choked to death on a torte! And anyway, there's more in my doctor's bag. Take your time.'

Filippo is first put to work mixing paint, which causes him no trouble. Fresco painting is not like painting boards: the pigments are simply ground into water and painted directly onto a thin layer of fresh plaster, the preparation of which is an art in itself. Art is required for everything. Behind the drop cloths around Felice Brancacci's chapel, life itself is art. Despite the painter's talk of swearing, Maestro Masaccio works mostly in the midst of an intense silence, which only erupts into the noisy banter Filippo had heard that first afternoon when a piece is finished. The two assistants take him under their wings without any fuss, no doubt, thinks Filippo, because of my habit. One of them, a slender, quick-eyed man of around Masaccio's age called Andrea di Giusto, is from Florence, from the Unicorn neighbourhood just across the river, the other one, Ruggerio, is older and is more of a plasterer and carpenter, and speaks with a heavy Grosseto accent. It is Ruggerio who mixes the special plaster for the day's work, the *giornata*, and smooths it inside the lines drawn by Andrea on the plaster that has been drying on the wall for weeks. Although it is Andrea who watches the maestro with intense, almost dog-like devotion, who outlines the people and scenery in red chalk and fills in areas that demand little skill, like draperies and sky, Ruggerio has an artistry all of his own. Filippo likes Andrea better – he is quick-witted, funny and knows all the gossip from the city – but he develops a deep admiration for the older plasterer. He is the sort of man who would, in Filippo's other life, have seen the ragged boy sketching in the marketplace and paid him a couple of denarii for a small picture of the Virgin. Men like Ruggerio are the fabric of the city: as ignorable and as fundamental as its bricks and paving stones.

Masaccio has almost finished the Tribute Money. He is filling in the background: the sinister mountains that roll back from the lake shore in folds the colour of drowned flesh; the turquoise wavelets of the lake itself. A storm is brewing. The balance of Heaven and earth is disturbed: the paths of Christ and Caesar are beginning to converge. Masaccio is whistling as he paints. He has been unusually energetic this morning: laughing, joking, waving his brush about like a *condottiere*'s baton.

Filippo is crouched beneath the scaffold, mixing some of the cold green for the lake, when he feels a presence looming over him. He looks up to find the prior looking down at him like a more or less friendly buzzard.

'Fra Filippo? Maestro Tommaso? A brief word.'

The whistling stops abruptly. There is a creaking and a scraping, and Masaccio drops down to the floor. He is blotched with green and grey, as if he's just played a particularly vicious game of *calcio*.

'What comes after this panel, maestro?'

'I think we will have reached a natural pause in our work,' Masaccio says, picking a crumb of plaster from the corner of his eye with a fingernail. 'Ser Felice tells me he is awaiting more funds, and ...' He pauses, and glances at Filippo almost furtively. 'I have had a letter from Maestro Masolino, just this morning, who tells me he is on his way to Rome and wants me to come and help him with a commission there.'

'Indeed? For whom?' The prior, Filippo might swear, is very slightly impressed.

Masaccio pauses again. 'For His Holiness.'

'Good Heavens! What … What a blessing, my son!'

'It is, indeed. My master is to paint an altarpiece for Santa Maria Maggiore, apparently.'

'Such an honour. But – it pains me to ask – what of us? What of Ser Felice?'

'As I say, this panel is all but finished. Another day, or two at the most. The next thing to be painted, as and when, will be Saint Peter's crucifixion on the other wall.'

'Good. Excellent.'

'But as to that, I understand from Ser Felice himself that he is …' Masaccio blinks diplomatically. 'Awaiting certain funds.'

'Aha. Yes, he hinted something of the sort to me,' says the prior. 'So you are looking at a pause, as it were, between finishing this and your master arriving in Rome?'

'Hopefully not, Reverend Father!' Masaccio grins, shakes his head. 'I have some potential clients. I don't know how long Masolino will be, and I must keep busy, you understand.'

'Would we could all find money in the mouths of fishes,' says the prior, nodding at the fresco. 'I do understand, maestro. Still, you will not have to search the denizens of the Arno for coin. I can offer you another commission here in the Carmine.'

'Really?'

'Happily. Fra Filippo?' Filippo gives a start. He has been digesting Masaccio's thunderbolt: summoned to Rome, by the pope himself! Unless that's a lie, he wonders, to get back at me for what I told Ser Giuliano? No, that is not his master's style. Will he take me? I am his assistant. But no, that isn't the arrangement he made with the prior … 'Fra Filippo, are you present?'

'Yes, Reverend Father. Sorry.'

'You will of course remember when we had this church consecrated five years ago?'

'I do, Reverend Father.'

'I was here too,' adds Masaccio. 'Working for Bicci.'

'Ah: that is very good. So you will both remember what a grand ceremony it was. A magnificent *Sagra*. We saw the great men of our city honour us with their presence. Signor Soderini, Signor de Medici, Signor Brancacci...'

'I think Brunelleschi was there. And Donatello,' says Masaccio.

'And the archbishop,' Filippo adds.

'They were. Many — most — of the great men of our city were there to honour our church and our great Order. Messer Soderini has decided to pay for a fresco of the event here, in the cloister. A work which you, my dear Maestro Tommaso, will be able to bring to life better than anyone, I daresay, in the whole of Italy.'

'I am flattered, Reverend Father.' Masaccio bows politely.

'My position does not permit me to flatter, maestro, but it enjoins me to tell the truth, which I have just done.' The prior gives Masaccio a warm smile. 'Messer Soderini — and myself — feel that all the great men of our city should be portrayed as they were and still are in life. All the great men who gathered to celebrate the Carmine, our church and, most importantly, the Order itself. Which brings me to my point. Though the Carmine has taken its rightful place at the very heart of Florence, too many of the laity believe that in the scheme of things, the Carmelites are upstarts. That we are a recent order. That, as you know, could not be further from the truth.'

'No, Reverend Father,' says Filippo loyally.

'Our founders were the prophets Elijah and Elisha themselves, of course, so far from being new, we are the most ancient of all the holy orders!' Fra Pietro slaps a hand down onto the planks of the scaffolding. 'We prefigure Christ Himself!'

'Do you?' says Masaccio, politely. Filippo sighs and braces himself for the inevitable lecture. And it comes: the prophets of the Old Testament, the hermits on Mount Carmel and their unbroken lineage, still following their rule when the Crusaders had found them centuries later...

'And the Franciscans? Two hundred years old, and giving themselves airs! The Dominicans are barely older than that!' The prior clicks his tongue. Filippo thinks he is about to begin a diatribe, but instead he clasps his hands in front of him as though to keep his emotions in check. 'Fra Filippo, you were with us when we made our procession to Siena last year.' The prior is leaning forward, studying him intently. 'And you will have seen the great altarpiece in our church there.'

'I did, Your Reverence.'

'With Elijah, and the early hermits on Mount Carmel? Good. But it is small.'

Filippo, who does remember being very far back in the church with the other young friars, nods again. He hadn't got anywhere near the altar, and he doesn't recall Elijah or anything else.

'It occurred to me, as long ago as the *Sagra*, that we need to tell our story here, in Florence,' says the prior. 'People are beginning to pay attention to the doings of artists. It is because of the Baptistery doors, I think, and that competition... Do you think so, maestro?'

'People love a competition,' says Masaccio. 'But they love beauty, and I think the doors made them proud of their city.'

'That may be. A rather vulgar affair, the contest, but then again it served God, and Maestro Ghiberti's doors are sublime,' the prior says. 'They have turned the eyes of the laity towards artistry, and craftsmanship. Beauty in the service of the Lord.'

'You have something in mind for the Carmine?' Filippo can't tell whether Masaccio is being polite. He knows his master is getting bored of this church. He has been talking, lately, about moving on, leaving Florence.

'Yes, I have a... a vision, an ambition for Santa Maria del Carmine. But not just an altarpiece. Something much bigger. A great cycle of frescoes.'

'I see, Reverend Father! Like the Franciscans have at Assisi,' says Filippo. The mere thought of the great church there, filled with the work of Maestro Giotto, makes him feel excited.

'Exactly!' The prior beams at him. 'And I believe it should be painted by one of our own.'

'Oh. You mean Maestro Bicci?' says Filippo, surprised.

'Not di Lorenzo, no. It will be an ordained friar. Someone who can tell the story from his very soul, because it is his own.'

'Who is it going to be, then, Your Reverence? Someone from Siena, do you mean?'

'Well, Fra Filippo.' The prior has propped his chin on his fingers again. 'It could be you.'

'*Me*, sir? Paint the *Sagra*?'

'Not the *Sagra*. For that, you can work with Maestro Tommaso. Learn as much as you can. Then, if your master thinks you are ready, you must join the Guild.'

'Good Heavens,' says Filippo sincerely, just managing to stop himself saying something much worse. The Arte dei Medici e Speziali... He will be a Guild member, like his father. It is almost too much to take in.

'He's ready now,' Masaccio is telling the prior. 'There are far less qualified painters on the loose here in Florence. Daubers. Smearers. The Guild will be lucky to have our Fra Filippo.'

'So you'll stand for him, maestro?'

'With joy, prior.'

Filippo barely listens as the details of the *Sagra* fresco are discussed. It is to be in the cloister, above the door that leads into the church. It is to be in *terra verde*, simple shades of green, a style that is fashionable in Florence that year. Not very big, but full of detail. The prior keeps repeating that he wants the faces of the dignitaries to be clearly recognisable to everybody, and Masaccio is assuring him that the figures will look more real than the living models. He is thinking how, at last, he is going to do something that would make his father proud. A Guild member – and one of the Greater Guilds at that! The most prestigious of them all ... Perhaps the wool merchants, the bankers, the silk merchants might disagree, but, yes, Tommaso di Lippo would have been proud beyond reason, of that Filippo is sure.

'So, maestro, were you going to tell me about His Holiness?' Filippo asks when the prior has left them to their work.

'Of course I was.'

'Good. I was thinking that I'd given you ideas. With what I told Ser Giuliano in Pisa.'

'No, it's completely true. They say His Holiness is rebuilding Rome. There will be work for everyone.'

'Even me?'

'Not this time,' says Masaccio, patting Filippo's arm. It is obvious that he is feeling slightly guilty. 'But ... You are an artist. Always have been, always will be. No matter what happens with your Order. The Carmine can't hold you for ever.'

'I was ready to leave the other night, but now that I'm back, I can't see how I could ever have believed I could.'

'Well, I've met plenty of men who used to be monks. Used to be. I'm not trying to give you ideas, Pippo ...'

'But you are, though, maestro!'

'I simply think that there will come a time. When you've painted Prior Pietro's great Carmelite fresco, for instance: what then?'

'There are a lot of walls.'

'And when you've painted on every one of them? The world is bigger than the Carmine, Filippo. You know that. You of all people.'

'It's supposed to be the world itself, you know,' Filippo says. '*Our* world. We renounce the other one.'

'Is that really true, though? I wouldn't ask any of the other brothers, Pippo ... No. I'm sorry. Forget I mentioned it. And anyway, we have this *Sagra* to worry about now,' Masaccio says kindly. 'Green ... Not much fun.'

'It will all be in the drawing,' mutters Filippo. 'The crowd. The foreshortening will have to be just right.'

'Exactly!' Masaccio, who has clambered back onto the scaffold, sits on the edge so that his feet dangle close to Filippo. 'You see? You are ready for the Guild. A crowd scene, lots of faces ... Your speciality, in fact. I shall be sure to give you some good ones.'

'Oh, yes?'

'We'll go and look at the real thing. Most of them are still alive, I expect. It's going to be dull as stale bread, all that green. We'll need to have some fun.'

'I think it's going to be exciting,' says Filippo. 'Painting in the cloister, all those famous people ...'

'Just wait and see,' Masaccio tells him. 'Messer Soderini isn't going to pay us for excitement. Still, you'll learn something valuable about the artistic life.'

'What's that, maestro?'

'As I said, wait and see.'

14

'I'M SEEING GREEN IN MY sleep,' mutters Filippo. The green crowd is marching across the cloister wall, thicker by the day. 'It's bloody endless.'

'I told you so,' says Masaccio, grinning. 'Anyway, I think we are done for today,' he decides. They go to the outer yard to wash their brushes and clean the plastering tools.

'I need something to inspire me,' Filippo complains. 'Don't you find it dull? It's so stiff, the composition. Not your fault, maestro,' he adds. 'I know it's what Messer Soderini wants. But wouldn't it be nice to put in a bit of drama?'

'Like what?'

'Like ...' Filippo considers. 'A pickpocket. Or a rabid dog.'

'Not exactly the tone we are after, Pippo. A pickpocket, though ... odds on there was at least one at work that day.'

'I probably would have known them,' Filippo says. 'What about it, maestro? Just a face and a hand, peeping out from behind Ser Brunelleschi?'

'When it's your commission, you put in all the thieves and dogs you like, all right? But I want us to get paid for this. We don't want to annoy Francesco Soderini, of all people.'

Filippo sighs and looks down at his hands, the colour of olive leaves. Then he has an idea.

'If you asked the prior, do you think he'd let me go over to Santa Croce, to look at the Giottos?'

'I expect he would. Why?'

'I always used to go there in the old days, when I didn't

want to draw any more people. It got really dull – a bit like this. Sitting and watching people walk past all day long, hoping that someone would want a drawing. And that they wouldn't try and cheat me.'

'I know just what you mean. It's usually the Baptistery doors, for me. Giotto, though: there's no better example for a painter, as far as I'm concerned. I'd come with you, but I have to meet someone.'

'So you'll have a word with the prior?'

'As soon as we're done with this.'

'Who are you meeting?' Filippo asks, slyly.

'None of your business.'

A little later, Filippo is crossing the Arno, wondering idly about the maestro's meeting. Business? Something in the way Masaccio had told him makes him think not. An assignation, then. The thought is intriguing. Man or woman? This is Florence, after all, and Filippo hasn't been able to ignore the fact that there are very few women in his master's paintings, the Madonna excepted. But then he remembers Masaccio's eyes lighting up when Filippo had told him about the girl, Simona, of Montopoli. And then there are the painter's moods.

Everything Filippo knows about love is what he remembers from overheard conversations when he lived outside the cloister. His own emotions had first pushed themselves into the light in the sterile quiet of the Carmine. His younger self had listened, huddled around campfires or sitting on church steps, to countless tales of braggadocio and heartbreak, and what seemed like a lot of cruelty, but he had been too young to really understand what was being said. There had been Cati Serragli ... And Mamma. If he had any notion of what a broken heart looked like, it was the devastated woman who couldn't raise her head off her pillow, who couldn't recognise her own son. Love had seemed to him, on balance, to be something best avoided. Recently, though, he is not so sure. He has had wild dreams of running away from the cloister, of finding Cati or of riding up to the inn of Montopoli on a magnificent mule and carrying Simona off to ... There is never any satisfactory conclusion to these fantasies.

The thought that his master might be suffering the pangs of love is intriguing. Who might she be? He tries to imagine her as he strolls along: strong features or delicate? Strong, he decides, crossing Piazza della Signoria. Square jaw, wide mouth ... But what about the Madonna in Pisa? Hard to think of a more delicate face. Perhaps the master had painted her from life. He tries to imagine Masaccio with a pale, slender girl, fading like a cut lily. It doesn't seem likely. Perhaps ...

He is walking along Borgo dei Greci when he hears footsteps coming up behind him. The street is not busy and out of instinct he turns, in time to see someone duck into a passageway. He shrugs, carries on. But then the steps come again. When he turns, no-one is there. He feels quite safe: who is going to rob a friar? He has nothing to steal. Children, probably. Still, his feet start to go a little quicker of their own accord. When he comes out into the Piazza Santa Croce, he looks again, and there is a man hanging back in the lengthening shadows where the street ends. Someone who wanted to ask his advice, perhaps? It happens. People want prayers, intercessions. Well, it couldn't have been important.

The frescoes in the Peruzzi Chapel are just as he remembers them. He stares for long minutes at Saint John feasting beneath an odd tent-like structure, while the moon rises overhead. Here is an old friend: the angels pulling John up to Heaven through a hole in the roof. In the Feast of Herod, the fair-haired women catch his eye, and he wonders, again, about Masaccio. But that isn't why he came here. He kneels down in front of the altar and lets the beauty of the long dead painter's vision bathe him in its otherworldly beauty. The angles of the strange buildings, the lustrous skies, the mountains lit by a sun very different from the one that shines over Florence: he lets it all soak in, until the hairs are standing up on his arms. This is what is missing in the bloody *Sagra*: the mystery. The unnerving touch of the Divine.

Filippo has promised Fra Pietro that he will be back for Vespers, though. Wandering across the piazza, he imagines that he is walking beneath that deep, fathomlessly blue sky, under those unearthly roofs. Which gets him thinking about the piazza in the Brancacci Chapel, and that Borgo di Greci is the very street where Saint Peter might be healing men with the touch of his shadow.

He is so absorbed in this meditation that he doesn't hear the footsteps coming up behind him until a hand grabs his shoulder. His old instincts engage their rusty gears and he spins and ducks, steps back with his arms flung out, and recognises Albertino.

His one-time friend is in the same tightly cut black suit of hose and tunic he had been wearing when Filippo had seen him last, outside the Buco. His dagger is in its sheath.

'Albertino!' says Filippo, warily. 'Have you been following me?'

'Didn't see me, did you?' Albertino's mouth makes a half-hearted attempt at a sneer, but Filippo can see at once from his pale, stretched face that there is no fight in him, and that the contempt in his voice is as thin as varnish.

'It's ... it's good to see you.'

'I bet.'

'What do you want with me, old friend? More harsh words?'

'You ...' Albertino shakes his head roughly, making his long, stringy hair lash his shoulders. 'Not today. Pippo, I need ...'

'You in trouble, Albertino?'

Albertino laughs, too loudly. 'Yeah,' he says hollowly. 'I'm in a bit of trouble.'

'With the Buco?'

'Trust a friar ... No. Money. I've been having a bad patch with the cards.'

'Oh.' Filippo can understand that. Albertino has always taken a bet, but Filippo remembers him playing with more fury than caution or skill. And no luck to speak of. 'Have you lost a lot?'

'More than I had.'

'What does that mean? We never had anything at all in the old days. What did you have?'

'I've been doing all right. Enough for some proper wagers. Enough...' He draws himself up and thumps his chest proudly with a fist. 'I had a good purse, all right?' Then he slumps. 'Anyway, it's gone.'

'And now you're in debt.'

'To a couple of ponces in the Vineggia. You know that place?' Filippo shakes his head. 'Rich boys. They aren't going to let me off. They'll do me in if I don't pay them back. Cut my dick off. That's what they said.'

'Talk,' says Filippo, soothingly. 'Just talk. You don't need me to tell you.'

'Not with these boys. They've done it before. I know someone...' He taps his face with his finger. 'They took one of his eyes out.'

'Everyone's heard a story like that,' says Filippo, though he is thinking: I haven't, not for years. And I wish I wasn't hearing this now.

'It's not a story, Pippo! Look!' He brushes back his hair, and Filippo sees what he has missed before: Albertino's right ear is a nub of tightly wrapped bandages, tar-black with dried blood. 'They cut what was left of it off right there, in the fucking tavern! I've got to pay them back!'

'What can I do, Albertino? You know I don't have any money to give you.'

'Oh, Christ!' Albertino groans and to Filippo's horror, he slumps to his knees in the street. Heads are turning. But then Filippo realises what they are seeing. A sinner and a man of God. The man of God is him. They think he has power. He stares down at Albertino's trembling back. In a mild panic, he closes his eyes in prayer. And behind his eyes, he sees the Virgin Mary, as Masaccio has painted her in Santa Maria Novella. Her hand up, pointing. Here is our burden.

He gathers the front of his habit and squats down in front of

Albertino. When he puts his hand on his old friend's shoulder, it is nothing but sinew and bone beneath the wool of the tunic.

'We can do something, Albertino,' he says. 'Something . . . I'll talk to the prior. Or the *commesse*. They'll remember you.'

'The widows? They always hated me,' sniffs Albertino.

'I don't think they *like* anybody. But they help. They do.' An idea floats by and he grabs it. 'All right. Not the widows. Did you know . . . Of course you don't. I'm a painter now. A *Frate dipintore*. My master is Ser Tommaso. Masaccio. He's a good fellow. If I ask him, I'll wager he will take you on as . . . something.'

'A painter? I can't paint,' says Albertino, a hint of peevishness in his despair.

'You won't have to. You can mix plaster. Hold ladders. I don't know: you can hammer a nail, can't you?'

'Anyone can do that.' Albertino raises his head. His face is almost yellow, except for his eyes, which shine wetly from great rings of reddish black. 'Do you really think he'd say yes?'

'I don't see why not. For a few pennies at first, but you can lie low over in the old parish. When the maestro takes to you – he will, he likes everybody – you'll soon make enough to get those bastards off your back. Come to the Carmine now. I'll find you somewhere to sleep.'

'I . . . I've got something to do,' says Albertino, but he is smiling, wiping tears from his face with dirty fingers. 'Tomorrow morning, though? First thing! Your master: he's a good man, you say?'

Filippo nods. 'As good as they come.'

'Not the sort for my trade, then?'

'No!' Filippo is taken aback.

'I only meant . . . I don't want to shame him. You know. If he's been . . .'

'Don't worry.' Why should I be shocked, he thinks. This is life. This is the burden. 'He isn't the sort to worry about that.'

'Tomorrow morning, then? Will you be there?'

'Albertino, where else would I be, in God's name?'

His friend laughs. He stands up, and Filippo thinks he seems lighter, as if a fraction of his burden has lifted. He wipes his face, tries to slap some colour back into it, winces at some throb of pain from his damaged ear.

'You're a diamond, Pippo,' he says. 'See you tomorrow, then? And you better pray for me. Hard as you can.'

'I will,' Filippo says, remembering the last time Albertino had said those words, taunting him, his hand on his dagger. And because this makes him feel a little ashamed, he crosses himself and makes the sign in the air in front of Albertino, who grins, trying for bravado, but Filippo can tell he is still terrified.

'See you, Pippo!' Albertino takes to his heels and ducks into a side street. Filippo looks around and sees that a small crowd of people have gathered. Some are nodding, but all are regarding him gravely. He doesn't know what to do, so he spreads his hands as if to show they are empty, clasps them in front of him and, head down, walks away as briskly as he can. Which is slower than he would like, because his legs are weak and shaky.

He gets back to the Carmine in good time for Vespers, but when he goes to find the prior, it turns out that Fra Pietro has gone to Fiesole for the night. After Vespers, he prays for an hour in front of the high altar, and later he does not sleep for a long time, but kneels on the floor of his cell, asking the Virgin to help Albertino.

★

The next morning Filippo lingers by the outside door of the church after Prime, but when Albertino does not appear he reasons that this is a desperately early hour for someone of Albertino's ways. He has still not come by Terce, when Masaccio arrives. After the service, Filippo changes into his painter's tunic and joins the maestro in the cloister. Masaccio tells him to begin drawing the outlines of the church and the other buildings in the piazza.

'Maestro, I met a friend last night on my way back from Santa

Croce,' Filippo says as he is leaning his ladder against the wall. 'I was wondering... We could use another pair of hands, couldn't we? To get this job out of the way?'

'I don't think we do,' says Masaccio. 'It's fairly straightforward. You and I are managing it perfectly well between us.'

'I mean, if we had someone to mix the *giornata*, for instance, you could be painting and I could be doing the outlines.'

'Not for this job,' says Masaccio absent-mindedly. 'The next one, maybe.'

'Oh.' Filippo scratches his chin. 'Maestro, I ask because, well, I promised him I would. He's in a bit of trouble.'

'Is he, indeed?' Masaccio is measuring out verdigris into his green-stained mortar. 'What sort of trouble?'

'He's a friend from my... my old times,' says Filippo. 'I came here, but Albertino stayed out in the streets. He hasn't picked the best paths to follow. I expect most of them are the ones I'd have had to choose, so I can't blame him. He does some things... Small stuff, gambling. Anyway, he's always been bad at cards, and now he owes a couple of bravos some money. They've cut off one of his ears, and if he doesn't pay...' He points vaguely below his waist.

Masaccio winces. 'Poor fellow. How much does he owe?'

Filippo shrugs. 'I don't know. Might be a lot, but I don't see how it could be, and he might be exaggerating. More likely it's a little bit, but the men he owes just want an excuse to hurt someone. And call it a matter of honour, no doubt.'

'The world is full of bastards,' says Masaccio, crushing pigment. 'So this... what's his name?'

'Albertino.'

'Is he trustworthy?'

'I'll make sure that he is.'

'And you've made him no promises.'

'Not exactly.'

Masaccio winces again. 'What does he do, to make enough

money to lose? He's not a thief, is he? I won't have a thief working for me.'

'No – not as far as I know,' says Filippo, who knows nothing of the sort. He ponders what to say next, and decides that he can't lie to his master. 'He cruises for trade at the Buco.'

He braces himself for laughter or disgust, but Masaccio just raises his eyebrows. 'Does he, indeed. I think that must be even worse, as a money-making exercise, than painting.' He rubs his thumb across his cheek, leaving a viridian smear. 'And you want to save him from that, do you, Pippo? That's very fine of you. So, is he honest, this Albertino? No, of course he isn't. But...' He considers. 'All right. Because you think he's worth saving, I'll take a look at him. That's all I'm saying, mind. Only because you think he's worthwhile. We could, I suppose, justify an extra body on this wall: I'm as sick of it as you are. And there isn't much for him to screw up. All right. Bring him in.'

'Thank you, maestro! He's coming in today!'

Masaccio sighs. 'I thought he might be. In the meantime, let's get on with this.'

15

But Albertino does not make an appearance at the cloister that day. 'Not worried about first impressions, is he, your friend,' says Masaccio. 'Tomorrow morning. After that...' He wipes his hands pointedly.

'I'm sure he'll turn up,' says Filippo anxiously. He spends half the night on his knees again, praying to the Virgin, trying to convince her that Albertino is a good soul, or ought to have been good, if Fortuna hadn't turned her wheel the wrong way for him every time.

Albertino's mother had been a prostitute, he remembers, but an almost respectable one, if that were possible, kept by a couple of rich men in a set of rooms near Sant'Ambrogio. Albertino had been sired by one of them and, shortly afterwards, his father had been exiled from Florence, and the other one had decided to run for high office and abandoned the woman. Soon, she had caught consumption and died, leaving Albertino completely alone. He had already been living rough for two years when Filippo, at six years old, had found him throwing stones at the swollen body of a dog that was turning in an eddy under the Ponte alla Carraia. Albertino had already begun to collect an odd assortment of rejected, abandoned and lost children around him; Filippo had been too independent to let himself be drawn in to the inner circle, and Albertino had seemed to respect him for it. As they grew, Filippo had taken to wandering around San Frediano and then further out into Oltrarno, drawing pictures, begging, wheedling food out of people, while Albertino had been more systematic: he divided his gang up into those who were good thieves, those who were pitiful beggars, and those who had some other talent which might bring some food down to the riverbank or into whichever abandoned house they were camping in. Most of the gang had died of the plague when Filippo was ten years old. Disease had thinned the ranks of Oltrarno's beggars and urchins to the point where it was quite easy to keep starvation at bay. Filippo had spent more and more time with Albertino, Nuzzio, the Cockerel and the others, hatching plans for robberies they never quite got around to, or launching raids into the Scala neighbourhood. But Albertino had begun to change even before that evening when the Scala had come onto their ground and killed Meo. Tonight, in his cell, trying to keep the image of his master's Virgin in his mind's eye, he wonders whether his friend had already started to hang around the taverns and the bathing spots in the river, because he had begun to see a hardness creep into his manner that was something other than the armour they all wore to survive; a knowingness that Filippo hadn't understood then and hardly understands now. Why is it all so difficult? He asks the Virgin, and she simply looks at him with her grey eyes and points to the calamity that has happened behind her.

It is halfway between Prime and Terce the next day. Filippo is drawing a window on the cloister wall, one of many he has done today: simple outlines, but he is laying out a section of the Sagra where Via Santa Monaca recedes into the distance behind the crowds celebrating the consecration. Each window must be drawn strictly according to the laws of perspective, and it is fiddly, exacting work.

Filippo is particularly jealous of his master today. Masaccio is doing a line of faces, and they are all people they both know: Maestro Masolino, Ser Brunelleschi, Donatello the sculptor. Much more diverting than endlessly receding windows.

Masaccio squints at the face he is painting. 'I think I've got Brunelleschi's nose right. What do you think, Pippo?'

Pippo climbs down his ladder and examines the wet paint. The architect's face, slightly simian, slightly badger-like with its sharply protruding nose and receding chin, seems fine to him.

'Looks more like Ser Filippo than the real thing,' he says. He hears voices in the yard behind the cloister: raised and urgent voices, and then the hammering of feet on flagstones. A dishevelled figure bursts into the cloister and runs towards Filippo, with a couple of older friars puffing angrily behind him. The man almost runs into Filippo and collapses, gulping air, against the painted wall. It is Nuzzio, his pock-marked face running with sweat.

'They've got Albertino,' he gasps. The friars huff up and begin to scold, but Filippo puts himself in between them and Nuzzio. 'I know him, brothers,' he says, firmly. 'I'll take care of this.'

'I'm going to fetch Fra Pietro,' says one of them, peevishly.

'Good idea,' says Filippo. 'Nuzzio, what do you mean? Who's got Albertino? The men he owes? Have they hurt him?'

'No! The Eight! The night officers have taken him.'

'For sodomy?'

'Oh, God … If only! It's much worse. The worst. The worst …'

'What the hell, Nuzzio …' Filippo hurriedly lowers his voice. 'For Christ's sake, tell me what's happened!'

'Albertino's in the Magistrate's Prison, Pippo. They're going to try him this morning, and then he'll hang. He's asking for you.'

'Hang? What for? Has he killed somebody?'

'Worse,' Nuzzio says again, shivering. 'Blasphemy! He … he threw a handful of shit at a shrine of the Virgin. The one on Via della Ninna, by the church. He was seen. *I saw it myself*, Pippo,' he whispers, and rubs his eyes, as though whatever they have seen has burned them. 'People went after him. They grabbed him. They would have killed him right there, except The Eight came. They took him off to the prison.'

'But why?'

'Why did he do it? Stupid, stupid bastard … He owed a lot of money to these two *bravi*—'

'I know. He told me.'

'Well, he'd just turned a rich trick at the Buco, and – you know Albertino – he thought he'd win back all the money he'd lost. But he didn't did he? Every hand was dirt. Always is, with Albertino, but he never seems to learn. Christ...' He rubs his eyes again. 'By the time he left the table they'd taken all his money, and then they took his dagger as well. He loved that thing, Pippo, but he staked it on one last hand! It's too late now. He won't need it.'

'Go on, Nuzzio.'

'Well, he cursed Our Lady really badly in front of the whole house. That got a few people standing up. So he told them all to fuck themselves, went out... And then he saw the Virgin up in that shrine. Had a bit too much to drink – more than too much, because he started screaming that she was mocking him, that she'd done him over. Then he bends down and picks up a big clod of horse shit and flings it at her.' His voice drops to a tortured whisper. 'Got her right in the face. And it...' He gulps. 'It stuck. It was *horrible*, Pippo! I never thought I'd see...' He buries his head in his hands.

'They don't usually hang people for blasphemy,' Filippo says. He finds he is stroking Nuzzio's back as though he were a distraught animal.

'But everybody saw! And more and more kept coming. They started calling for his blood,' says Nuzzio. 'Saying he was a thief and a gambler and, worst of all, a bugger, that they'd all seen him going in and out of the Buco with men, corrupting everyone who walked past...'

At this moment the prior appears. Filippo explains as best he can what has happened. Fra Pietro's eyes widen and he shakes his head.

'And you know him, this Albertino?'

'Since I was a boy, Reverend Father. He's asking for me. Can I go to him?'

'I would rather that the Carmine was not involved in this,' says Fra Pietro.

'But I saw him two days ago. He wanted me to pray for him. He was desperate for me to help him. I've known Albertino for a long time, Reverend Father. He's not an evil man. He's just had a bad life, and from what Nuzzio here tells me, he's not in his right mind.'

'You won't save him from the noose,' says Fra Pietro. 'If the mob wants The Eight to hang somebody, The Eight will do it.'

'But I can comfort him,' says Filippo quietly, remembering the damaged man sobbing on the cobblestones at his feet.

The prior takes a deep breath, lets it out. 'If you think you can,' he says at last.

'I do.'

'Then go.'

Nuzzio leads Filippo at a desperate pace through the streets towards the prison. More than once, Filippo finds himself running behind him, and as the day is hot and he is in both habit and heavy cloak, he is out of breath and footsore by the time they reach the Via del Proconsolo. There is a crowd in the street in front of the Palazzo del Podestà, the Magistrate's Palace, headquarters and prison of The Eight. They are kicking their heels sullenly, looking up at the windows of the tall, brutally crenulated building, and making a hum like a giant hornet's nest. There are guards in front of the gate leading to the inner courtyard. They sneer at Nuzzio, but when he points to Filippo they relent and let the two of them pass. Filippo has never been inside this place before, though he has passed it many times and shivered. Nothing good ever came of being caught by The Eight. Stories of the terrible things that happened to you if you ended up inside these walls were part of any gathering of street children, and every now and again a corpse might be seen dangling from one of the upper windows, to confirm that all the stories must be true. But for the first time, Filippo realises that his robes protect him. The guards are not looking at him suspiciously: if there is anything to be read into their glances, it is a sort of mild gratitude. His kind are needed here. He is welcome. And it appears that he is protecting Nuzzio, who seems less afraid. They find an official, who frowns when he hears Albertino's name and shakes his head in disgust. A guard is detailed to guide them, and they are led up one flight of stairs and then another, to a small, windowless room under the beams of the roof.

'He's going to trial in a quarter of an hour,' says the guard. Filippo enters the cell but when Nuzzio tries to follow, the guard grabs him by the collar. 'Not you,' he says. The door is kicked shut behind him, and through it Filippo can hear Nuzzio protesting in a high, frightened voice. It is almost dark, but the light of a rush lamp spreads a wan, jaundiced glow over the man sitting huddled on a low stool in the corner of the cell. Albertino looks very young and small, far smaller than Filippo would have thought possible. The man who had attacked him that night outside the Buco, who had followed him the day before yesterday, had been far taller than him, and worryingly ageless. But now Filippo feels as if he has been allowed to peer back across his life to when he and Albertino had dreamed up plots to steal a side of beef, or to trick Palla Strozzi's wife, richest woman in Florence, into adopting them. But in those days, Albertino had never sat hunched over like that, rocking. He had never cried, but Filippo can hear him sobbing quietly now.

'Albertino? It's Pippo.'

Albertino lifts his head, and Filippo is shocked by how frail he looks, how ill. His face is creamy white like the fat around a cow's heart, and as shot through with thin red veins. A thick daub of filth runs from one temple to his mouth. He has a black eye and there is crusted blood around his nose. Mud cakes his hair, and his damaged ear has bled a dark trail down his neck and into his ripped tunic. Filippo manages not to gasp. Instead he turns and hammers on the door.

'Bring me water and a cloth,' he demands, when the guard

opens it. 'Quickly!' There is a jug of water standing outside another door on the bleak landing. Filippo points to it, the guard fetches it. When the door is shut, Filippo takes the water over to where Albertino is crouched. He dips the corner of his cloak into the water, lifts Albertino's face gently with his hand and begins to dab away the dirt, which turns the water in the bowl dark crimson with blood.

'You heard what I did?' says Albertino. His voice is scarcely more than a rattle. Filippo nods, wipes away more dirt.

'I meant to do it,' Albertino rasps. 'Pippo, I've heard people say I couldn't have known what I was doing, but I did. Do you hear me?'

'I do, Albertino.'

'So you can't forgive me. I can't forgive myself. I want them to hang me, Pippo. I deserve to die a hundred times. I would have killed myself by now ...'

'Don't say that.' Filippo dips the cloak again, begins to wipe away the blood on Albertino's neck.

'But I would have, if I'd been able to get away. I cursed the Holy Mother for letting me lose that game, and then I did her harm!'

'She has forgiven you.'

'How can she?'

Filippo closes his eyes and sees the old Virgin, her back straight, her jaw set firm against despair. 'Because she has seen far, far worse. If you are sorry, she'll forgive you.'

'I will go to hell.'

'Do you want to?'

Albertino lifts his head and grits his teeth, and a flicker of his old self moves beneath the ruin of his face. Then his shoulders slump. He shakes his head. 'No. I don't.'

'So let yourself be forgiven.'

'Do *you* forgive me?'

'Me? I'm nobody. But yes, I forgive you with all my heart.'

'I don't know what to do, Pippo. I don't know! I've never said sorry. To anyone.'

'Did you ask me for forgiveness just now, or was that just … words?'

Albertino hesitates. He looks into Filippo's eyes, and his fear is almost unbearable.

'I asked,' he whispers.

'And I forgave you,' says Filippo. 'Now ask Our Lady, just as you asked me. Don't hesitate.'

Albertino screws his eyes shut and rocks back and forth, back and forth. 'I don't know the right prayer.'

'Are you sorry?'

'I am! Blessed Mother, I am!' He begins to sob as he rocks. 'I am so sorry! I am a wretched man! I threw shit in your face, Mother, and I'm so sorry!'

Filippo takes Albertino's face in his hands. 'There: you've done it. Now you have to repent, Albertino. Quickly, before they come for you. Can you do it?'

'I'm not strong enough,' whispers Albertino. Filippo dips his cloak again and brushes the cool water across his friend's brow.

'You've always been the strongest one,' he says. 'Remember when you stood up to that bastard of a carter in Borgo San Jacopo? Do that now. Show the Devil your face, and tell him to fuck himself.'

Albertino stares at Filippo, then smiles, showing a bloody stump where a lower tooth has been knocked out. He puts up a thin, almost weightless hand and holds Filippo's wrist. Water drips between their fingers. 'Will you hear my confession, Fra Filippo?' he says, shakily.

'I will.' Filippo closes his eyes again. 'My friend, my son. I will.'

When the door opens, it seems as though a day has gone by, though Filippo's hands are still wet, and when he nods at the guard and puts out his hand for Albertino, his friend stands up straight. A deep tremor shakes him, and Filippo takes his hand. Albertino clenches it with ferocious strength. Then he nods.

'I am ready,' he says.

The Eight hold their court in a surprisingly small, modest room lower down in the palazzo. There really are eight of them, Filippo has time to think, and then he is trying to stop the guards from shoving Albertino. To his amazement, when he looks them in the eyes they look sheepish and stand back, pointing to where Albertino should stand in the middle of the bare wooden floor. Filippo is still holding his hand.

The eight magistrates, dressed in long robes, some in black, some in red, hats with long trails hanging down across their shoulders, are lounging on benches set up beneath the room's single window. They are all middle-aged, all of the same rank and wealth. And how strange that those things should make them look so much like each other, Filippo thinks. They have the bored, impatient air of men who would rather be doing something productive with their time, like making money. Filippo has seen that look on countless faces, on men who have stalked past the beggar boy waving his drawings at them, far too eager to get back to their counting-houses and contracts to waste their time on pictures. But Albertino has barely stood still before the oldest magistrate, who must be the podestà himself, leans forward, plants his elbow on his knee and demands:

'Albertino of San Frediano?' A clerk, a small, grey-haired man whom Filippo has not noticed before and who is perched behind a high desk near the door, begins scribbling in a large book.

'Yes, Your Honour.' Albertino's voice is thin but steady. The grip of his fingers is tight around Filippo's hand.

'Do you have any other names?'

'I've never had that good fortune, Your Honour.'

'You are charged with ...' The podestà glances at a ledger held by one of his red-clad colleagues. 'With a most damning catalogue of offences. Chief of which is that of dishonouring the Virgin Mary.'

The magistrate with the ledger nods and reads out a short account of Albertino's crime, so knotted up in legal flourishes that Filippo stops listening to his voice. The scrape of the clerk's pen is almost as loud as the man's words.

'How do you plead?'

'Guilty, Your Honour.'

The podestà raises his eyebrows and mutters something to the man on his other side. 'To the other crimes. You are accused of sodomy, of practising this most unnatural of vices habitually, at the tavern known as Il Buco, at certain places beside the river and in sundry low houses in the parish of Santo Stefano al Ponte.'

'I plead guilty, Your Honour. And to gambling, and stealing various articles of money and clothing from men who paid me to lie with them, and for blaspheming at the card table.' The words tumble out. Albertino gives Filippo's hand a final squeeze, and lets go. 'I repent with all my heart. I do not ask for mercy, but I ask the Holy Virgin Mary to forgive me.'

The clerk's pen scrapes, scrapes, and stops.

'Is this so?' The podestà turns to Filippo. I am not the one who is accused, he tells himself, though half a short lifetime of running from The Eight has left his insides feeling hollow with unease.

'It is, Your Honour,' says Filippo. 'This man has made a full confession to me and repents, truly and earnestly. I'm certain that his repentance is genuine.'

The podestà leans back and the other seven men gather around him. There are a few moments of whispering, shorter than the saying of a pater noster. Then the eight men resume their places. They look just as bored, Filippo observes.

'Albertino of San Frediano. You have pleaded guilty to all the crimes of which you stand accused. It is therefore the decree of this court that you pay with your life. You will go from this room to the chapel, and then you will be taken to an upper floor and hanged from a window, your body to remain hanging until the fourteenth hour tomorrow.' The podestà turns to Filippo, who is trying to understand what he has just heard. So much precision.

Such mundane detail. 'As his confessór you should know that ordinarily he would be taken to the gallows outside the walls, but there are concerns about the crowd outside in the street.'

'Can I stay with him?' Filippo slips his arm through Albertino's. He senses that his friend has used up all his strength and that there is hardly anything left inside the body standing beside him.

The podestà nods, puzzled. 'That is your function, is it not?'

'I don't... Yes, it is. Of course it is.'

The podestà waves a finger at the guards. They open the door and one of them slips out of the room. When the guard returns a moment later Filippo almost jumps out of his skin, because the man is followed by two apparitions swathed in long black robes, black capes, and with tall, pointed black hoods over their heads. It takes him a moment to realise that he has seen these men, or their brothers, countless times before: just two members of the Misericordia, the Confraternity who bury the bodies of the poor and – yes, now he understands – escort condemned men to their deaths. He has seen these strange black-clad figures gathered around the little corpses of too many of his friends, and been thankful to them for the tenderness they always showed, when, just a few minutes before, people had been walking past the dead boy or girl without even looking down. Even so he feels the palms of his hands grow damp.

But Albertino, when he turns and sees them, doesn't even flinch. The *Neri* – the Blacks, so they are always called – position themselves in front and behind him and, in sombre train, they walk through open halls, through a loggia that looks out onto the central courtyard, and through another doorway. Filippo smells stale incense and snuffed candles and knows this is the chapel before he has stepped into the narrow, high-vaulted room. The *Neri* take Albertino by the arms and lead him up to the altar. One of them whispers in his ear but Albertino is already kneeling. Filippo kneels beside him. He doesn't know what he should do so he puts his arm around Albertino, who looks into his eyes and with a grateful smile buries his face in Filippo's white cape. Filippo takes his head gently in his hands, taking care not to hurt the injured ear, bends his head and begins to murmur the Rite of Absolution.

'*Dominus noster Jesus Christus te absolvat...*' As he says the words which he has learned but never used, he has the growing sense that he is being watched. '*...et ego auctoritate ipsius te absolvo ab omni vinculo excommunicationis...*' He raises his head towards the altar, and sees that there are paintings on every wall of the chapel. Figures, a crowd of gold-haloed saints; God above, floating in a painted sky of the deepest blue which is full of its own life and light. He knows it at once, and lets the beauty fill the words he is speaking. '*...et interdicti in quantum possum et tu indiges.*' As he makes the sign of the cross, he feels Albertino's breathing slow and grow calm against his chest. '*Deinde, ego te absolvo a peccatis tuis in nomine Patris, et Filii, et Spiritus Sancti. Amen.*'

'Is that it?' says Albertino, his voice muffled by the cloak.

'That's it,' Filippo says. He feels suffused with something. With the gift of an otherworldly blue sky. The blue of Heaven. Of Giotto di Bondone. 'Do you truly repent, Albertino?'

'I do. Everything is mended now.' He takes a deep breath. 'I want to go, Pippo. Can we go?'

Filippo looks up at the *Neri*, sees nothing but four pairs of eyes glinting through black cloth. He nods, and quickly, silently, the two figures bend down, take Albertino gently but expertly under the arms and raise him to his feet. He resists them, but when they see that he is trying to turn towards the altar they relax their grip enough for him to make the sign of the cross and bow. Then, very quickly, they turn and march him to the door. Outside in the wide gallery, a small company of armed men are waiting, with two more *Neri*. Without waiting for Filippo, they start to walk Albertino very quickly across the tiled floor. Filippo hurries after them, but they have already stopped in front of one of the great windows. A plain wooden bench has been shoved against the wall beneath it, and a man is standing on it, a stout, grey-whiskered man dressed like a mason. He has the looped end of a rope in his hands, and the other end is wrapped and tied around the central mullion. Albertino is almost there, and Filippo has to run to get in front of him. Albertino's face is turned upwards, towards the ceiling vaults, which are painted in garish blue, studded with gilt stars. And he is smiling.

Filippo has to watch as the guards grab Albertino and lift him, as if he weighs no more than a sheaf of wheat, up onto the bench. He has to, because this is what it means to take a vow. To *keep* a vow. He clasps his hands as the noose goes around his friend's neck, but he doesn't know if he is praying or not. He feels the Virgin's grey eyes on him, and what her upturned palm is pointing out is Albertino, standing against the light throbbing in from Via del Proconsolo, or is it the noise of the crowd that is throbbing, as the grey-whiskered man twists a cord expertly around Albertino's upper arms, pinioning them roughly, pulling the knot tight, and almost in the same movement winding another cord around his wrists.

'*Te absolvo a peccatis tuis te absolvo a peccatis tuis in nomine Patris, et Filii, et Spiritus Sancti. Amen.*'

'Pray for me, Pippo!' Albertino's voice is clear and strong, and Filippo raises his hand to bless him, but the soldiers have pulled him off balance, heaved him up as the bench rocks beneath him, and dropped his shoulders down on the windowsill, face up. There is a roar from down below in the street.

'*...in nomine Patris, et Filii, et Spiritus Sancti. Amen.*'

But Albertino is gone. With a casual grunt, the guards have shoved him out into space. Filippo's heart beats once, twice, then the coils of rope around the stone mullion clench, there is a dull twang, and Filippo feels a shock go through the floor and up into the soles of his feet, though there is no way that Albertino's poor wasted body could have dislodged so much as a flake of plaster from this great brute of a building.

'Pippo!'

Filippo turns, numb, to find Masaccio running up the stairs.

The painter hurries across the gallery, his feet tap-tapping on the tiles. The sound seems deafening to Filippo, though it is almost drowned out by the hooting of the mob down in Via Proconsolo. He unclasps his hands and points, vaguely, to the window. The men are already climbing down from the bench. Two of them pick it up and carry it off. One of the *Neri* comes over and pats Filippo on the back.

'He made a true repentance?' The man's voice is muffled by the sinister black hood, but he sounds pleasant enough. Filippo just nods.

'I'll make sure that is properly known.' He looks towards the window and shakes his head. 'Your first, I'm guessing?'

'First?'

'Execution.'

'Oh. Yes.'

'Well done.' The man pats him again and walks off with his companions.

'Wait!' Filippo calls. The man turns, and the peak of his hood bobs absurdly. 'Will you look after him — after?'

'That is our duty,' says the man. 'The truth is, though, that no-one else will care.'

'I do. He was my friend,' says Filippo, quietly.

Masaccio takes his arm firmly and starts to lead him towards the great staircase. 'The prior told me to come,' he says. 'The whole city is talking about that Albertino.'

'He was my friend,' says Filippo again.

'You were *his* friend, Fra Filippo. Did I overhear? He repented?'

'He did. He wasn't bad. Just unlucky. That's all it takes, you know.' Filippo wipes his eyes with his sleeve, and is surprised to find them dry. He thinks he should be weeping hard enough to turn these stairs into a waterfall, but that will come later.

'There are Giottos here,' he says, so he doesn't have to listen to the mob.

'What? Where?'

'In the chapel.'

'Oh. Yes, of course there are. I've never seen them.'

'You wouldn't want to,' says Filippo quietly. 'Not that way. Not like Albertino did. I almost told him. I was giving him absolution...' He shakes his head. The thought of that is too big to deal with. 'And I almost said: look up at the sky. Look up at the maestro's blue. That's where you're going.'

Masaccio talks to an official and they are let out of a side door away from the crowds.

'I'm taking you home,' says Masaccio.

'Home?'

'The Carmine.' They walk along in silence, giving Via Proconsolo a wide berth. Masaccio leads them up to the Duomo, and then west. They turn left and head down towards the Ponte alla Carraia, Filippo following Masaccio's solid figure through the crowds, letting the faces drift past him. As they are crossing the river, he stops in the middle of the bridge and leans on the parapet, looking across at the Oltrarno bank.

'That was where we found the dead woman,' he says. 'In those reeds: that was where Meo was killed.' It is a litany he is reciting for himself. 'Where that dead tree is... that was where Albertino groped Angelo's sister. We all slept down there under the pier after the *calcio* on San Giovanni's Day. Nuzzio, Il Cucciolo, Federico, Pagolo, Angelo, Il Gallettino.' Masaccio has come to lean beside him. 'Albertino. And me.'

'Come along, Pippo. The prior will be worrying about you. Let's get you home.'

Filippo looks up at the sky, which has turned a wonderfully deep, fathomless blue. The tears start at last, but his heart is rising inside him. He smiles, and feels tears gather in the corners of his mouth. 'It's all right, maestro,' he says. 'I am home.'

16

THE NEXT DAY FILIPPO IS helping Ruggerio the carpenter saw up some lengths of plank for a new scaffold, when Nuzzio appears, edging around the church door, wide-eyed with apprehension. He looks as if he expects to be struck down by a blast of fiery disapproval from the altar behind him in the church. When he sees Filippo he raises his hands in relief.

'Pippo!' he hisses, walking crab-like along the wall. It would be funny at any other time, Filippo thinks, but after what has happened... The vengeance of the Lord is terrible. And the vengeance of The Eight is even worse. He straightens up, brushing sawdust from his habit.

'È, ragazzo,' he says, searching for the San Frediano accent he seems to be leaving behind him these days. 'Have you come to pray?'

'No. I mean, not yet. Can you come with me for a bit, Pippo?'

'Not really. I'm working.' Nuzzio looks past him, frowning, at Ruggerio's big frame hunched over a stack of lumber.

'Didn't know monks did carpentry,' he mutters. Then he grimaces and gestures, desperately, for Filippo to follow him.

'I'll be back in a moment,' Filippo tells Ruggerio, and finds Nuzzio lurking in one of the side chapels.

'You're welcome here, you know,' he says.

'I don't know,' says Nuzzio darkly. 'Listen. It's about Albertino.'

'Of course, Nuzzio. I was there. It was... quick.'

'Yeah, well, not as quick as all that.'

'You were there?' Filippo is aghast. 'You watched?'

'Course. We couldn't let our mate die alone, could we? We were all there in the street. He made a good end. We're all proud of him. And...' He looks around nervously. 'That's why I'm here. The *Neri* pulled him up a couple of hours ago.'

'And I suppose they've buried him by now.'

'Ah. They haven't. Not yet. There's some bother about finding a place to put him in the ground. Because, well, of what he did. Meanwhile, they've put him in the Bigallo.'

'That makes sense, I suppose,' Filippo says. The Bigallo, an odd little building close to the steps of the Duomo, is the head-quarters of the *Neri*, where they bring the city's unclaimed corpses and lay them out in the usually vain hope that someone – a relative, a friend – will take them for burial. It is one of the choice entertainments of the street children to go and inspect the day's haul. Sometimes, Filippo remembers, the marble tables were all empty, and other times there would be a silent company of shapes straight or hunched under stained sheets. He shakes his head at the memories. 'I don't think I can do anything,' he says. 'The body belongs to The Eight now. The *Neri* will take care of it.'

'I know, I know,' says Nuzzio. 'It's just that he's there, and the boys and me were talking...You and your drawings, Pippo. You can draw him. Draw Albertino.'

'I...' Filippo blinks. 'You mean, draw Albertino's body?'

'That's it.'

'Why, Nuzzio?'

'To have something of him,' says Nuzzio softly. 'He was always the best of us, until – well, you know that. We'd like to have something. You were his friend too.'

'I don't think...'

Nuzzio lays his dirty hand softly on Filippo's arm. 'Please, Pippo,' he says, his voice starting to crack.

'Wait here.' Filippo climbs the ladder to where Masaccio is working. 'Can you spare me for an hour, maestro?' he says. 'It's important. To do with ... with yesterday. I'll be back directly, I promise.'

'Is everything all right, Pippo?' Masaccio looks concerned.

'Everything's fine. I just need to do something for Albertino. And, maestro, please don't tell any of the brothers, or the prior. Especially not the prior.'

'I won't, Pippo. But be quick. Are you sure there's nothing wrong?'

'Nothing worse,' says Filippo with a feeble grin. He picks up the satchel he has recently been given by Ruggerio, just a simple sack with a strap to hold his drawing tablet, some scrap paper, chalks and charcoal. Carrying it reminds him of the old days, and now, following Nuzzio through the streets, the feeling is stronger than ever.

The Bigallo still has the power to make Filippo's skin crawl. The building itself does not make sense: it had once had a top half, but a fire had taken that off and it has never been rebuilt. The skinny pillars of the loggia do not support anything. But it is the shadows behind the pointless columns that seem to breathe a cobwebby chill out into the bustling square in front of the Duomo.

The last time he had come here, it hadn't been to gape at the corpses, but to look at the fresco of the Virgin that Bernardo Daddi had done in the last century. Bicci had brought him. Filippo had liked the way that Daddi had put a pigeon's-eye view of the city under the Virgin's skirts, and the way the old painter had used light, but compared to his beloved Giotto, the work had seemed muddy and old-fashioned. Now, the Virgin gazes down on him from her wall, gigantic and bored. She is meant to be calling the little orphans of Florence to shelter under her cloak, but judging by the look on her face she has just discovered that she doesn't like people all that much, let alone children. Even so, Filippo says a prayer under his breath and makes the sign of the cross as he and Nuzzio approach. A few brothers of the *Neri* are standing around, looking at them through the slits in their black hoods. Filippo tries to imagine the faces beneath. Ordinary faces, he thinks. Notaries, book-keepers. Butchers ... No, I hope there are no butchers. Huddled beneath the Virgin, a knot of faces he recognises. Federico, the pox-ravaged Bonafortuna, Il Cucciolo. They are whispering among themselves but when they see Filippo they nudge each other and Federico beckons. They lead him through a door and down a short corridor. They pass frescoes – not very good ones, at that, Filippo can't help noticing: poor imitations of Maestro Giotto – and then they come out into a large and dim room lit by narrow windows and a few candles.

Anyone who has grown up on the streets of Florence, espe-cially around the slaughterhouses and tanneries of Oltrarno, is accustomed to the smell of death. Even so the air of the room they have entered almost makes Filippo gag before he manages to swallow his disgust, because though it is cool, there is a stench that wafts in invisible threads across his face. It is coming from the far end of the room, where a dozen or so trestle tables of rough wood stand in a row. Long, cloth-shrouded shapes cover three of them. Two of the corpses lie under sacking. The third is swathed in fresh white linen.

'That's him,' says Nuzzio, pointing to the unnaturally bright form under the linen. 'We bought the cloth. We're trying to buy him a grave, but no church will put him in their ground. Are you ready, Pippo? He isn't pretty.'

'I'm ready,' Filippo says, although he isn't. Nuzzio must sense this, because his fingers wrap themselves gently around Filippo's wrist, while with his other hand he pulls back the sheet from the face of the corpse. Filippo finds himself looking into a pair of milky eyes sunk deep into blue-rimmed sockets. Albertino's mouth is open and his neck is stretched unnaturally, and bruised a deep blackish-red.

'*Quod vos estis ego fui, quod nunc sum et vos eritis,*' Filippo mut-ters. The others look at him questioningly. 'I was what you are, and what I am you shall be,' he says. The words his master had painted beneath the Holy Trinity in San Lorenzo have come unlooked-for into his head, but whereas in the fresco they seem like a serious but merciful lesson, here they seem completely empty of mercy. But then, the maestro hadn't used the palette of death: putty, liver, jaundice yellow, bruise green.

'Can you do it?' Nuzzio whispers. 'We won't blame you if you can't.'

Filippo doesn't reply, but fishes in his satchel for paper and a stick of chalk. He clears his throat, fighting the nausea hovering in his diaphragm. What can he draw? What can he show that is not pure horror? This piece of wreckage had been a man two days ago, who had knelt in front of him and begged for God's forgiveness. Well, has he found it? Because the only evidence of mercy that Filippo can see is in the faces of Albertino's friends. Isn't that enough? He closes his eyes, sees the old Virgin in San Lorenzo and imagines her pointing to the body in front of him. This is our burden.

'I can do it,' he says.

The chalk hovers above the paper, as if unwilling to be a part of this ugly business. But his hand forces it down, traces a hesitant line, then a more confident one. He draws, forcing himself to look at Albertino, and when he looks down at the paper he sees he has begun to draw someone else. Or is it? The face being formed out of red chalk is not dead, apparently: not sleeping either, but at rest. Lying back against the warm sand of a riverbank, smiling faintly at the memory of some mischief, or at the prospect of more to come. Filippo blinks away the tears that are pricking his eyes, and tries to reverse the decay and the torment.

'I can't do more,' he says at last, shoves the paper at Nuzzio, who takes it silently, studies it, holds it out for the others.

'That's him,' says Il Cucciolo. 'We knew you'd do it properly.'

'Did I? It's how I remember him … But I don't remember him very well. I don't know if he ever looked like that.'

'I think he did,' says Nuzzio. 'Didn't he, boys?'

'Doesn't matter. This is how we want him to be, here,' says Il Cucciolo, thumping his chest. 'Before he got stitched up by those ...' He begins to curse angrily, tears streaming down his face, and another man, someone who Filippo doesn't recognise, takes him by the arm.

'Come along. Let's go and have a drink, eh? For Albertino. He wouldn't care about a drawing, but he'd like us to have a drink.'

'That's right,' says Nuzzio. 'He'd want that. But he'd have liked the picture as well. You know he envied you a little bit, Filippo? Your drawings. Said it was easy money, but when he tried to draw faces they looked like rotten apples.'

Filippo winces at the image, which is too close to the mark here in the charnel house. 'He tried to draw people?' he says.

'*Tried*. When he couldn't, he said it was stupid, but I think he was really jealous of you, Filippo. He thought what you did was like magic.'

'A trick, you mean, like a conjuror?'

'No, real magic. He was a bit afraid of it, tell you the truth. It was how you made people look blessed, you might say, no matter how pig-ugly they really were. Thought you were better off in the cloister, because all sorts of funny stuff goes on in there.'

'It doesn't, you know.'

'Sure about that? Because you've changed, Pippo.'

'I'm sorry, Nuzzio. People do.'

'Nah. I don't care. Come and have a drink for old Albertino.'

'I should get back to work ...'

'Just one.'

Filippo looks over at the marble plinth where his old friend is lying. Someone has pulled the sheet back over his head and something like peace has been restored. The drawing in Nuzzio's hand is more real, now, than what is lying over there. That was what they had wanted from him, after all. He's done his best.

'All right,' he says. 'Just one drink.'

★

They buy a big clay flask of cheap stuff from a wine shop on Via del Oche. 'Let's go this way,' Nuzzio says, as they leave the shop. 'You've got to see something.' He leads them down through the Piazza della Signoria and into the alleys beyond.

'We're not going to the Buco?' asks Filippo, suspiciously.

Nuzzio chuckles grimly. 'Don't worry,' he says. 'Look: we're here.'

They are in a small alley behind the Palazzo Vecchio. The church of San Pier Scheraggio is close by, and here, on the corner of Via della Ninna, a crowd is milling about. As Filippo watches, people come and go, and every few moments someone kneels at the corner itself and lays something down on the cobbles. Nuzzio nudges Filippo, urges him forward with a jerk of his chin. Filippo goes closer and realises where they are. Above the street, set into the angle of the walls, is a stone alcove, and inside it, an ancient Virgin in carved wood. He had stopped here the night he had got back from Pisa. And this must be where Albertino picked up a lump of dung and sentenced himself to death. He edges towards the crowd. Candles are flickering in the shadows beneath the shrine, and bunches of wild flowers are mounded against the bricks. The crowd swells, surges. A wiry man with a big black beard is wandering around, lecturing people in a loud, educated voice. Another man, a grey-stubbled labourer, notices Filippo and nods respectfully towards the Virgin.

'The *bardassuola* threw shit at our beloved Mother, and see what happened!'

'What did happen?' asks Filippo reluctantly.

The man gives him a surprised look. 'The filth hit her right in the face, and a piece stuck...' He shakes his head, clicks his tongue. 'And then it rained, didn't it? All last night... How it poured down! Well, when the sun came up this morning, what did we find? The filth on her cheek is still there, but look! Go on!'

Filippo squints. The Virgin's face is very worn, the wood scoured into soft, worm-pocked pleats. Her nose is half gone.

Flecks of red paint still speckle her lips and centuries of lead paint have stained her cheeks a faint white. And there, on the left cheek, a star-shaped brown stain.

'The stain?' Filippo says sceptically.

'A rose! Perfect, isn't it? Our Lady takes the dung of the evil-doer and makes a flower! The first one to see it, an old widow with consumption, up at dawn ... Well, what do you think? She saw the rose on Our Lady's face and the consumption lifted off her chest like a dirty crow and flapped away!'

'A miracle?' Filippo is half listening to the labourer, half to the bearded man, who seems to be saying something about the Medicis.

'You knew all along, brother! Of course you did!' The labourer claps him on the shoulder. 'And you know what they're saying?' Filippo shakes his head. 'That the dirty little bugger who did it — with the Devil guiding his hand, according to them who saw it happen — he's been forgiven by her. They say an angel swooped down from above and carried his soul off to Heaven as he was hanging from that window, even though the horned ones thought they had him ...' He sighs, his face a loose smile of pure enchantment. If you'd seen what I've just been staring at, would you smile that way? Yes, you probably would, Filippo thinks, hearing the crowd mumble, the bearded man still giving his speech to anyone who catches his eye. He is tempted to take out his drawing tablet and sketch the old man, because he is so peaceful, so bewitched by whatever it is he sees up there on the statue. Instead he slips away to where the others are waiting for him, thinking that he'd like to believe in this miracle as well, but ...

'What do you think?' demands Federico.

'What do you mean?'

'You're a priest.'

'I'm a friar. You mean, do I think it's a miracle? Do you?'

Federico shrugs. 'It's Our Lady, isn't it? She can do anything.

Albertino got what he deserved, but now she's forgiven him. He got lucky in the end.' The others nod in agreement.

'Then it's a miracle, isn't it?' says Filippo. He wishes he could be that sort of believer, but he never has been. Albertino had gone to his death with some sort of peace in his heart – perhaps that was the miracle. I saw it happen. That old man, finding so much joy in a dung-stained piece of wood: a miracle? Perhaps. His joy, that is, not the story. Filippo has always wanted to believe the stories, the magic tricks, that tell you that life is like the Ascension Day pageant, full of hidden cogs and gears that bring angels swinging down from the roof and whisk saints up into painted clouds. But that just makes you believe God is the machinery and the paint, when He's the man you've never met, standing out of sight, watching the ropes go up and down, hoping they don't break. The real miracle … Filippo narrows his eyes as they come out into the sunshine on the riverside. He feels the heat on his face, wrinkles his nose at the charnel-house stench rising from his clothes. It's this, he thinks. The world is beautiful. We are beautiful. Even at our worst, at our most desperate, when we are suffering, or raging, or blinded by our own ignorance. In love, or dead on a stone table. The trick is to see it. No … No. The trick is to look. Always to look.

Nuzzio leads them down to the river's edge between the two bridges, their old home. People stare at the young friar in the company of ruffians, but Filippo ignores them. It isn't difficult: he still has the smell of death in his nose and two faces in his mind's eye: Albertino as he is, and Albertino as he never had quite been. His robes don't mean all that much. He hasn't really changed after all. Stretched out near the water, the dirty sand trickling between his toes, he drinks and passes the jug around, drinks and passes, and talks about days like this a long time ago, about friends who have gone and how the world is changing. But they won't change. Oh, no: this will never change. There will always be the river, and bad wine, and good stories.

When he gets up to leave, it is already well into the afternoon. Midday prayers have come and gone. He wanders into the church and finds that he doesn't need to explain himself to Masaccio and the others. They understand. Which is good, because Filippo finds that he doesn't want to make excuses. There is nothing to apologise for, after all. This is who he is: a mongrel, a badly cooked dish of vagabond, friar, maker of pictures. It's exhausting trying to be something different, he has decided. Sooner or later, you end up turning green under a sheet in the Bigallo, or floating down the Arno, being nibbled by eels. If you're lucky, somebody will care enough to bury you. He retreats into a corner next to the altar and starts grinding cinnabar into red powder. This is all there is to life, anyway, he thinks. This is all there needs to be. He works the pestle in the mortar. When this is done, there are brushes to be washed, a knife to be sharpened. Work. An ordinary miracle, but quite enough, he realises, to fill a whole life.

17

Filippo stands under the archway of his father's old house, listening to the flap of laundry trying to dry in the freezing air, and to the subdued cooing of pigeons. One neighbour is chatting to another from upstairs windows in the rough, rich dialect of San Frediano. As he does whenever he comes to this place, he finds it hard to believe how much he hates it here. The memories swarm too thickly. But he's behaving like a child, he tells himself, and says a prayer to the Virgin. Prayers, though, have never seemed to work here. It is a tomb; no, it is a mortuary, with hopes lying like abandoned corpses under dirty sheets. The upstairs neighbours, though, seem happy enough: one is joking about her husband's manhood, and the other has just made a heavy-handed pun about eels. Filippo chuckles despite his mood. Perhaps his prayer has been heard after all.

Leonarda opens at his second knock. She looks ill: her eyes are sunken, and the pale skin of her cheeks is sallow and chapped. Her shoulders are slumped: nothing good ever comes knocking at this door. When she sees Filippo she brightens and a little flush comes to her cheek, and this makes his own heart jump.

'Filippo ...' she begins, but he takes her hand and steps inside.

'I've come to do something,' he says.

'Mamma is sleeping. Otherwise you could see her. I'm sure she would be happy to know you're here.'

'Would she?' He swallows his bitterness. This is not why he came. 'It's me who's happy to be here, sister,' he says. 'But first I have to explain.'

Leonarda's face falls. 'Oh, no, Pippo! You're in trouble!' Her hands clench beneath her chin.

'No, no. Listen! I'm a painter now.' He straightens his back, holds out his pigment-stained hands for her to inspect.

'But you're still wearing your habit,' she whispers, confused.

'You can be both,' says Filippo. 'It's like a miracle, isn't it? I haven't been to see you because...'

'Because what? You never come.' It is not an accusation, just the truth.

'I've been in Pisa,' Filippo goes on, because there is no point in denying that Leonarda is right. 'I met a painter, called Masaccio. If you've seen the new frescoes in the Brancacci family chapel, well, that's his work. I was in Pisa, at the cloister there. And I helped him with his work. I painted something for him. An altarpiece.'

'You painted an altarpiece, Pippo?' Leonarda plainly doesn't believe a word of this.

'Four panels. Not the most important ones, but still. I got paid as Ser Masaccio's assistant, and, well...'

'What are those?' Leonarda interrupts, frowning suspiciously at the bag of tools, the wooden trug full of pigment jars, the brushes...

Filippo takes a deep breath. 'I'm going to paint a fresco for Mamma.'

'I don't understand.' His sister is still frowning at the painting things, and he sees she has both hands clenched.

'There's nothing to understand,' he says hurriedly. 'My master has gone back to Pisa for a week or so. I asked him if he could get the prior's permission for me to come here. I thought that something on her wall might... might cheer her up.' As soon as he has said that, he regrets it. Antonia Lippi is far beyond the reach of cheering up. And to his horror, Leonarda starts to laugh, though it is closer to sobbing than to laughter. She has her fingers pressed against the thin skin of her temples.

'I'm sorry, Pippo,' she says. 'Yes. Why not? Mamma won't

even notice, but…' She laughs again, her body clenching as if cramped. 'Yes. It will be good to have you in the house.'

Only when Filippo has brought his things inside does he realise how small the apartment really is. It seems to have shrunk since he was last here, as though the damp as started to make the walls contract. On this winter's day the mildew looks darker, the smoke stains more tarry. To his relief, his mother is asleep, or at least she is lying back with her eyes closed, and does not move when he slips into her room and puts his tools and paints against the wall. Reluctantly, he lays the palms of his hands against the flaking plaster. The wall is damp, faintly slick with mould and soot and cooking grease, with the emanations of his mother's breath. He shudders.

When Filippo had imagined painting a fresco in his mother's room, the idea had come to him, quite suddenly, of these imperfections gathering into the perfection of a Crucifixion. He had been surprised by this: conceptual thinking is not encouraged in the cloister, and had been quite useless in his life on the streets. But here it is: an idea. He has had an idea. Even the prior had seemed impressed.

'Light from darkness?' he had asked, thoughtfully.

'Yes … Yes! But also the sacrifice, coming out of the filthy walls, the … the …'

'Contrast?'

'Exactly! I want to show her that God is with her, even in that place. Especially there.'

But here, confronted with the miserable reality of this hated place, he sees that the brooding Crucifixion he has imagined – austere, pitiless (he will admit it: a shameless cribbing from his master's Trinity in Santa Maria Novella) – would be an act, not of love but of cruelty. It would turn the crushing gloom into horror. Filippo sits down gingerly on the very corner of his mother's bed. She does not move.

He still wants to paint something. His mother needs something to look at. This room is empty of the smallest spark of beauty. It is a tomb for the living. No wonder she has slipped so far into her own darkness. Perhaps something bright, something hopeful might find its way into that darkness. He needs to bring light. He must bring hope. His mother's finger twitches, and even that tiny movement causes him to flinch. Her mouth is slightly open, and her shallow breathing sends little puffs of steam into the cold air. He pulls the old quilt up to her chin, covering those thin, unconsciously twitching hands. This quilt had been sumptuous, long ago: the best wool and silk, brought home by his father like a magnificent hunting trophy. He remembers creeping into his parents' room and lying down on it, carefully, feeling the sheen of the silk beneath his little hands. Holy Mother ... How deep had he buried that memory? But all his most distant memories are full of colour and sensation. As his mother had faded, so had the colours. He sighs, and his breath is a gout of white steam. His sister rattles a pot in the other room, and she must be stirring the meagre fire, because a thin trickle of smoke, reluctant smoke from dead charcoal and damp twigs, slithers into the bedroom. The pigments, neatly ordered in their trug, catch his eye. Leftovers from the Brancacci frescoes, they are mostly the cheap, dull ones: green earth, raw umber, Mars brown, terra verde, a murky red ochre, terra di Siena, azzurro della magna, a small vial of yellow orpiment. Earth colours, mostly, but in here they blaze with life. The orpiment is almost too bright to look at. Its intensity seems to diminish his mother's frail presence even more.

He gets up and goes into the other room. Leonarda has put on a long apron of undyed homespun, patched and scattered with burns and stains. She is squatting in front of the hearth, blowing into a smouldering arrangement of twigs. Some charcoal has rolled onto the floor tiles. Filippo picks up a piece and starts to sketch, absent-mindedly, on the scoured surface of the narrow table. The outline of his mother's face, the jutting jaw line, the spread of her hair across the pillow. He adds a mouth, a nose, but ... These come from memories. He draws the eyes.

His mother, asleep, seventeen years ago. This isn't the woman lying next door. And then again, it is. In his eyes, in his heart, she is still there, like this. She must be. Beauty is hiding in her, like it hides in everybody. Beauty does not die. It waits to be called forth.

'Pippo…' Leonarda, standing, has seen the black lines on her freshly scrubbed table. But Filippo grabs her, hugs her tight. He has just realised that the fresco he will give her will be a celebration. A Nativity, he thinks… No. An Annunciation.

The rotten plaster comes off all too easily: the sickly ochre drops away in flakes and curls, the plaster beneath crumbles away in damp grains and tangles of horsehair. Leonarda stands in the doorway wringing her hands, but Filippo has promised her that he will clean everything up, make everything good. But the dust is rising. He had wanted to replaster the whole wall, using his newly learned skills: do a job that would make Ruggerio proud. But now he sees that will be impossible with his mother lying here. So he has marked out a rectangle and cut into it with as much care as he can. Even so, the wall is falling apart. He'll need Ruggerio's skills if he's going to put things to rights.

Ruggerio himself has brought a sack of plaster, lugging it up the steps on one broad shoulder, terrifying Leonarda when she opens the door to his knock. Filippo calms his sister down, makes introductions, leads the big man inside to look at the wall. Ruggerio clicks his tongue when he sees the rotten plaster.

'Rather you than me,' he says, but he gives Filippo instructions on how to mix a strong under layer, how to stop the rest of the plaster from falling away. 'But it'll take weeks to dry in this place,' he mutters. 'Cold *and* damp…' He looks down at Monna Antonia, who has done no more than turn her head slightly away from all the noise and dust, and at the pale, thin figure of Leonarda, who seems on the point of tears. 'Let me think,' he says, and leaves. Filippo goes back to scraping plaster from the bricks that he has revealed, but an hour later Ruggerio knocks again, and Leonarda opens the door to find him standing beside three large bundles of firewood.

'Some old scaffolding I had lying around in my workshop,' Ruggerio explains as they bring the wood inside. 'I was going to give it to the cloister, but ...' He nods shyly to Leonarda. Ruggerio has daughters her age, Filippo knows: both of them married, comfortable. They undo one of the bundles and splintered pieces of a ladder emerge. The sluggish fire bursts into life. Heat spreads through the tiny apartment almost at once. Ruggerio leaves, with a promise to bring more wood tomorrow. Leonarda sinks down onto the bench, the apartment's only seat, and stares at the fire, lost in amazement. The flames pigment her face a healthy pink. It is an illusion, Filippo knows, but just to see his sister warm herself seems like a miracle. He sets about mixing plaster, and by the time he leaves, the wall is patched and the first coat of the under layer is done.

The next day the plaster is not dry, but Filippo notices that the pile of firewood is much the same as when he had left.

'You have to burn it!' he tells Leonarda. 'Don't worry – I know Ruggerio. He seems like a bear but his heart's like a freshly baked cake. He'll bring you wood for ever now. Burn it! Warm this place up!'

In another day, Filippo has trowelled on the next layer of plaster. His mother is awake, propped up against her pillows. Her head lolls to one side and she seems to be staring at her left shoulder. Filippo forces himself to ignore her, as he has been doing. She is his patient, he has told himself. She is his patron. She is ... anyone, except his mute, unblinking shell of a mother.

Finally, the wall is ready. Filippo knocks on the door after Terce, a bucket of fine plaster for the *giornata* in his hand. Women are staring at him from the windows that line the yard. They know who he is, of course, and he knows what they say when the door shuts behind him: poor Tommaso di Lippo's wayward son, taken in by the Carmine – the Lord Himself is the only one who knows why they took pity on such a disgusting little urchin... Let them say what they like, he thinks, kissing his sister's cheek. Once upon a time he might have wished they might go to hell, but what could be more hellish than this place? As he carries his bucket into his mother's room he says a quiet prayer to the Virgin that all of them be saved. The woman lying in bed blinks at the ceiling as he walks in, her eyes focused on nothing at all.

Here is the blank wall, the pinkish oval of plaster with bulging edges, a yard wide and almost another yard high. Waiting for him to begin. But now that he is here, he doesn't know what to do. The idea for an Annunciation had seemed so perfect four days ago, but he has never really thought about making one. He knows the form, of course: the Angel Gabriel on the left, reverent and considerate with his tall lily stalk; the young Virgin accepting the news with varying degrees of wonder, joy or resignation, depending on the skill of the artist. Bicci di Lorenzo had just completed an Annunciation triptych when Filippo had left for Pisa, which with his recent training he cannot see as anything but hopelessly old-fashioned. Filippo sits on the corner of the bed. He has grown used to Mamma over the last few days; she no longer fills him with dread or longing. She is a member of her own silent order, he has decided, sunk so deep in meditation that her concerns are no longer those of the world. This is her cell. It is fiction, he knows, but it works. He reaches out and pats the hard rise of her shin beneath the bedcovers.

'What should I do?' he mutters. He stares at the plaster, imagining Bicci's stiff, mannered figures. How is the angel meant to stand? He seems to remember conventions, rules, but rules have never really stuck in his head. He gets up and goes into the other room. His sister is crouched in front of the fire, which is crackling away hungrily, eating up Ruggerio's dry lumber. When she hears him she rises and turns. Her face is flushed bright pink from the fire and she gives him a shy, almost furtive smile, as if embarrassed that he has caught her enjoying the heat. Filippo laughs out loud.

'Thank you, Narda! Thank you, Mother!' His sister is shaking her head in bemusement as he runs back to the bedroom – he is there in three strides – finds a stick of red chalk in his trug and begins to draw.

★

The Angel Gabriel has a broken nose and a missing earlobe. He stands with the awkwardness of someone who only finds themselves in fine company when something has gone wrong, but this time he is delivering good news, not waiting to be scolded, so his almost girlish mouth, strangely out of place below that crooked nose, is trying hard not to smile. The hand that grips the rigid stem of the lily is white, and perhaps that is also why the angel is smiling, because the boy whose face Filippo has borrowed for Gabriel belongs to Albertino, whose hands had never been clean.

The Virgin, of course, is Leonarda, as he had seen her warmed by the fire, by the joy of a sudden turn in the path of life which has brought her to a place she has long since ceased even imagining. That something so simple – a fire with wood to spare, to pile on until the stones of the hearth grow too hot to touch – can be so transforming... What is the difference between the great miracles and the small ones? Filippo has been chewing this over as he paints. Here on the wall, Narda is not quite smiling – Filippo has not seen his sister smile, not exactly, for more years than he can count. But the face in the painting is about to: its muscles have rediscovered this forgotten talent, happiness is rising, and the great realisation, that with the news she is hearing comes the weight of the universe, has not yet struck home. Filippo is discovering that paint and brush can be merciful. He wants to lift a burden from Narda, not add a new one.

214

Angel and Virgin stand against a plain background the colour of the summer sky at dawn: robin's-egg blue with a faint, spreading wash of gold. He isn't completely satisfied: the faces are too smooth, too artless for his liking, and Gabriel's hair looks as though it is modelled in soft clay, as though the angel is wearing a sculpted wig. But he doesn't know how to do it better. He must pay more attention to Masaccio. The wings are wrong as well: the feathers should look like peacock eyes, but he's not entirely sure what those look like. There is a man who sells game in the Santo Spirito market, and Filippo had made a detour there one morning to study the dangling pheasants. Is it all right for an angel to have pheasants' wings? They look exotic, though, and noble in their way.

Angel and Virgin are posed beneath a domed roof held up by four pillars, a pavilion of sorts, the kind of curious half-building that Giotto imagined in his frescoes. Beyond, Filippo has painted the horizon beyond Florence: the familiar mountains. The pavilion stands on a paved square, on which figures are passing to and fro. Two children are squatting just outside – are they playing something in the dust, or just waiting? – and a bearded man is peering, amazed, around one of the columns. Filippo is not really sure what these people are doing in his painting, but it seems to him that a proper fresco should have a crowd. And besides, it will be good to bring in a little of the outside world to this narrow little room.

'I've finished,' he calls to Leonarda. The pigments, what is left of them, are back in their trug, the plastering tools waiting by the door. He is sweeping the floor with a worn-out broom, chasing nuggets of plaster and nubs of dried paint from under the bed. His mother has not moved for hours. She had been sitting up, eyes half-closed, but now she is sleeping, and only a faint tick of pulse by her right eye shows that she is alive at all. Has she seen any of the strange goings-on of the past week? She must have, Filippo thinks. But nothing has happened. No great awakening, no sign, in fact, of anything working inside his mother's head. He sighs. After all, it isn't a very good painting, he thinks to himself. What did I expect? I'm not Saint Peter, to be raising women from the dead. The thought makes him shudder, and he crosses himself. When he looks up, Leonarda is standing in the doorway.

Tears are streaming down his sister's face. Her hands are pressed together as if in prayer.

'It isn't all that good,' Filippo mutters, but Leonarda doesn't seem to hear him. She is staring at the fresco as though she has never seen it before, though she has watched it take shape day by day. They have hardly talked. Filippo's time outside the Carmine is strictly rationed, and he has tried to use every second of it. And besides, what would they talk about? They are both monastics, in their way: this apartment is Leonarda's cloister as surely as the Carmine is her brother's. Their lives are nothing more than routine. They can't bring each other the casual gifts of conversation: gossip, prices, a bargain found, some news overheard. He has listened, every now and again when his concentration has ebbed, to Leonarda working in the other room, cooking, scouring pots, scrubbing. There has been evidence of sewing and mending. They have not eaten together: the cloister has long since trained Filippo's stomach to go without, and he has not wanted to see how little his sister has to keep her alive. He has tried not to watch her spoon gruel into his mother's mouth, tried not to hear the unwilling smack of her dry lips, the laboured gulp as she swallowed. Well, he is done now. He won't have to hear it again ... But should he not, perhaps, have taken the spoon from Narda, tried to feed Mamma himself? It hadn't occurred to him, and now it is too late.

'It isn't so bad, is it?' he says to Leonarda, making a joke he knows is feeble. Or perhaps it really is that bad. It hasn't cured his mother, after all.

'No, Filippo. It's ... I can't say it. It is a miracle.' She covers her face for a moment, then presses her hands together again. Filippo realises that she really is praying.

'No, no, no ...' he begins, but Leonarda steps around the corner of the bed and grabs him, hugs him more tightly than he could have thought possible. She'll waste all her strength, he thinks, but he is hugging her as well, carefully, because her bones feel so delicate beneath his thick hands. Does she recognise herself? He opens his eyes and peers over her shoulder. The Virgin does not, after all, look all that much like his sister. She is slightly plump, well fed, dreamy. There are comfortable gaps in this woman's life. It isn't Narda. Or perhaps it is Narda as her brother wishes she could be. And how strange, if that's true, that Narda doesn't see it. How sad. But, in a way, how fortunate. 'I'm sorry, Narda,' he whispers.

'Why?' She pushes him away fondly, looks into his face, her own face streaked red with tears. 'What have you got to be sorry about? Unless you didn't paint this – was there someone else in here all this time?'

'No, no. It was me.'

'Then what? It's wonderful. I'm going to fetch Father de Simone. I want him to see it.' De Simone is the priest of the church of San Frediano. 'I want everyone to see!'

'I want Mamma to see it,' Filippo mutters.

'Oh ... Oh, Pippo.' Leonarda hugs him again. 'She knows. Honestly. She does. I can tell. And now ... It will be as if she's in church ... no, in the Duomo! It's as if you've made her a bed right in front of the high altar. You've brought Our Blessed Lady to keep Mamma company.'

'I just want her to ...' But Filippo can't say what he wants, because he does not exactly know. 'I should get back to the cloister,' he says instead, wiping his eyes on his sleeve. 'I don't want to miss Vespers.' He makes himself busy, rattling the pigment jars in the trug, squinting critically at Gabriel's ear, which isn't quite right, but is as good as he can manage. He goes to the door, picks up the bucket of tools.

'Will you be back tomorrow?' Leonarda asks.

'No, I don't think so. I ... I've been pushing my luck with the prior, you see, and I don't want to make him angry.' He grins, despite the pain in his heart. He had thought he might bring healing, but ... 'And my master will be back from Pisa, maybe tomorrow, or the next day. I have to make sure everything is ready for him.'

'Will you bring him here?'

Filippo pauses in the doorway. The thought, strangely, has not occurred to him. 'I suppose I could,' he says uncertainly. 'Yes. I'll ask him. I'll see if he wants to come. He's a very busy fellow.'

'Come back soon, Pippo.'

'I'll try.' He turns and almost runs down the steps, nearly colliding with a portly woman festooned in bed sheets she has just taken down, who is lurking near the street entrance. Bring the maestro ... No, no. Impossible. He doesn't want Masaccio to come here, to smell the mildew, hear the mean, gossiping tongues. To feel the walls press in on him.

Masaccio does not return the next day, or the next. Filippo goes about his daily routine, unusually grateful for it.

18

In the event, it is almost another week before Masaccio comes back to Florence. Filippo, who has been trying to slip away whenever he can to spend time in Ser Felice's chapel, finds him planted in front of the Tribute Money, still in his muddy riding cloak.

'Welcome back, maestro,' Filippo says. Masaccio jumps.

'You startled me! Hello, Pippo. I've been thinking about this...' He steps back and looks up at the panel. 'I think I have it, but...'

'You do,' says Filippo. 'Everyone says so.'

'Do they? Good.' Masaccio frowns.

'Did everything go well with Ser Giuliano?'

'What? Oh, yes. It was fine. Fra Antonio approved of the saints. Ser Giuliano paid up.'

'And... the things I told him?'

'It seems that Fra Antonio already gave him another story. That you were mistaken about the pope. It was a cardinal, or something. Much easier to explain. I just nodded my head.' Masaccio tugs at an earlobe. 'You'll have to forgive me, Pippo. I am worn out. But I haven't forgotten about your money.'

'Oh, yes, my wages...' Filippo tries to sound as if he has barely given it a thought, but it is plain from Masaccio's sigh that he hasn't succeeded.

'I need to talk to the prior about what to do,' he says, pinching the bridge of his nose wearily. 'Because as you said, I can't just give you money, can I? You'll be breaking your Rule. Tomorrow, though, Pippo. Or perhaps the next day.'

'Don't worry, maestro,' Filippo says soothingly. 'But ... There is one thing! I've done a painting.'

Masaccio looks puzzled. 'Really?' he says. 'Where? In the cloister, I suppose?'

'No, not here. In my mother's room. I wanted to do something for her. Something to lift her spirits.'

'What did you paint?'

'An Annunciation.' Filippo hangs his head, feeling the disappointment of the other day flooding back. He shouldn't have said anything. 'At least, I tried,' he adds hurriedly, 'But it's no good. And Mamma hasn't even looked at it. I shouldn't have bothered. I expect I'll go back and paint over it.'

'Nonsense. I'm glad you've been keeping your hand in,' says Masaccio kindly. 'It's good to practice. And it was a generous thought, Pippo. I'll have to see it, of course.'

'No, no! It isn't worth a moment of your time.'

'Have you forgotten, Pippo, that I'm your master now? I *have* to see it.' Filippo sees that though Masaccio is smiling, he is completely serious. 'Tomorrow morning?'

'Well ... I suppose so.'

★

Filippo spends a sour night. The thought of Masaccio in his mother's apartment troubles him. He thinks, too, about his master's strange mood, which had seemed to be something deeper than the fatigue of a couple of days' riding. He has noticed it before: during the week in which they had finished the Tribute Money, Masaccio had drifted off, two or three times, into some distant, gloomy place. He would stand, silent and tense, on the scaffolding, or wander off into the church. Andrea and Ruggerio had obviously been used to these spells, and now he comes to think of it, what was it Filippo had heard Donatello say, that day in Pisa? 'Are you in one of your moods?'

Filippo turns over on the unyielding mattress and pulls his blanket tighter. People have their ups and downs. The maestro is no different. I expect it is money that's worrying him. I don't want to take him to Mama's house, though perhaps Prior Pietro won't give me permission to leave the cloister. Holy Mother, please make him refuse...

But the prior is all too happy to let Filippo show his master the fresco. Indeed, he delivers a little sermon about the confluence of piety and filial duty. So Filippo leads Masaccio reluctantly down Borgo San Frediano through a fine, freezing drizzle.

'This is it,' he mutters outside the archway that leads to his old home. At least there is no laundry flapping, and all the old shrews are huddled up behind their shutters. He follows Masaccio up the slippery steps and winces as his master raps briskly on the door. Leonarda opens almost at once. A gust of warm air billows around her, and instead of mildew, Filippo catches the scent of wood smoke and cooking food.

'My sister, maestro: Donna Leonarda. Narda, this is my painting master, Ser Tommaso di Ser Giovanni di ...'

'Simone. Di Simone di Cassai,' says Masaccio, bowing quite elegantly. Filippo rolls his eyes fondly at his master, but sees, to his surprise, that Masaccio has struck a most uncharacteristic pose: right foot pointed, left hand on hip, as though he were one of the overdressed bravos that preen and strut about the Piazza della Signoria, almost bursting out of their tight tunics whenever a pretty woman comes into view. As the stone landing is very small and treacherous with green lichen, Filippo's main concern is that Masaccio will go over backwards and break his neck, which will give the neighbours something to talk about for the next hundred years.

'People call him Masaccio,' he says. The painter shoots him a look, but Leonarda breaks into a smile so surprisingly wide that it is Filippo who nearly loses his balance.

'Do you have someone to clean up after you, then, Ser Masaccio?'

Masaccio blinks, seems to change his mind about something
and clears his throat importantly. 'Pippo tells me he has painted
a fresco for your mother, Donna Leonarda. I have come to
inspect it.'

'That sounds very official!' Leonarda steps back inside and
motions graciously for them to enter.

'Well, I am his master,' says Masaccio, 'and as such, I'm re-
sponsible for everything he does.'

'But it's just a painting in Mamma's bedroom!' says Leonarda.

'Even so, Donna.' Masaccio draws himself up to his full height,
which is not considerable. He looks around, but there is nothing
to see: bare, streaked walls, the opening to the kitchen, the door
to the bedroom, which stands open.

'It isn't a palace, Ser Tommaso,' Leonard tells him. 'But it is
our home.'

Masaccio looks at Filippo, who shakes his head minutely and
rolls his eyes. 'I warned you, maestro,' he mutters.

'About me, Pippo?' Leonarda says brightly.

'Oh, for Heaven's sake ... Here, maestro. It's in here.' He
steps into his mother's room and beckons to Masaccio. The
painter follows, and Filippo almost feels him jump when he
sees the motionless, white-faced woman lying in the bed. 'That's
Mamma,' Filippo says, tight-lipped. 'Don't worry. She doesn't
know we're here.'

But Masaccio isn't looking at Monna Antonia. He is staring
at the wall.

'Isn't it wonderful?' says Leonarda, and Filippo is flushed with
gratitude for her loyalty. 'Well? What do you say, Ser Tommaso?'

'Do you ... I don't suppose you have any wine, Donna Leonarda?' Masaccio is bending to inspect something: Gabriel's hand,
perhaps, or the folds of his tunic.

'Oh. I'm afraid not.'

'I expect I drank the last of it, eh, Narda?' Filippo breaks in, too jovially, he knows, but his sister gives him a look of intense gratitude.

'Oh. Oh! Of course. Never mind. How rude of me.' Masaccio straightens up, seems to notice Monna Antonia for the first time. 'So this is your mother, Pippo.'

'My mother. *Our* mother,' he replies. 'I wanted to do something to lift her spirits, because ... When doctors could be paid for, they said it was melancholy, because our father died so unexpectedly. I thought—'

'Melancholy has sharp claws,' says Masaccio. 'It does not give up its prey so easily.' Filippo looks at him intently, but his master is studying the Virgin's face. 'She is very beautiful,' he murmurs. 'Yes ...' He turns, seems to shake the heavy mood of the room from him with some effort, but then he grins. 'It is excellent, Pippo. You have my stamp of approval. This could only have been made by your hand.' He glances at the Virgin again, then at Filippo's sister. 'No-one else draws like your brother, Donna Leonarda.'

'He's always done it,' she replies. 'But what a compliment, Pippo! From a real painter like Ser Tommaso!'

'*Pippo* is a real painter, Donna. And this is a real painting, whatever that means. Has your ... Your mother must have seen it?'

'She doesn't see anything,' says Filippo starkly.

'Oh, Pippo, she does. Pippo doesn't know her like I do,' says Leonarda. 'I mean no harm by that,' she adds. 'He has his life in the cloister, doing important things. Holy things. It's my lot to be here. She does see, although I think it isn't in the way that you or I do. I don't know what it is she sees, but I know she has looked at your painting. I came in just this morning and I swear her head was turned towards it.'

'Just an accident, I expect,' Filippo says briskly. 'Right, maestro! We should be getting back to the Carmine, or the prior will have me flogged.'

'Pippo!' Leonarda makes the sign of the cross.

'I'm going to bring him here,' says Masaccio.

'Who?' Filippo starts to edge towards the door, willing Masaccio to follow.

'Prior Pietro.'

'No! Absolutely not, maestro!' Filippo stares in horror at Leonarda, but his sister is wringing her hands in excitement.

'The prior is your sponsor, Pippo. He believes you have a great talent. This proves it. Of course he must see what you've done.'

'Oh, God...'

'Pippo, it's an honour! He can say a prayer for Mamma while he's here.'

'Donna Leonarda is quite right. I'll try and bring him tomorrow. Will that be convenient?'

'Every day is convenient, Ser Tommaso.'

Filippo all but drags Masaccio out of the apartment and into Borgo San Frediano. 'Don't bring the prior, maestro – please,' he says, chewing nervously on a fingernail. 'It... It wouldn't be good for Mamma. Too much excitement. And Leonarda isn't as strong as she looks either.'

'Nonsense. Your sister is fine, and it can only be a blessing for your mother. And that was unmannerly, Pippo, shooing me out like that. I didn't get to say a proper goodbye to Donna Leonarda.'

'You're going to see her tomorrow,' snaps Filippo rudely. Masaccio looks at him, and bursts into laughter.

'I'm sorry, Pippo. I really am. But you have nothing to be ashamed of. Listen to me. I lost my own father when I was five years old. He was big and strong, successful in his work – a notary is what he was. Smallpox. I don't remember what he looked like, Pippo, but I remember the smell of smallpox. It's sweet.'

'I'm sorry, maestro. I didn't know.'

'I didn't tell you. My mother, well, she married again, and

when I was sixteen *he* died. I've seen melancholy. I know what it does. And I've seen poverty.'

'Everyone has *seen* poverty...' Filippo kicks a lump of greying cabbage stalk that is lying on the cobbles. It skitters away across the wet stones and a small girl, walking hand in hand with her mother, sees it and gives it her own, inexpert kick. Something about the little girl's eagerness, her clumsy determination, lifts his spirits. 'To tell you the truth, maestro, it wasn't the poverty I minded. I've never minded it. Never cared one way or the other. It was the — you were right, maestro, Mamma is afflicted by melancholy. That was what I couldn't stand. Because I didn't understand it. I'm not a person of dark humours. I can only pity her, you see. I can't feel with her.'

'You are lucky, then,' says Masaccio.

'I know.' Filippo sees that his master is walking with his neck hunched against the drizzle, his mouth set, sullen. 'Sometimes I think that luck isn't much use if you can't share it, though. Just because I'm happy doesn't mean that Mamma is.'

'Or your poor sister.'

'Leonarda? I've never seen her so happy. I think she liked you, maestro.' Filippo gives Masaccio a lopsided grin: he isn't quite sure what to think about this yet.

'She was your model for the Virgin, wasn't she? Not easy to recognise. You gave her an ease and a grace she can't have in real life. That is what you do, Filippo.'

Filippo spreads his hands, equivocally. 'Is it?'

'That's your gift. I've just realised. It isn't the hand that draws your line, Pippo: it's the heart.'

'I don't like to see people unhappy, that's all. I want them to be as they *should* be, not as they are.'

'Whores? Thieves? A blasphemer, like Albertino? That's him as Gabriel, isn't it?'

'I didn't think anybody would recognise him. Yes, that's Albertino as he was. And no, maestro, he was never quite like that. But inside, that was him. That's everybody.'

'Really?'

'That's how I see it, yes, maestro.'

'With all the misery of this world?'

'No matter how stained something is, there's always something bright underneath.'

They are crossing the square towards the Carmine. 'I'd like to believe as you do, Pippo. As far as I'm concerned, by the way, you're qualified for the Guild. But there's one last thing I want to do with you before you take your oath.'

'Certainly. What is it?'

Masaccio leads him, not into the cloister but in through the main door of the church. At the Brancacci Chapel, Masaccio slaps his palm against the wall and points up to the blank panel beside the Tribute Money. 'Do you remember what's going there?'

'Adam and Eve expelled from Paradise, isn't it?'

'I was going to leave it for Masolino – to complement Adam and Eve over there,' says Masaccio. Filippo doesn't look up at the naked couple. He tries not to, these days. 'But it's a small job. No more than a week. I've been planning it for a long time anyway. You will help me: no-one else. Then you can take your oath.'

Filippo is intrigued and there is a prickle of worry as well: his master is not his usual self. Hasn't been, really, since coming back from Pisa. If they are going to start this new panel straight away, perhaps there won't be any more mention of the fresco in his mamma's room...

But to his disappointment, the prior collects him from the refectory early the next morning, and when they go out into the clear but frosty piazza, there is Masaccio and another man whom Filippo recognises at once: Donatello the sculptor, who slaps him heartily on the back and earns himself a disapproving frown from Prior Piero.

'What's he doing here?' Filippo hisses to Masaccio as they are walking. Behind them Donatello and the prior are having a surprisingly lively chat about something.

'I was talking to him last night, and he asked after you. I said he should see your painting, and he agreed. You should be flattered.'

'Oh, yes, I suppose ... Just don't tell anybody else, maestro. Promise me.' But Masaccio just laughs.

Filippo is biting his lip as Leonarda opens the door on the little party. There are heads in almost every window, staring at the prior. It strikes him that they will believe that his mother is dying, that Prior Piero is here to give her the last rites. The thought just deepens his unease. Leonarda's jaw goes slack when she sees the prior. She curtsies politely to Ser Donatello, and they all bustle in with as much dignity as they can muster in the narrow little space. Donatello goes straight to the fresco, but it lifts Filippo's heart to see that the first thing the prior does is kneel beside his mother's bed, take her hand gently and whisper something into her ear. Monna Antonia's face gives no sign that she hears him, that she sees any of them. She stares, unblinking, at the ceiling.

'I told you,' Filippo hears Masaccio tell the sculptor.

'He's come a long way from those plump little saints in Pisa,' Donatello mutters.

'I'm here behind you, gentlemen,' Filippo reminds them, but he is ignored.

'The luminosity ... He learned that from you, of course,' Donatello says.

'No. That's the interesting thing. That is his. You know my style.'

'You are the master of *presence*,' says the sculptor. 'These figures are almost ... Hmmm. Weightless. Yes, I see it now. And Gabriel's face — what a face! The sort of angel you might find hanging around by the bridge.'

'Not that you would know about that,' says Masaccio, hurriedly, nodding towards the prior, who is rising to his feet. Donatello just chuckles.

Prior Pietro folds his arms. His head falls to one side. Filippo watches him nervously. Masaccio watches. Donatello scratches his beard. The prior breathes deeply.

'I think you can see, once and for all, that you were right about Fra Filippo, Reverend Father,' Masaccio says quietly.

'Oh, yes. Indeed.' The prior strokes his chin with the ball of his thumb. He turns to Filippo. 'I congratulate you, my son. The painting is well done. Very well done. But as an act of charity, of love, I would say it is done even better.' He turns to Leonarda, who is peering in from the corridor. 'Do you like it, my dear?'

'Yes, Reverend Father! Who couldn't like it? It's as if the Holy Mother has come down to live with us!'

'A blessing for your poor mother. And for you.'

'It is, Reverend Father. I ... I didn't know Pippo could do this! He was always in trouble, you see, and his drawings, well ...'

'That was a long time ago,' says the prior, soothingly.

'Yes. He's grown up.' And suddenly she begins to cry. Filippo puts his arms around her, and she pats his hand where it rests on her shoulder. 'Don't mind me, Pippo. I'm happy for you, that's all.'

'Let us go now, gentlemen,' says the prior. 'I believe we are crowding Donna Leonarda out of her own home. I am sorry we have inconvenienced you, my child.'

'You are most welcome, really! Let me fetch some bread. I have a little wine ...'

'I am afraid I have business at the Carmine,' says the prior, gently. 'Ser Tommaso has work to do ...'

'Always!' Masaccio bows. Donatello looks around and blinks, as if he has just discovered that four men are crammed into a tiny room, and that a white-faced woman is lying motionless behind him.

'And I have to meet someone in Santa Croce,' he says. They all squeeze out into the narrow corridor, huffing and puffing and contorting themselves politely, and Filippo can't help but notice the way that Leonarda is watching Masaccio, her mouth pursed into a delicate bud. He smiles to himself. Despite the crush, the apartment seems less oppressive, somehow. Perhaps it is just the warmth of the fire. Perhaps it is the sound of voices, the prior saying a low blessing to Leonarda, Masaccio sharing some small joke with his friend the sculptor. But a burden seems to have lifted from him as well, and when they are trooping down the steps outside, he looks up and waves regally to the neighbours.

★

The next day, Filippo wakes up worrying about his sister. She isn't used to all this fuss, he thinks, and she's delicate. He hopes that yesterday's visit has not upset her, or – God forbid! – had a bad effect on Mamma. He asks the prior if he can slip out for an hour. Permission granted, he runs into Masaccio coming in surprisingly early to work.

'You're going to your mother's place? Excellent! I'm meeting some people there. We'll go together.'

'Who are we meeting?' asks Filippo, even more worried now. Masaccio is striding urgently across the piazza and Filippo has to struggle to keep up with him in his heavy robes.

'A couple of Donatello's acquaintances,' Masaccio tells him. 'He was quite impressed, our stone-chipper.'

'You know him well, don't you?'

'He's a good, good friend. I wouldn't have got that job in Pisa without him – he sponsored me, you know. And in a way, he's my real teacher.'

'I thought Masolino—'

'Masolino took me under his wing when I needed a master to get me into the Guild. He's generous beyond belief. Says I'm *his* teacher now, which is …' He considers, doesn't finish his sentence. Which is true, Filippo says to himself. I can see it, you can as well. Masolino knows what he's talking about.

'So Donatello …' he prompts instead.

'Donatello is the genius of our age,' Masaccio says. They

229

are hurrying up Borgo San Frediano. The sun is forcing itself through fine grey clouds and Filippo notices a few spring flowers growing in between bricks and stones. 'Like Giotto was a hundred years ago, Donatello is today. Or maybe there hasn't been anybody like him for a thousand years! I don't know. He's like one of the ancient ones reborn. He shapes stone as if it were cloth – or flesh. One day, painters will be able to put something on a wall or a board, and anyone seeing it will think they were looking through a window into the real world outside. And they'll have learned how to do it from Donatello. Study him, Filippo, like I have. When I'm in Rome, promise me you will.'

'I promise,' says Filippo. 'Gladly. A very pleasant assignment, maestro. I'd rather go to Rome with you, though.'

'I understand that, Pippo,' Masaccio says, heavily. 'Next time ...'

'What's going on?' Filippo stops inside the gateway that leads to his mother's building. A small crowd of people is gathered in the courtyard at the foot of the steps that lead up to her apartment. Some faces he recognises – a few neighbours, an old woman who has always lived across the street – but others he does not.

'No idea,' says Masaccio. They push through the crowd. The neighbours recognise Filippo, of course, and start nudging and muttering to one another. Has something happened to Mamma? His knees feel weak as he runs up the steps. The door is ajar and he pushes it open but it catches against something. He forces his way in and finds he is crushing an amused-looking man between the door and the wall.

'What is happening in here?' Filippo demands. The man, who is wearing fashionable red and whose greying hair is receding jauntily from his temples, is about to say something, but at the sound of Filippo's voice, Leonarda's head appears in the doorway to her kitchen. She beckons to him furiously. He hurries over, seeing with alarm that his mother's room is full of people.

'Leonarda! What in God's name ...'

'Don't swear, Pippo!' Leonarda giggles nervously. She is as

white – whiter, in fact – than one of the sheets hanging over the courtyard, but she does not look frightened or ill. She seems, in fact, quite elated.

'Tell me, Narda! Is it Mamma?'

'No! It's your painting. Your wonderful painting.'

'I don't understand. Is Mamma all right?'

'She's fine! And she has a visitor. Guess who it is!'

'Oh, Christ.' Filippo breathes again.

'Stop swearing, Pippo. Guess who's come? You never will!'

'I don't know, Narda! The pope?'

'Filippo! Don't be silly. It's … Oh!' She steps back and curtsies. Filippo, growling with irritation, turns around, angry words gathering in his throat, only to find himself face to face with a thin man, his face beginning to harden into early middle age, wearing a black tunic and a plain black hat. There is something about the man's pendulous earlobes, his narrow, pointed nose …

'And you must be the painter?' the man says, nodding graciously at Leonarda who, Filippo sees, is pointing at him with a trembling finger. His voice is low and cultured though rather rough, as if he spends most of his time shouting, but something about him lets Filippo know that this man never shouts, no matter what the occasion. Filippo recognises him now. Who wouldn't recognise Cosimo de' Medici?

Not quite forty, Cosimo's hair is already turning grey. He has a long, lean face, made longer by a finely sculpted nose that curves down to meet the slight up-curve of his chin. His grey eyes are cool and calm although Filippo sees immediately that they miss nothing. An unassuming figure, on the face of it: a well-off lawyer, you might think if you passed him in the street, or perhaps a doctor. Hard to imagine him disturbing the thoughts of the Albizzi family, who still think they are in charge of Florence, yet disturb them he does, and they hate him. Now he is regarding Filippo with an almost wistful expression. Hard to believe that when his father dies, which will happen soon, as everyone is saying, Cosimo de' Medici will become one of the richest, most powerful men in Florence. In all of Europe. But the deeper he looks into those grey eyes, the easier Filippo finds it to believe.

'I did the painting, yes,' Filippo says, because although there are a great many polite things he ought to be saying, he can't remember any of them.

'Fra Filippo Lippi. I heard all about your fresco from my friend Donato Bardi. I hope you don't think I'm being rude, forcing my way into your mother's house like this.'

'Force, sir? I'm ... I'm sure you didn't do that,' Filippo stammers.

'One tries not to be overbearing. But I am glad you are here. Would you do me the honour of showing me your painting?'

'Of course, sir.' With a thunderstruck glance at his sister, Filippo follows Cosimo into the other room. There he finds Donatello, who grins at him toothily through his beard; Masaccio, and the man in red, who introduces himself at once as Poggio Bracciolini, at the young friar's service.

'I told you, Ser Cosimo, that this young Carmelite shows promise, did I not?' Donatello winks at Filippo. Near his leg, Monna Antonia's pale face lolls against her pillow, eyes half-closed, a discreet, silvery bubble of spit resting between her lips. No-one one is paying her any attention. Perhaps that's just as well, thinks Filippo.

'And you were right, as always, Donato. So, young man. Where did you find your inspiration? The scene is familiar.'

'From the Baptistery, sir,' says Filippo, though somehow he understands that Cosimo knows exactly what he is going to say. 'Ser Ghiberti's Annunciation on the north doors.'

'Indeed. What better example could you have found? The faces ... Our Lady is modelled on your delightful sister, I think.'

'That's right, sir. I took the liberty ...'

'Another good choice. And Gabriel? He really is intriguing. A real person too, I think? Drawn to life?'

'From memory, Ser Cosimo. A friend from many years ago. He ... Well, he's dead.'

'Then you have an excellent memory.'

'It's not exactly how he looked. But I did my best.'

'Yes.' Cosimo gives him a piercing look. His eyes are a perfect grey. 'I believe you did.'

'You know, Cosimo, I think perhaps we should leave these people alone now.' The man in red is standing in the doorway. 'We are disturbing the poor invalid.'

'Well said, Poggio. My dear friend is a connoisseur of books and a hunter of rare treasures,' Cosimo tells Filippo. 'He is also quite the most courtly man in Florence. Yet again he must remind me of my own execrable manners. Shall we, gentlemen?'

They shuffle out into the corridor, startling Leonarda, who retreats into her kitchen. 'Filippo!' she hisses. 'Someone else was here earlier. I need to tell you ...'

But at that moment, Donatello throws his arm around Filippo's shoulder and pulls him back into the gathering. 'What do you think of your pupil, Ser Tommaso?' Cosimo is asking Masaccio.

'I am taking him before the Guild on Friday to be sworn in as a member,' says Masaccio, and Filippo's chest swells when he hears the pride in his master's words.

'So he won't be my pupil for much longer, which is entirely fitting. He's something of an amazement, our young friar.'

'Congratulations, Fra Filippo,' says Cosimo. 'I expect to hear your name bandied about.'

'I think that might depend on where you happen to be, sir,' Filippo says, starting to relax in the embrace of all this praise. 'They'll always talk about me down this end of the Borgo, I expect, but by the time you reach Santo Spirito ...'

'Reputation, young man. Cherish it. Nurture it. Don't let it out of its cage until you are quite sure it will find its way back to you,' says Poggio Bracciolini.

'Thank you for the advice, sir,' Filippo says, sincérely. 'But you see, I'll be a ... what is that title, maestro?'

'*Frate Dipintore*,' says Masaccio. They are standing on the steps now, and what seems like the whole of the Dragon neighbourhood is staring up at them.

'That's it. Friar-painter. I'm going to work in the Carmine. I expect that's where my reputation will stay as well.'

'I wouldn't be so certain of that, brother,' says Cosimo. They make their way solemnly down to the courtyard, and Filippo thinks of the stern-faced, long-robed men in the *Sagra*. I should paint this myself, he thinks, but not in green. In the Borgo, he finds that Cosimo has gently led him away from the others, so that the two of them are walking a few paces behind.

'I don't feel myself entirely welcome down here in the Dragon,' Cosimo says. 'But when Donato told me I had to see something, well, I trust our Donatello. He was right, as he always is.'

'Thank you, Ser Cosimo. You know, my father always spoke highly of the Medici.'

'Did he indeed?' Cosimo chuckles. 'I doubt that, but thank you anyway, Fra Filippo. This is Soderini territory. I'm sure your father was a good and honest man, and loyal to his parish. Hmm.' He clasps his hands behind his back and looks down at his shoes. 'Loyalty. It's a valuable thing, young man.'

'I think so,' says Filippo seriously.

'There was something that happened earlier in the year,' says Cosimo. 'An unfortunate incident with an image of the Virgin. Some young ruffian insulted an image of the Virgin near San Pier Scheraggio. Hanged the next day from the Palace of the Magistrates, as he deserved. But one hears that, before his sentence was carried out, a young Carmelite prayed with him in his cell, stood by him during his trial, heard his full confession and brought forth a genuine repentance. They say that miracles have been happening around the shrine where the crime took place, not the least of which, to my mind, is that the unfortunate young man is said to have been saved by the grace of Our Lady and spared the fires of hell. Now the trial and execution were done in rather a hurry...' Cosimo touches the tip of his long nose with his forefinger and furrows his brow. 'And it's my understanding that the records of The Eight are not very thorough. But I thought it interesting that this young man, who grew up an urchin down here in Oltrarno, should have been attended *in extremis* by a friar of his own age, from his own neighbourhood. I saw the man hanging, by the way, and though his face... One can only imagine. Still, it was clear he had found repose. Rather a striking face. Quite distinctive. Not, strictly speaking, angelic.'

'I couldn't help it, Messer Cosimo,' says Filippo, worried. 'I wasn't expecting anybody else to see the painting. Just me, and my sister, and well, my mother doesn't really see anything. He was a good friend – Albertino was his name. He wasn't a bad man, my lord. Just very, very unlucky. So unlucky that his luck only came back after he'd died.'

'What caused him to do what he did? Gambling, wasn't it?'

'As I said, he had no luck, though yes, he loved to gamble. Funny how those two things often go hand in hand. Anyway, he was in trouble with a couple of men he owed from the gaming table. But then he had to go back, didn't he? Had to give it one last play. They took him for everything, of course. I think something just broke inside him. He'd had a hard life, you see. On the streets, and then working at the Buco...' Filippo shakes his head gravely. It could have been me, he wants to say. It would have been me.

'I'll paint over him, though, shall I?'

'Why? I'm not chastising you, young man. I'm admiring your loyalty. But do you really think angels should have the faces of street urchins? Should saints be blacksmiths, or dyers, or cooks?'

Filippo takes a deep breath. 'Jesus was a carpenter,' he says.

'So he was,' says Cosimo. 'Look. Our friends are getting away from us. Can I give you a word of advice as we catch them up?'

'Please,' says Filippo, dreading what it might be.

'Poggio is right about reputation. But don't hold yours too

close. We poor souls across the Arno would be sorry not to enjoy your gift.'

'I'm going to paint a history of the Carmelites in our cloister,' Filippo says.

'A cycle? Like Giotto.'

'I doubt that very much!'

'Still, one day you will be finished, and when the world comes looking for you ... Don't turn it away, young man.'

★

The prior is waiting for Filippo in his study. As soon as he had stepped into the cloister, hoping to slip away into some quiet corner, a novice had found him and all but dragged him to the prior's door. When he goes in, he finds that the prior is not alone. Another friar is sitting beside his writing table. A tall, thin man with a squared-off nose and an underbite, Fra Albizzo d'Azolino de' Nerli looks pugnacious but carries himself with the self-assurance of the nobleman that he is.

Though the Carmine is a small community, thirty-five friars and ten novices, Filippo has never spoken to Fra Albizzo. The Nerli are the richest family at this end of Borgo San Frediano, and among the richest in Oltrarno. Fra Albizzo pays for the lavish Crucifixion feasts the Carmine holds every year and is often in the company of the prior. So Filippo doesn't know what to think when he sees the two men, both of whom have the abstracted air of men who are planning something that a lowly creature like Filippo will never comprehend.

'Good morning, Fra Filippo. I hear you have been in exalted company.'

'I suppose I have, Reverend Father,' says Filippo. 'Very unexpected, I assure you.'

'I expect you know Fra Albizzo de' Nerli.'

'By face and of course by reputation,' Filippo says, bowing politely.

'And I know you, Fra Filippo. I remember Tommaso di Lippo – your father,' he adds, as though Filippo might not remember. 'He was in the Confraternity. He died…When did he die?'

'Seventeen years ago,' says Filippo. Surely he knows all this, he is thinking. He knows exactly who I am. But what does he want?

'You were just at your mother's rooms, I understand?'

Filippo nods. 'I was there this morning, in fact. With Prior Piero.'

'How kind of you, brother.' Filippo turns to the prior. 'Did you go to see my mother?'

'I took Fra Albizzo to see your fresco,' says the prior.

'Really? Why? That is to say, I'm flattered by all this attention being paid to my work, but it doesn't deserve it. I don't deserve it.'

'I asked to see it, young man, because there has been talk in the building,' says Fra Albizzo. 'And in the Borgo.'

Filippo rolls his eyes. 'The neighbours are not kind. The whole place was my father's house, in the old days. It is a sad thing to say, but people, given the chance, always seem to relish the misfortune of others. So it is with my poor mother and sister.'

'I know the story,' says Fra Albizzo.

'I expect you do, sir. The house is sold off now. The widows of the *commesse*, in their kindness, give my sister just enough to rent a couple of dirty little rooms on an upper floor, but… Mamma is not well. She hasn't been right since Papa died, and it's only getting worse. I thought that giving her a painting to look at might do something good for her health.'

'Still, there has been a disturbance.'

'Oh. Well, that was never my intention. I simply wanted… I wanted to cheer my poor mother up, and bring something holy into her room. It was only ever intended for her. And I thought I had your permission, Reverend Father.'

'You did, Fra Filippo. Unfortunately…'

Fra Albizzo interrupts him. 'And now I hear that Cosimo de'

Medici – *Cosimo de' Medici!*...' He curls the name around in his mouth as though it belongs to something appalling and yet admirable: some exotic, man-eating beast from India, perhaps. 'Messer *de' Medici* and his retinue have trooped across the river to see it. A painting in a shabby little room. Extraordinary.'

'It is rather a good painting,' says the prior, diplomatically.

'Be that as it may, Reverend Father. Young man, I have been assuming, all this time, that you know who your mother's landlord is. Do you?'

'I'm afraid not,' says Filippo, irritated. 'I have never been part of my mother's business dealings – or those done on her behalf, I should say.'

'Well, I am. I own the building,' says Fra Albizzo, tapping his fingers decisively on the table top.

'Oh.' Filippo blinks. 'I had no idea.'

'You don't take an interest in your mother's affairs?'

'As a friar in holy orders, brother, I'm not really in a position to do that, am I?'

'Perhaps not,' Fra Albizzo concedes grudgingly. 'But anyway, the matter is this: I am no longer able to rent those rooms to Monna Antonia and Monna Leonarda.'

'What? Why not?' Filippo clenches his fists. His whole body is rigid with anger and disbelief, but who is he standing before? Two friars, two grave-faced men in Carmelite robes. 'I don't understand. Because of the painting?'

'No. It is business, Fra Filippo. Your mother's rent, paid by the *commesse* though it is, would have been cheap even thirty years ago. Added to that, your mother is bedridden and your sister is in no position to maintain the rooms as she should. It is the least one might ask, surely, in return for a few pennies, to have the place kept decently?'

'I could paint it!' Filippo says desperately.

'You are a Carmelite friar!' says Fra Albizzo sharply. 'Not a house-painter! The dignity of your office...'

'And yet you are a friar and a landlord, who wants to throw two helpless women into the street!'

'I am a Nerli!' Fra Albizzo narrows his eyes. His knuckles have gone white on the table.

'And your noble blood gives you an exemption? Reverend Father, is this right?'

'There isn't a great deal I can do,' says the prior. There is sympathy in his face, though.

'It's because of Messer de' Medici,' Filippo says. 'Isn't it? Politics as well as business, brother? What is the point of these robes, eh?'

To his amazement, Fra Albizzo winces. 'Yes, politics!' he says angrily. The prior lays a hand across his wrist. 'There is no escape. The curse of our city. Damn it all.'

'Fra Albizzo does not, in his heart, want to act against your poor mother,' says the prior, gently.

'Then don't,' says Filippo bluntly. 'Why should you? Out of spite, because Ser Cosimo took a look around their shabby rooms for half an hour?'

'You are not stupid, Fra Filippo, though you are uneducated,' Fra Albizzo tells him. 'You know that the families of Oltrarno – the Uzzanos, the Soderinis, the Brancaccis … Yes, the Nerlis, do not look happily on the Medicis and the way they are becoming a power in our city. I won't speak of it. I despise these things. It is not simply because Cosimo de' Medici came to my building, though that is extraordinary in itself. I had already taken action before I knew of his visit. It is because there are whispers – nothing is worse than a whisper, Fra Filippo: nothing! – that your Gabriel has the face of a certain Albertino da San Frediano. Yes? The notorious blasphemer? There is a small cult springing up around the statue he defaced. I am not the head of my family. My brother, as I'm sure you know, is most involved in the governing of our city. It is his fear that this cult, with Medici backing, will find a toehold here in San Frediano.'

'Because of my fresco?' Filippo shakes his head in disbelief.

Because of Albertino? he wants to demand. Because of my friend?

'A painting can be a thing of great power,' the prior is saying.

'Do you believe this, Reverend Father?' Filippo is trying with all his might to keep the rekindled anger out of his voice.

'Actually, I do not. The so-called cult won't last out the summer, and if it does, it won't spread beyond the parish where it started. And I know Ser Cosimo – my position here has led me to have many dealings with him. He is the precise opposite of a man who would involve himself in such foolishness. But what Fra Albizzo is trying to say ...'

'I am not acting out of spite,' snaps Fra Albizzo suddenly, jabbing his forefinger down onto the table. 'But others are. There is nothing I can do. I am sorry, Fra Filippo.' He stares grimly ahead of him. Then something seems to give in his face. The lines soften. 'Truly. I am. Your father was a good man: pious and respectable. I enjoyed his company. And I should say that I didn't buy his house after he died: I inherited it quite recently from a cousin. Families ...'

'The Carmine is your family, Albizzo,' says the prior firmly.

'If it's just business ...' Filippo scratches the bridge of his noise with a fingernail. A minute ago he had been imagining his paint-stained fingers wrapped around Fra Albizzo's neck. But suddenly he feels sorry for the man. And his mind is spinning like one of Ser Brunelleschi's machines, hoisting up scenery and lowering angels. He imagines himself painting over Albertino's face – it will happen, anyway. Squatting beside Albertino behind Santo Spirito, throwing the dice. One throw. He can almost hear Albertino's voice: go on, then, *cagniuola* ... 'Before Christmastide, Maestro Tommaso the painter told me you had offered to rent him a house in the piazza here.'

'So I did.' Fra Albizzo shrugs. 'He did not take me up on it.'

'Have you rented the house?'

'As things stand, it is still empty. There is some interest.' Fra

Albizzo glances at the prior, as if he is uncomfortable discussing such things here.

'I should like to rent it from you,' says Filippo.

Fra Albizzo looks at the prior, then at Filippo.

'Rent? With what, young man?'

'Last year, I painted four panels of an altarpiece commissioned by Ser Giuliano degli Scarsi of Pisa. For which Maestro Masaccio owes me four and a half florins. You mentioned a rent of one florin a year, I believe, so ...'

'Rent for whom?' says Fra Albizzo to Filippo. His manner is softer, suddenly. He seems to have stepped down from his aristocratic plinth. Is it the mention of money? Filippo wonders.

'For Monna Antonia, my mamma, of course,' Filippo tells him. 'And my sister Leonarda.'

'I ...' Fra Albizzo sighs. 'This does seem to be an admirable solution. But I am sorry: there seem to be far too many difficulties.'

'Like what?'

Fra Albizzo turns to the prior. 'This young friar would be overstepping the Rule, by going into a financial contract ...'

'You do, though, brother,' says Filippo. 'You rent to Mamma and who knows how many others? You were going to rent the place to my master. Honestly, I don't see the difference.'

'But there is. You see ...' Fra Albizzo is irritated. He's going to patronise me in a moment, thinks Filippo, and then I'll mess things up.

'Of course, I understand that you own a lot of houses around here, and this is a bit of a trifle for you, but it would be a true act of kindness. And, you know, rent. In advance, brother.'

'In advance, you say?'

'It will have to be,' Filippo says, feigning reluctance. 'I can't hold the money, can I? The Rule ...'

'I was under the impression that Ser Tommaso was going to give the money over to the Carmine as a donation,' says the prior. He is plainly trying not to smile.

'But has he, though, Reverend Father? I don't think the maestro parts with money that easily.'

'Now you come to mention it, he has not.'

Filippo grins. 'So you see, Fra Albizzo, the rent will have to be upfront. Four and a half florins, for ... six years.'

'*Six years?*' Fra Albizzo splutters. The prior bursts out laughing. Albertino chuckles somewhere in Filippo's heart.

'I assume you have special rates for members of the Order,' Filippo says. His toes are so tightly curled in his sandals that he can no longer feel them, but he is keeping a straight face. One throw ...

'Well, Fra Albizzo? Do you have special rates?' the prior asks innocently.

'I ... I ...' For an awful moment, Filippo thinks that the friar is going to slap him, because his face has gone bright red and his mouth is tight. But instead, to his amazement, Fra Albizzo lets out his breath and begins to chuckle. 'Five and a half years,' he says. 'Until Saint John's Day of 1432.'

It is Filippo's turn to breathe again, and uncurl his toes. 'That seems reasonable,' he says, with a small and polite bow of his head.

'Very reasonable,' says the prior, quickly, because Fra Albizzo has begun to colour again. 'I will have a contract drawn up. I think you are doing an excellent thing, Albizzo. Tommaso di Lippo was a good friend to the Carmine. The Confraternity of Saint Agnes lost a stalwart when he died. And to bring his poor invalid wife closer to the church ... Yes, a suitable thing.'

'So we are making an agreement?' says Filippo. Now that it is done, he feels almost dizzy with emotion.

'We are,' says Fra Albizzo. 'Prior, you might have a stern word with young Fra Filippo about his business practices. Rather too sharp for a Carmelite brother. But ... I cannot fault his filial devotion. I think you are right. Most suitable.' He smiles and holds out his hand. 'To our contract.'

Filippo grabs, shakes heartily. 'This is wonderful!' he says.

'Never have I seen a man more happy to be relieved of four and a half florins,' says Fra Albizzo.

'I haven't seen them, have I?' says Filippo, looking at the prior. 'If I'd had the gold in my hand... No. You have no inkling of how happy this makes me, Fra Albizzo. The Lippis have always been friends with the de Nerlis and... and...' Best to stop, now, he tells himself.

'I shall send for the notary,' says the prior. 'Back to work, Fra Filippo. I shall want a report from you tomorrow on the progress of your work. If that is all...?'

19

'F<small>ILIPPO!</small>' L<small>EONARDA STANDS IN THE</small> doorway, dressed as always in a plain white smock. She is pale – even more so than when he had last seen her.

'*Tommaso?*' A voice, thin as whey, from the bedroom. Leonarda shuts her eyes for a moment, sucks in her breath.

'She's asleep,' she says. 'This is what she does. She asks for Papa. She's dreaming, I suppose.'

'Perhaps she won't, any more. Perhaps she'll get better.'

'I don't think so, Pippo, but I know you pray for her, so there is always hope.'

'I've got something better than prayers! I mean, there's nothing better than prayer,' he corrects himself, makes talons of his hands in frustration. He has been rehearsing this speech for hours, and it won't come out properly. 'Holy Mother, help me!' he exclaims. 'I've used my wages from Ser Masaccio to rent a house. From Fra Albizzo de' Nerli.'

'But you live at the Carmine.' If Leonarda were less tired, Filippo sees she would be exasperated. He takes her hand and rests it against his cheek. When was the last time he did this? He doesn't remember.

'No, sister! For you and Mamma!'

'I don't understand. Fra Albizzo wants to evict us. That's what I was trying to tell you when...'

'Don't worry, sister. About anything. Fra Albizzo ... He says it was all a misunderstanding. There's a whole house, just for you and Mamma. You have it for five and a half years, paid for. And after that ... Don't worry about after. It's beautiful — small, but clean and the sun comes in for most of the day. And you don't need to worry about anything. I'm Masaccio's assistant now: he pays me, but what can I do with his money?' He tugs at his habit. 'I'll give it over to you. All of it.'

'Where?' Leonarda is staring at him, her eyes huge. She thinks she's imagining this, thinks Filippo. 'Where is your house?'

'*Your* house. It's in Piazza del Carmine, on the west side. You can bring Mamma to church whenever you like!'

To his horror, Leonarda presses her palms against her face, over her eyes. Her fingernails dig into her forehead. 'I'm becoming like Mamma at last,' she sobs. 'I knew it would happen. I'd catch it sooner or later.'

'You can't catch what Mamma has,' says Filippo. 'You aren't mad, and neither am I. Look. Here's your contract, drawn up by Prior Pietro and Fra Albizzo, properly witnessed and everything. The rent is paid: all of it, in advance. You can leave here, Leonarda! You can leave right now!' He grabs a wrist, wrenches her hand away from her face and stuffs the contract into it. 'Look, my sister!'

Leonarda looks. She carries it to the door and stands on the stone landing for a long time as the neighbours hoot and cackle above her.

'Do you promise me that this is real, Pippo?'

'I promise. Shall we tell Mamma?'

'She won't ...' Leonarda shakes her head. 'She won't understand us.'

'Let's tell her anyway.'

★

'Draw,' says Masaccio, picking up a length of red chalk and holding it out. When Filippo takes it, he taps the roll of paper which holds the design, and walks off.

Filippo studies the design. He has seen it before, or parts of it, as it had taken shape yesterday evening in the candlelight. To the left, the gates of Eden. Above, the Archangel Michael, hovering on a square of his own robe, a great sword clutched in his hand. He hangs above the naked couple who walk uncertainly towards the edge of the paper. Everything is drawn with careful detail apart from the heads of Adam and Eve. Odd, thinks Filippo, but I suppose time is short. He's probably doing the heads now. He sets to work, and by midday prayers he has most of the design transferred to the wall. Masaccio is waiting for him when he gets back from the refectory. Filippo mixes plaster and puts up the *giornata* for the background and the gateway. By the evening Masaccio has filled it in: the stark brown undulations of the desert, the grey walls and battlemented arch, a triangle of blue sky between Adam's shoulder and the Archangel's robe, into which thirteen rays of shining silver light are shining, a reminder of the splendour Man will never see again in this life.

The next day, Masaccio does the angel, his robes a billow of implacable, dazzling orange, one hand pointing sternly, the great sword, almost too big for the delicate celestial bearer, picked out in silver. 'We'll burnish it later,' Masaccio tells him. He has been oddly quiet. Usually he is animated when he works: his limbs restless with energy, whistling tunelessly between his teeth, but as he fills in the angel's face, the silence of the church seems to be gathering around the two painters. Archangel Michael looks gentle, almost ethereal beneath thick blond locks, but his mouth is curled in disgust.

They begin early the next day. Filippo puts up the *giornata* for Eve and Masaccio starts straight away, working from the feet up, feet that are shrinking from the touch of burning sand. Eve's hand covers her sex, her arm is across her breasts. She has grown sleek and plump on the fruits of the Garden, but now the sun of the world is burning her for the first time. This is all as Filippo has outlined it, but the face hangs above, a blank oval.

Filippo wanders out to use the privy. When he gets back, Masaccio is leaning in close, hiding the last section of the *giornata*. His brush is moving furiously, dabbing and slashing. His shoulders are hunched, the lines of his body are tense and awkward. Every joint seems to be locked except for the wild motion of the right arm and hand. Filippo has never seen his master paint like this. Filippo finds that he has caught Masaccio's tension. He stands below the platform, craning his neck to see, listening to the whisper of the brush and the creak of the scaffold. People come and go in the church. Candles are lit. Women chatter somewhere back near the main door. A mass is said in a side chapel. But it has emptied again, fallen silent, before Masaccio comes to the edge of the platform and beckons him with a crooked finger. He looks exhausted, squeezed out, his pointed features sharpened, his eyes dull. Filippo scrambles up the ladder. Masaccio steps aside and leans against the wall.

'There,' he says.

'Maestro ...' Filippo begins. But his mouth hangs open, silent, because he is looking at another open mouth, a blank, black void. Eve has thrown back her head, face clenched, eyes meeting the glare of the sun for the first time, feeling mortality flooding into her, as sour as vinegar. She is howling with pain. Realisation is burning her. Guilt has hollowed her out. That is the void behind that dreadful, yawning mouth. The painter's brush has licked and stabbed at the wet plaster. The face is almost crude, but it is also horrifyingly, wonderfully real. The calm, beautiful woman on the wall across the chapel, who has delighted his dreams, has destroyed herself. Filippo discovers, just in time, that he has backed away from it almost to the edge of the platform.

'Watch it,' says Masaccio, grabbing his wrist, pulling him back to safety. He heaves a sigh and sits down, legs dangling into space. Filippo drops down next to him.

'Well?' asks the painter.

'I don't know,' says Filippo.

'You don't like it.'

'Like, maestro? Do you want me to like it?' He stares up at the ceiling of the chapel, receding into shadow. 'It frightens me. But it's good. It's incredible.'

'Thank you.'

'People will hate it.'

'Because it's ugly?'

'Because it's real. Do people come to church to see real pain?'

'There's plenty of suffering in every church, Pippo. Crucifixions, martyrdoms.'

'But they don't look real.' Filippo fingers the heavy cloth of his sleeve, thinking. 'I saw a woman once, when I was small. She'd been sleeping on the steps of Santo Spirito with her baby, and when she woke up she found the little boy had died in the night. I was sleeping across the street. That was the expression on her face. I don't want to remember the sound she made, but ... I can hear it anyway.'

'She was like Eve, then.'

'Yes, she was. I understand, maestro. But it's still hard to see.'

'I've never seen the things you've seen, Pippo.'

'Then how can you paint them?'

'Because that's the reality of things. That's how the world is, underneath.'

'There's always hope, maestro! There's redemption!'

'You can't have hope without suffering. Anyway, tomorrow is Adam. First thing, Pippo.'

Filippo watches anxiously as his master climbs down the ladder. The painter seems completely exhausted. But when he is standing on the tiles, he stretches, splays his fingers towards the roof, and grins lopsidedly up at Filippo. He pulls off his smock and throws it into a corner.

'Tomorrow,' he calls.

'Tomorrow, maestro.' Filippo sits for a minute more, but he finds the thought of that twisted face behind him unnerving, so he too goes down. It will soon be time for Vespers. He blows out the candles in the chapel, happy to consign Eve to the shadows.

★

Masaccio paints Adam from the feet up as well. Filippo stands beside him, shaking his head at the speed of the work, marvelling at the ease with which his master is forming Adam's body, the ridges of muscle across his belly, the matter-of-fact accuracy of his *ucello*, dangling there for all to see. Adam isn't hiding his privates. From the drawing, Filippo assumes he will be beseeching the Archangel with open hands.

'No-one's ever painted a body like this, maestro,' he says.

'I know,' grunts Masaccio.

'How did you learn it?'

'From Donatello. From old Ghiberti. From the dead.'

'The dead?'

The maestro shrugs, but from the tightness of his shoulders Filippo knows this is pretence. 'In the Bigallo. If you give the *Neri* a donation they let you look at the bodies.'

'I know,' says Filippo, shuddering. Adam doesn't look dead. He looks very alive, though his body is doomed now.

'It was Adam and Eve who gave us the Bigallo and places like it, I suppose,' Filippo says. 'And they're walking towards death. I see that now.'

'We all are,' says Masaccio. He paints in silence for another half-hour, then calls Filippo, who is sitting down by the chapel altar, sketching his bare foot. When Filippo is on the platform, Masaccio hands him his brushes.

'You're going to finish him,' he says.

'Me?' Filippo's stomach lurches.

'Your last apprentice piece. Tomorrow we're going to the Guild. But you need to do this first.' He doesn't say anything else, but turns away and climbs down the ladder. When Filippo looks over the platform, he has already left the chapel. Filippo is alone with the headless, armless Adam.

He stands as long as he dares, aware that the plaster is drying, that the *giornata* is waiting. The arms tucked into the chest, here, he thinks. Palms up, begging... He closes his eyes, trying to imagine the face, but instead he hears a woman's horrified, hopeless scream. What would I do, beside a woman I love, knowing what I know? Of what she has done? Of what I have allowed? I am just as guilty. This is the burden. Unbearable, but it must be borne. Do I turn to the angel, beg him to forgive me? Take Eve, but let me back into Paradise? Spare her, but take me? Or simply beg him to tell me what we need to know: how much will we suffer? For how long? And most of all, why? In God's name, why? The brush hovers. He glances across at the opposite wall, at bearded Adam, solid and unaware. You don't know about the future. You don't remember the past. Well, now you see all of it, my friend. Filippo finds that his hand is shaking. He searches for a face, an expression, but all he sees is Albertino, dead in the Bigallo. There is too much suffering here already, surely? How can he add to what Eve is already howling to her new, empty world?

He cannot. He begins, slowly at first, then with more confidence, to paint. Adam's hands do not beseech: they curl against each other, and into their pitiful shade the man drops his face. A thumb pushes at an eyelid. The corner of his mouth, just visible, curls up in a rictus smile of despair. Filippo makes the shoulders, heavy with muscle, give their whole weight to the task of burying the man's face into the sepulchre of his own flesh, once immortal, now already seeded with death. It is all he can do, Filippo knows. He is exhausted by the sheer mass of what he has painted. When Masaccio comes back up the ladder, Filippo is leaning his forehead against the cold stone of a corbel. He can feel the paint drying on his hands, stretching the skin.

He knows he should wash the brushes now, but he hasn't the strength.

'Oh, Filippo,' says Masaccio. He stands with his arms loose at his sides.

'It's no good,' says Filippo. 'You'll have to redo it tomorrow. I couldn't match your Eve, maestro.'

'No, no, Pippo.' Masaccio comes and wraps his arms around his pupil's shoulders. 'I see what you've done. I understand.'

'I took the coward's way,' Filippo tells him. 'What you wanted ... I couldn't do it.'

'What did I want?'

'Suffering. Terror.'

'That would have been my way, Pippo. I know, now, that it isn't yours. You haven't let me down. This is grief. This is ... humanity.'

'I couldn't show his face.'

'You did the only thing you could. You gave him dignity.'

'But is that right?'

'It's God's gift to us. Or our gift to ourselves. In any case it's what keeps us trudging through the desert, eh? You have passed my test, though it wasn't a fair one. I already knew you would. I knew what I'd find.'

'What was that, master?'

'A simple thing. Much neglected. Highly praised, rarely practised.' Masaccio picks up one of the brushes that is lying beneath the panel. He spits on his palm, agitates the bristles in the moisture, begins to touch up the curls of Adam's hair. 'I mean compassion, Pippo. That's all.'

'Not skill, then?'

'Oh, you have that, all right. You'll have a thousand pupils of your own. Skill, artistry, a perfect eye ...' Masaccio dabs at Adam's ear, fills some shade beneath his hands. Filippo sees that he is making the painting his own, subtly: the master's prerogative. 'Here they are, side by side: my vision of the world, and yours,' he says as he works. 'I wondered if you would imitate me. I need to show the pain of it all – all this. You understand, don't you? When I look around, I see that everyone is either angry, or lustful, or tired. Or bored – the tedium of life, Pippo. How to paint that, eh? How to make boredom holy.' He squats down, mixes some more paint. 'But to you, there's beauty behind everything. I wonder which of us is right? I fear I am. Most people, in their hearts, would agree with me, and that seems to confirm my thesis.' He stand up, squints at the wall. 'You've done the hands well. Better than mine. Yes, I think I must be right about the world, but even so I hope ...'

'We could both be right, you know,' Filippo says. 'Shit on the outside, perfect on the inside. Like the statue. Albertino's statue.'

'That would be too easy.' Masaccio laughs, but he is not smiling. 'What does it matter anyway? We are painters, not philosophers. Chasing money, just like the rest of the mob. Seeing what we can get away with.'

'I've never been good at learning. I never seem to listen, not even to you. There's never been a painter like you, maestro, and yet I'm still not paying attention. I'll try, I promise. When you get back from Rome ...'

'No! For God's sake, Pippo! After tomorrow, you will be a painter in your own right. Follow your road, not mine! I should have learned from you.' He sighs, turns away from the painting. 'I'm going to tell you one more thing, as your maestro. It isn't complicated, so listen, for once in your life. Just this. You are a good man, Fra Filippo. Accept it. A good man.'

20

'Does your mamma like her new lodgings?' Masaccio is leading his horse along the Siena Road, and Filippo is strolling beside him, enjoying the autumn sun, although the road dust rises and falls beneath the horse's hooves. The summer of 1428 has been oppressively hot. The plague has licked at Florence, though it has moved on now. It feels good to be out here beyond the walls, climbing the low hills towards San Casciano among the ripening olives and the oaks, green leaves rusting to warm brown. Filippo thinks of pigments: terre di Siena, malachite, the most expensive ultramarine for the sky. No, he decides that should be Egyptian blue. Cheaper by far: this is a scene he wants to forget. Saying goodbye is not a thing he likes to do. And in the days just passed, as Masaccio has been making his preparations to leave, Filippo has come to realise that he will miss the stocky, sharp-faced painter dreadfully. 'I'll be back before next summer,' Masaccio had assured him for the hundredth time as he had fastened his belongings onto the back of his horse. 'You'll need a hand with your great Carmelite fresco, won't you?'

'And Ser Felice's chapel needs to be finished,' Filippo had said, pointedly.

'Exactly. He'll be sending me unpleasant letters the whole time I'm gone.'

'Speaking of which, will you write to me? I want to hear about Rome. I've heard stories...'

'All of which are true, I assure you, and worse even than that,' Masaccio had laughed. 'You would love Rome, Pippo. Too much,

I expect. Better you're staying here and making Prior Pietro happy. But yes, I'll write.'

'Pippo?' The horse's hooves plod on. The dust coils and eddies. Masaccio nudges Filippo out of his thoughts. 'Your mamma? She likes Fra Albizzo's house?'

'She does. Although she can't speak.' Filippo grabs at a stalk of dead, dry fennel, snaps it off, twirls the rattling spokes of the flowerhead. 'Or won't. But I can tell. And my sister's like a different person.' The two women had moved in the day after Filippo had brought his sister the news. Fra Albizzo, out of the kindness of his heart, had arranged for his mother to be carried to her new home on a stretcher draped with a Turkey carpet and padded with silk coverlets – though when Filippo had thought about it, the men in Nerli livery who had carried the stretcher had been making an unmissable point about Nerli power and Nerli wealth to the people of San Frediano. Well, so be it. Filippo knows he has got an extraordinary bargain for his florins. The house is not large and is one of the oldest in the piazza, but the Nerlis have kept it well. There are two floors, fireplaces in each room, a kitchen hearth. The whole house has been newly whitewashed inside. The south-facing windows look out over a garden planted with date palms, orange trees, olives, bay trees and rows of scented herbs. When she had first gone inside, Leonarda had stood for perhaps a quarter of an hour at one of the upper windows, just looking down into this green square, listening to the sparrows and watching a large ginger and white cat roll around on one of the gravel paths.

'The air is sweet,' she had said, eventually.

'It's just air. This is how it's meant to smell,' Filippo had said.

Monna Antonia had been installed in the larger of the two upstairs rooms. She had showed no interest in the proceedings. The liveried men crowding into her old room had not produced a single flicker of emotion. When they had carried her down the stone steps of the courtyard like a pale queen on her stretcher, the neighbours craning out of every window and crowded into

256

the yard, she hadn't even turned her head, just stared up unblinking at the limp washing above her. Her stately procession along Borgo San Frediano had brought forth nothing more than an exhausted sigh or two. Filippo had seen her carried up the stairs in the new house between the two Nerli men and laid down in the bed, an old, dark piece left over from before the Black Death but, like everything belonging to the Nerlis, well looked after. The screens on the window had been opened, and the sound of voices had risen from the piazza: hawkers, children rolling hoops and spinning tops; a bored dog tied to a barrow, barking for attention.

'This is your new home, Mamma,' Filippo had said, and she had done nothing but sigh again, close her eyes and settle her head on the clean white pillow. But, he thinks now, perhaps that had told him something after all. Had she let go, ever so slightly, of whatever dark thing she had been clinging to for all these years? He thinks he saw a tiny release of tension, nothing more than the snapping of a spider's thread, but could that not mean something? But when he has seen her since, in the brief visits he is allowed by the prior, a half-hour here and there between working on a new panel in the Brancacci Chapel – Saint Peter raising Saint Theophilus from the dead, which won't be finished until Masaccio gets back from Rome, much to Ser Felice's annoyance – and the implacable routine of prayer, he thinks she is changing. She seems younger, somehow. Her hair is perhaps more streaked with grey, but a certain tightness has left her forehead. Her eyes move more quickly, and he has seen them dart towards the window when a particularly loud noise comes up from the square.

Leonarda, though, had apparently seen much more. 'She is better, Pippo: so much better!' she had assured him, and Filippo had wondered into what minute calibrations of shade his sister has divided her drab world: where an imperceptible shift towards white can seem like a miracle.

One day, though, he had come in to find Monna Antonia standing by the window. He had jumped in fright: her thin, white-draped form had seemed uncanny, ghost-like, even in the strong daylight. He had gone over to her. 'Mamma?' he had said, but she had not answered him. He had followed her eyes, darting here and there across the piazza. She had been looking, really looking. There is an animating spirit inside there after all, he had thought.

A few days later, Leonarda had brought her into the church. She had walked with agonising care, placing one foot in front of the other as though the stones of the piazza were burning coals. Filippo had been drawing a part of the Saint Theophilus scene, and Monna Dianora had come to tell him that his mother was there. He had hurried down the aisle, taken her other arm, led her up to the high altar, where she had stood, swaying gently, in front of the Madonna del Popolo. Even though the church had been busy, Filippo had felt enveloped in silence. But – perhaps it had been his imagination – there had seemed to be something companionable about it. An almost imperceptible warmth, with his mother as the source. She had turned, finally, and they had led her back to the house.

'I thought of painting her another fresco,' Filippo says, picking seeds from the fennel head. 'But Fra Albizzo might get upset, mightn't he?'

'Best not to push your luck,' Masaccio agrees. 'Especially after the bargain you squeezed out of him. What happened to your mamma's old rooms?'

'The Nerlis are pulling the whole building down,' says Filippo. He knows he should feel something about that, but he doesn't – perhaps a faint relief, but nothing more. Albertino as the Angel Gabriel: at least you were an angel for a little while, my old friend, he thinks. I can always paint you again. I won't forget.

'My father wouldn't have minded, in any case,' he tells Masaccio. 'He thought progress was good.'

'Your old home, though?'

'No. It hadn't been that for a long time. I hated it. My home was always outside those walls, not inside them. I'm glad it's gone. I hope they build something better, though. Let the light in.'

They have reached the top of a gentle rise in the road. Beyond, it dips down and rises, more steeply, towards Tavernuzze on its ridge.

'I'll go on, then,' says Masaccio. He stands, the horse nuzzling his shoulder, dust swirling around him like smoke. 'If you land any big commissions, write to me.' He grins, but Filippo shakes his head and throws his arms around the painter, hugging him as tightly as he dares. Then he turns around and hurries down the road towards the city. Something makes him stop halfway down the hill. He looks back, and sees that Masaccio has mounted his horse and is just setting off. A cloud of dust is rising between them.

'Thank you, maestro!' Filippo puts his hands around his mouth and bellows as loudly as he can. 'Thank you!' If Masaccio hears, he gives no sign. Besides, the dust is piling up into a billowing wall, and soon the hilltop is completely obscured.

Filippo turns back towards Florence, shimmering in the crease of the mountains. It is early afternoon by the time he walks through the Porta Romana. The guards nod respectfully as he passes. For all they know, he's just walked all the way from Rome, a travel-stained holy man.

He is expected at the Carmine, of course, but there is nothing he wants to do except go down to the river and sit with whoever he might find there. He won't find any friends, though. Nuzzio is in the Stinche prison for some minor theft. The plague's sticky tongue has swept Federico out of the world. Il Cucciolo has left with a band of mercenaries. Bonafortuna has simply disappeared. But who else can he talk to? They are the only people who might have understood. He had told them when he had lost his father, and they had nodded wisely, because they were all orphans too. Now that he feels as if he has lost another father, who is going to comfort him? He smiles at a little girl staring at him from a doorway. She sticks her tongue out and makes devil's horns at him. He bursts out laughing. Stop being so bloody miserable, he tells himself. You're alive. The sun is shining. All of this is your riverbank.

He is at the corner of Via del Campuccio. There is a sharp clatter above him, and he looks up to see a spiral of white and grey, wheeling and rising away from him into the Egyptian blue sky. He laughs again, and when he looks down, there is a girl walking towards him, a girl with a long, graceful neck, yellow ringlets bound up in a white scarf. She hears him laughing and smiles. Her lovely face, which he has drawn once, scratched out on a windowsill with a corner of slate ...

'I was watching the doves,' Filippo tells her. 'Aren't they beautiful?'

'Yes, they are, brother! They live in my aunt's garden. I love to watch them. They are so funny ... Though they eat all my aunt's herbs.'

'You're Giovanni di Salvi's daughter, aren't you? Giovanni the weaver?'

The girl looks at him in surprise. 'Yes, I am. How did you know?'

'I'm Filippo Lippi. Tommaso di Lippo the butcher was my father.'

'Oh! You're ...'

'Pippo lo Schizza. That *was* me, a long time ago. I'm Fra Filippo now. *Frate dipintore.*'

'What does that mean?' The girl frowns charmingly. She must have really disapproved of Pippo the Sketcher, he thinks, which makes him smile even more. But add some Latin ...

'Friar-painter,' he says. 'I'm an artist. A Guild member and everything.'

'Do you still draw people, though, Fra Filippo?' The doves clatter overhead, and they both look up. When they look down again, their eyes meet.

'Certainly!' Filippo pats the satchel that always hangs at his side. 'And by a piece of good luck, I have paper and charcoal with me.' He raises a speculative eyebrow. 'You don't mean...'

'If you've got time? It would be fun. You could... put me in one of your paintings.'

'I could. I will! Where shall we go?'

The girl turns and leads him into Via del Campuccio. 'I know a place,' she says. Filippo hitches his satchel across his shoulder. He glances up towards Heaven, half-expecting to see... what? There is nothing, just a distant blur of white where the doves have ascended, impossibly high, and the endless field of ultramarine. The girl's footsteps clip along the cobbles, receding. A woman walks past, carrying a pot of stew fresh from a baker's oven, trailing the spirits of beef and garlic and thyme. Two drunks are arguing. A ragged boy is about to steal an orange from a windowsill.

'I'll follow you,' says Filippo.